ONE DEAD WEDDING PLANNER

"Madeline?" Savannah called out.

There was no response as the music got louder and louder.

She glanced toward the door. She really had to get back to the ceremony, and yet . . .

"Madeline?"

She hurried toward the bedroom and noticed, for the first time, that the French doors leading out onto a small, enclosed patio were open. The music was coming from that direction.

"Madeline, are you there?" she said as she approached the doors. Just beyond them she could see the tiny, private pool . . . just big enough for the bridal couple to do a bit of skinny dipping, if they so desired.

The music stopped just as Savannah reached the doors.

From there, she could see the pool, adorned with floating white lilies and ivory candles. No doubt, thanks to Madeline. Savannah realized this was part of the "tidying up" she had been doing.

So romantic. Such a perfect setting for newlyweds.

At least, it should have been.

But for the body, floating facedown in the middle of it and the red blood staining the crystalline waters . . .

Books by G.A. McKevett

Just Desserts

Bitter Sweets

Killer Calories

Cooked Goose

Sugar and Spite

Sour Grapes

Peaches and Screams

Death By Chocolate

Cereal Killer

Murder à la Mode

Corpse Suzette

Fat Free and Fatal

Poisoned Tarts

A Body to Die For

Wicked Craving

A Decadent Way to Die

Buried in Buttercream

Killer Honeymoon

Published by Kensington Publishing Corporation

G.A. McKevett

Buried in Buttercream

A SAVANNAH REID MYSTERY

KENSINGTON BOOKS
www.kensingtonbooks.com

KENSINGTON BOOKS are published by

Kensington Publishing Corp.
119 West 40th Street
New York, NY 10018

All Kensington titles, imprints and distributed lines are available at special quantity discounts for bulk purchases for sales promotion, premiums, fund-raising, educational or institutional use. Special book excerpts or customized printings can also be created to fit specific needs. For details, write or phone the office of the Kensington Special Sales Manager: Kensington Publishing Corp., 119 West 40th Street, New York, NY, 10018. Attn. Special Sales Department. Phone: 1-800-221-2647.

Kensington and the K logo Reg. U.S. Pat. & TM Off.

ISBN-13: 978-0-7582-3813-9
ISBN-10: 0-7582-3813-4

First Hardcover Printing: April 2012
First Mass Market Printing: March 2013

10 9 8 7 6 5 4 3 2 1

Printed in the United States of America

Lovingly dedicated to Blanche McGivney Hald,
a beloved inspiration to all generations
to walk in beauty and in strength.

I want to thank all the fans who write to me, sharing their thoughts and offering endless encouragement. Your stories touch my heart, and I enjoy your letters more than you know. I can be reached at:

sonja@sonjamassie.com
and
facebook.com/gamckevett

Chapter 1

"This ain't exactly the roarin' hot time we had planned for this evening, huh, babe?" Dirk Coulter said to the woman at his side.

Savannah Reid couldn't take her eyes off the red wall of flames that had jumped the fire line half an hour ago and was rapidly consuming the town's community center. The building where she and the guy next to her were to have exchanged wedding vows an hour ago.

"Not even close," she said, slipping her arm around Dirk's waist and leaning against him. "I had much more ambitious plans for you this evening, big boy."

He put his arm across her shoulders and pulled her closer. His voice cracked a bit when he kissed the top of her head and said, "I'm sorry I couldn't get your wedding gown out, Van."

She blinked back some tears that had nothing to do with the smoke in the air or the ash falling like dirty snow around them and the crowd assembled to watch the battle. It was all-out war between the San Carmelita Fire Department versus Mother Nature, and Big Momma was winning.

"Hey, you tried," she replied. "If you'd tried any harder, I'd be bailing out my groom-to-be on our so-called wedding night, and that'd just be the cherry on the crap sundae."

"I only hit him once."

"Yeah, and that was one time too many, you knuckle-head."

Dirk flexed his hand. "A love tap . . . that's all it was."

"And if you and Jim weren't poker buddies, he'd have pressed charges then and there."

"Eh, he knows I'm a man under duress. If there's anything harder on a guy's nerves than gettin' hitched, it's having the place he's supposed to do it in get torched on his wedding day."

"Well, you be sure and mention that 'duress' business to him," she said, " 'cause here he comes now. And he ain't lookin' none too friendly."

An enormous fireman was elbowing his way through the mob, composed of countless other firefighters, copious members of the media, town cops galore, and an overabundance of run-of-the-mill gawkers.

When Jim Barbera reached them, he stuck his finger in Dirk's face and said, "I don't care if you *do* have a gold detective's badge, Coulter. Don't you ever lay a hand on me again like that or I swear, I'll—"

Slipping deftly between the two men, Savannah flashed the firefighter her best Southern belle, eyelash-batting, deep-dimpled smile. "Please don't hold it against him, Jim," she said in a soft, down-homesy drawl. "Dirk was willing to risk life and limb to go into that burning building to rescue my wedding gown. And I know you'd have done the same for that pretty little wife of yours . . . what's her name . . . Lilly? She's expecting, isn't she? And this is, what, your third youngun?"

"Uh-huh." Jim was trying hard not to succumb to

Dixie charm. "You shouldn't have let your man go into a burning building, Savannah," he grumbled. "Not for anything. That's the number-one rule."

Savannah could feel her dander rising. The dimples got a tad less deep, the smile a bit less wide. The drawl had a bite to it when she said, "In the first place, he ain't *my man* just yet, thanks to this blasted fire. And even if he was—knowing him like I do—I don't reckon I'll be doing a lot of 'letting' him do this or that. He's got a mind of his own and that's the way I like it . . . most of the time."

Fortunately, Jim got a call on his cell phone. He answered it with a predictable degree of gruffness, considering the conversation he was having, the smoke he had inhaled, and the fact that the fire behind him had totally engulfed the structure he and his company had been fighting to save.

"Yeah," he said into the phone. "Oh? Okay." He glanced around at the bystanders, then at Dirk. "Coulter's standing right here. I'll tell him."

He stuck the phone back into his pocket. "That was the chief," he said. "They're at the point of origin. It's the same guy again . . . a pentagram drawn in the dirt and a black candle in the center of it."

Immediately, Savannah turned toward the mob of spectators, and her eyes began to scan each face in the crowd, one by one. Nobody had to tell her what Jim and Dirk were thinking as they did the same. Odds were high that their arsonist with the creepy rituals was among them, watching with everyone else, enjoying the drama, the destructive fruits of his labor.

What was the point of unleashing hell on a community if you couldn't be there, firsthand, to watch the calamity?

This was his fourth fire in less than a month. They

had to catch him before he burned the whole county down.

After a long, dry summer, Southern California had enough problems with wildfires without a pyromaniac getting his jollies by setting more.

"The wind shifted two hours ago," Jim said. "And they announced it on the local news."

"He had to know it was coming this way," Savannah added. "Plenty of time for him to get here."

Dirk switched from his Grumpy, Thwarted-Bridegroom Mode to his usual—Harried, Cynical Police Detective Mode.

His modes didn't vary much.

"Let's socialize," he said to Savannah, "mingle a bit."

"Yeah, you do that," Jim told them. "I'm gonna get back to work, if I've got your word, Coulter, that you won't be trying to rescue any more bridal apparel."

But Jim didn't need to finagle any promises out of Dirk. Ruined wedding plans pushed aside for the moment, Detective Sergeant Coulter and his still bride-to-be were on a mission. They had an arsonist to apprehend and a strong, personal investment in his capture.

"If I get my hands on him," Savannah said, as they headed for the crowd of onlookers, "I'm gonna mash him like a spider on a sidewalk, until he's nothing but a big, greasy spot."

"No, you've gotta save me some."

Dirk took her hand and led her over the uneven, rocky ground with a paternal tenderness that was sweet and touching.

Three months ago—when both of their lives had been changed forever—all that loving concern had meant the world to her. His constant attention and unfailing devotion had been exactly what she had needed to survive her ordeal and heal the damage that had been done to her body and spirit. She never would have made it without him.

Two months ago, his endless support and help had been comforting, even convenient, as he had scurried about, running errands for her, waiting on her hand and foot.

But now, she was getting tired of being treated like a victim. She was a survivor. And all this solicitous hovering was getting to be a bit much.

Gently, she withdrew her hand from his. "Let's split up," she said. "We'll cover more ground that way. You work this end of the crowd, and I'll take the other end. Meet you in the middle."

Instantly, disapproval registered on his face in the form of his standard-issue showdown-at-high-noon cowboy scowl. "You're gonna go by yourself?" he said.

"Yes. I am. Just like I go to the little girls' room all by myself." She gave him a smile that was sweeter than her words. After all, he wasn't deliberately being a pain in the rear end; he meant well.

So, she wouldn't smack him upside the head . . . this time.

But he wasn't going to let it go. "I don't know how happy I am about you going off by yourself so soon after—"

"Then, darlin', you can just get happy in the same bloomers that you got unhappy in," she said as she started to walk away from him.

"Be careful!"

She smiled back at him over her shoulder, and lightly scratched the tip of her nose with her middle finger.

Chuckling, he shook his head. "Well, at least don't tackle anybody. You know what the doctor said."

As she left him behind and worked her way to the opposite end of the crowd, she tried not to think about what the doctor had said.

"Ms. Reid, you're a very lucky lady. Three of those five shots could have easily been lethal, had they been an inch or two to the right or the left."

No, some memories should remain on the shelf marked, "Best Left Alone."

"The worst is over, Savannah girl," she whispered to herself, as she had so many times during the past three months. "The worst is over and done with. Move on."

She passed a group of teenaged girls wearing far less than their mommas should have let them out of the house in. She checked them off her mental list.

Most arsonists were male. And the majority of them had practical reasons for setting their fires. Revenge, insurance fraud, or to destroy the evidence of other evil-doing . . . those were the most usual reasons for blaze-setting.

But Savannah remembered, all too well, the class she had taken while still on the police force, the points the arson specialist had made when profiling what he had called the "pure arsonist." Though rare, there were individuals who derived their own strange brand of sexual gratification from setting fires, watching them burn, and reveling in the secret joy of knowing they had created the ensuing havoc.

She ran down the mental checklist: 90 percent male, usually white, ages seventeen to twenty-six, with possibly some form of mental illness, substance abuse, previous felony convictions.

And she decided to add one more qualifier: mud-wallowin', slop-suckin' pigs, who ruin other people's wedding days.

Of those assembled to watch the mayhem, only a few

fit the description, and even fewer when she ruled out those young white men who were excitedly chattering with others about the drama before them.

Instinctively, she knew she was looking for a loner.

And at the edge of the crowd, she found one.

On the opposite side of the community center's parking lot, on a small hill dotted with sagebrush, stood a solitary figure—a young, Caucasian man, dressed in baggy, dark clothes, who looked like he had just emerged from his mother's basement for a rare outing. He was farther from the fire than the rest of the spectators, but from his elevated position, he had one of the best views in town.

Gradually, Savannah worked her way through the crowd to get closer to him and have a better look.

Leaving the rest of the spectators, she casually strolled across the asphalt parking lot toward his hill, trying her best to watch him without being too obvious. Instead of making a beeline for him, she turned left and meandered in the direction of a path that appeared to lead from the lot up to where he stood.

Concerned that he would spot her, she moved slowly, trying to stay behind any tall brush that would provide cover. Fortunately, he seemed so fixated on the scene below that he was oblivious to all else.

Drawing closer, she could see that he was young, probably early twenties. He was dressed all in black, and once, when he turned her way for a moment, she caught the glint of a large, silver medallion around his neck.

Her pulse rate quickened. She was pretty sure she'd seen a star on the pendant. Maybe a pentacle?

Ducking behind a tree, she reached into her jacket pocket, pulled out her cell phone, and gave Dirk a call.

"Yeah?" he said.

"Other side of the parking lot, on the hill," she whispered. "The guy in black, watching the fire. I think it's him."

"Where? Oh, yeah. I see him."

"Where are you?" she asked.

"On the far side of the crowd. Where are—? What the hell!"

She grinned. He'd spotted her. And even from sixty yards away, she could read his indignation in his body language. She gave him a little wave.

Instantly, he started to elbow his way through the spectators, heading in her direction.

"Don't even think about taking him yourself," he told her. "You wait for me."

Savannah's grin disappeared. "I know the drill," she said.

And she did. Having been a cop—his partner, in fact—she knew all too well about waiting for backup. But it was one thing to wait for assistance as part of the routine. It was another to have someone—especially a former partner—tell you to do so because he was afraid you couldn't handle a situation by yourself.

"Be very careful, Ms. Reid," she could hear the doctor saying. *"I know your work involves physical altercations from time to time. You can't afford to—"*

"Oh, shut up," she whispered to the voice in her head.

"No," Dirk barked back. "I won't shut up! You wait for me!"

Rather than admit she'd been talking to herself, she just said, "I'm waiting, okay?" and clicked the phone off.

He'll be here lickety split anyway, she thought to herself as she watched Dirk push through the crowd like a football player within a few yards of a Hail Mary touchdown.

Even if he has to mow down women, children, and a couple of grandpas to get here.

Poking her head out from behind the tree, she sneaked another peek at her suspect.

And saw him staring right at her.

Nailed, she thought. *Shoot f're. Now what?*

She stuck her best ain't-it-just-a-fine-day look on her face and came out from behind the tree. "Boy, this here's a steep hill," she said, strolling up the path toward him, pretending to be out of breath. "But it looks like you got the best view from up here. Mind if I join ya?"

The look on his face told her, yes, he minded. Very much.

He also looked quite excited . . . in a way that reminded her of when she'd walked into the bathroom and caught her younger brother, Macon, with a girlie magazine.

She took one quick glance down at the front of his pants.

Yep . . . highly excited.

He also looked highly annoyed.

"Get outta here," he said. "I don't want company."

"Well, now . . . that ain't very neighborly of you," she said, continuing to close the distance between them. "I just want a good look at the fire. That's all."

"Look at it somewhere else," he shouted, getting more agitated by the moment. "Leave me alone."

Then, under his breath, she heard him mutter, "You're *ruining* it."

As she drew within ten feet of him, she could see his medallion clearly. And, yes, it was a pentacle, a large, inverted one, hanging on a thick chain, in the center of his chest.

She wanted to glance back over her shoulder and see

where Dirk was now. But she didn't want to give away the fact that she had reinforcements on the way.

Besides, Dirk had to have seen her continue on up the path. And knowing him as she did, she was certain he was now racing toward them, grubby sneakers barely touching the ground as he ran.

He was a darlin' . . . if a pain.

She stopped about six feet away from the guy and studied him carefully. Approximately five feet, six inches tall, weighing at most a hundred and thirty . . . he wasn't a very large man. She'd wrestled much bigger. And won.

Even from that distance she could smell alcohol on him. His eyes looked glassy. His speech was slightly slurred when he said, "I'm not kidding, lady. You go someplace else to watch it. I was here first."

Taking one step closer, she fixed him with eyes so cold they would have given pause to someone more astute, someone less fixated on his sexual obsession.

"Exactly what am I ruining for you?" she asked him in a deadly, even tone.

"What?"

"I heard you say I was ruining it for you. What's that? The fire? Watching it?" She nodded her head in the direction of the blaze that had now completely engulfed the building below and was casting a lurid glow across the twilit landscape.

He said nothing, but his breathing became heavier, faster as he stared at her, rage in his eyes.

She felt a fury of her own welling up as she thought of the plans she'd had for this day . . . this night.

"You go setting fires to get your rocks off," she told him. "You don't give a tinker's damn what it costs others."

He gasped, his eyes wide. "How . . . how do you know? Who are you?"

"I'm somebody who knows what a crazy twitch you are," she replied. "You set these awful fires that destroy property, kill wildlife—and even people sometimes—and all because you've got crazy urges inside you that you can't, or won't, control."

He moved toward her. She braced herself . . . and wished she'd strapped on her weapon before leaving the house earlier.

"What's it to you?" he shouted in her face. "Mind your own damned business."

He tried to move past her.

She blocked him.

"Oh, it's my business," she replied, her voice soft and deceptively calm. "It's very much my business."

"Get out of my way!" He reached out and shoved her, hard.

A moment later, he was lying on the ground at her feet, curled into a ball, holding his head and moaning . . . a small trickle of blood running down his forehead.

She heard Dirk pounding up the hill toward her. She turned and saw him, panting, face red and sweating, his Smith and Wesson in his hand.

"You can put that away," she told him, nodding toward the drawn weapon. "He's down."

"Yeah," Dirk replied, gasping for breath. "I see that."

"She hit me!" the arsonist told Dirk as he knelt beside him and examined the damage to his forehead. "She's crazy! She hit me for no reason . . . really hard . . . with her purse!"

Savannah glanced down at her hand and realized for the first time that she was, indeed, holding her pocketbook. And apparently, without thinking, she had smacked him with it.

"For no reason, huh?" Dirk said, reaching down and

turning the pentacle medallion first one way, then the other.

"Yeah. No reason at all. And her purse was really hard!" complained her victim. "And heavy! I think there's a brick in it!"

Dirk shook his head. "Naw. I know what she carries in her purse. Usually just some nail polish and a few candy bars."

Savannah hefted her handbag a couple of times, testing the weight.

Yes, as a matter of fact, it *did* seem heavier than usual. It seemed a *lot* heavier.

She opened it and saw the gleam of her 9mm Beretta.

"Oh, yeah," she said. "I forgot I put that in there." She pulled out the weapon.

The guy on the ground gagged when he saw it and held up his hands in front of his face. "Don't!" he yelled. "Don't let her shoot me!" he said to Dirk. "I'm telling you, she's crazy!"

"Naw, she ain't crazy," Dirk said as he pulled a pair of handcuffs from behind his back and rolled his prisoner onto his face in the dirt. "She's just been stressed out lately. She's a bride-to-be. And you know how *they* get. It's a wonder she didn't shoot you."

"I'd forgotten I was packin' or I would've," Savannah told him, replacing her gun in her purse. "Believe you me."

Dirk snapped the cuffs on him, then yanked him to his feet. "Dude, if it weren't for you," he told him, "right now I'd be gettin' a piece o'—" He glanced at Savannah. "I mean . . . enjoying the bliss of my nuptial union."

"What?" The guy looked genuinely confused. "What's that?"

"Something you ain't never gonna know nothin' about." Dirk started down the hill, his detainee in tow.

"Unless you establish a close, meaningful relationship with your prison cellmate . . . which is a strong possibility," Savannah added, following close behind.

In the ever-deepening darkness, they had to choose their footing more carefully as they descended the path.

"Be careful, Savannah," Dirk said over his shoulder. "Watch your step through here."

For a moment, her temper flared. She made a mental note to have a serious sit-down with her groom-to-be. He was going to have to pull back on this overprotective crap, or they'd never make it through their honeymoon. She could already hear the chickie-pooh on the evening news: "Bride bludgeons groom senseless with bouquet! Film at eleven!"

She surveyed the scene below them—the exhausted firefighters, still battling in vain to save the community center, the spectators, some of whom were wondering if it would spread into their neighborhood and consume their homes. No doubt, countless animals were running for their lives, their own habitats destroyed.

She told herself that this guy's crimes had far more devastating consequences than just her postponed ceremony.

But when she thought of her beautiful wedding gown, now nothing but a pile of black ash inside that burning building, she had more than a passing fancy to plant her foot on that skinny little nerd's butt and send him tumbling down the cactus-strewn hill.

"Ruin my wedding day, would ya," she muttered. And instead, gave him a smack on the back of the head.

"Hey! What was that for?" he whined, trying to turn around to look at her while Dirk dragged him along

with even less tender loving kindness than was usually
offered by members of the San Carmelita Police Department.

"Oh, shut up," she said, "you dim-witted, devil-wor-
shippin', fire-startin' pestilence. And keep movin'."

Chapter 2

Having checked their prisoner into the San Carmelita Hotel and Resort, furnished with one steel-framed cot, decorated in neutral shades of gray—bars on windows and doors, no extra charge—Savannah and Dirk were homeward bound.

He drove the battered old Buick through the middle-class streets of her neighborhood, which seemed so serene in comparison to the other side of town, where they had just been.

But Savannah knew the peace and quiet were temporary. Chaos awaited her. Pure, unadulterated bedlam reigned within the walls of her humble home.

Oh, goody. She could hardly wait.

"You dreading going home, sugar?" Dirk said, obviously reading her mind.

"You have no idea," she said with a sigh. "It's been hard enough with the whole motley crew there for the past few days. But now . . . with what's happened today . . . they're gonna be busting at the seams with the sheer drama of it all."

He reached over, took her hand, and gave it a squeeze.

"It was your wedding that got flushed down the toilet. Not your sisters' and brothers'."

"Yeah, but you don't understand. Coming all the way out here to Southern California . . . this is the social high point of their lives."

"Well, what I don't understand—and sure don't approve of—is all eight of them and their kids piling in on you, all in that little house of yours. Don't they have motels in McGill, Georgia? I was only there that once, and I don't recall seeing one."

"A motel? Are you kidding? McGill doesn't even have a Walmart. Don't you remember? Folks there still travel by covered wagon and shop at the general store."

He shot her a quick, questioning look.

She chuckled. "Just kidding. McGill has a hanky-panky motel, like every other town in the country. But seriously, my family members can't afford to pay for a motel. They had to sell Waycross's extra pickup, cash in all the pop bottles they could lay hands on, and pawn Marietta's toy poodle just to come up with the bus fare."

"I still think they oughta rent rooms somewhere and get out of your hair. They know you're still recuperating and—"

"I'm okay now."

"You're a lot better, but you've got a long ways to go before you could say that you're really—"

"Stop it."

"I'm just sayin'—"

"Well, don't."

His face darkened. It was the expression she hated most. Righteous indignation. He frequently donned it when he knew darned well he was wrong.

"So, you're telling me," he said, "that you just want me to keep my concerns about your welfare to myself?"

"That's exactly what I'm telling you."

It's bad enough, she thought, *to have to listen to the voices in my own head telling me how worried they are about me. I don't need yours added to the chorus.*

"Listen," he said, adding that sitting-on-my-high-horse tone of voice that she hated to his I-know-better-than-you scowl, "I'm going to be your husband and that gives me the right to tell you whenever I think you're——"

"Whoa, good buddy! You better get it inside your noggin right now that things aren't going to change that much once you've slipped a wedding band on my finger. I'm still gonna do what I darned well want, dang-near all the time. When it comes to my personal business, you're welcome to state your case about it once, and then I'm gonna expect you to drop it."

He rounded the corner and headed down her street, his frown deepening. "And are you going to abide by the same rules?" he asked. "Like if I decide to get my Harley running again, you're gonna tell me once that you disapprove and then not nag me about it?"

"Get real," she said. "Of course I'm gonna nag you about it, night and day. That's what wives are for. It's part of our job description."

He pulled the Buick over to the curb, several houses away from hers, and turned in his seat to face her. He reached over and ran his fingers through her glossy, dark brown curls, his fingertips lingering at the nape of her neck.

Delicious shivers trickled through her body, reminding her of what they were missing tonight.

Damn that flea-bitten, mangy firebug anyway. She couldn't help hoping he was making lots of friends in that jail cell.

"So, after we get married," Dirk said, his voice low and deep in the darkness of the car, "you say not much is gonna change, huh?"

She grinned and turned her cheek into the palm of his big, warm hand. "Well, you'll have to change the oil on my Mustang and mow my lawn."

"Yes. And . . . ?"

"And I'll cook a lot of good food for you. But then I was doing that already."

"Yes. And . . . ?"

"And of course, we'll be having hot, sweaty, swingin'-from-the-trees, jungle sex three times a day."

Big grin. Big, big grin. Much better than the grumpy scowl any day.

"Now, that's more like it." Gently, he pulled her toward him.

Very gently.

Too gently.

With a sharp pang of sadness, she wondered if he would ever get over that feeling that she was infinitely fragile. Would that terrible fear inside him ever subside?

He kissed her, and the sadness and fear slipped away for several moments.

Not far away. But enough for her to enjoy the warmth of desire and deep affection for this man who had saved her life. A simple man who truly wanted nothing more than to be a good husband to her.

"I love you," he whispered.

"I love you, too," she replied.

And she did. She knew it even in places that still ached, parts of her that would never be the same.

Five gunshot wounds, he had told them when he'd brought her, bleeding and dying, to the hospital. Five.

It was a wonder she was alive, and right then, she was so, so grateful that she was.

"Do you wanna just come on home with me?" he said,

his lips close to her ear, his breath warm on her neck. "Just because the wedding went up in smoke doesn't mean we can't still have a honeymoon night."

"Sure," she said. "I'll come home with you."

"Really?" He looked shocked. Pleased, but shocked.

"You betcha. Right after you go into my house and tell my granny that I'm going to be shackin' up with you tonight, wallerin' in the squalor of fornication and—"

"All right, all right. Never mind." He pulled back and put the car in gear. "Seemed like a good idea at the time."

She laughed, leaned over, and kissed him on the cheek. "We've waited this long. What's another week or so?"

"Agony."

He drove on down the street and pulled into the driveway of her quaint, Spanish-style cottage. Every light in the house appeared to be on, and even with the windows rolled up, she could hear the Reid clan's ruckus.

"You don't have to walk me in," she said. "Just come by and get me as soon as you're out and about tomorrow morning."

"What do you wanna do?"

"Be somewhere else."

"Gotcha."

They kissed once more. Quickly. Granny Reid was probably looking out the window.

"Van," he said, as she started to open the car door. "That hot, sweaty jungle sex . . . are you really expecting that three times a day? Because I'm not sure if I can—"

"Oh, please. Get real. We're both over forty, for heaven's sake."

He looked enormously relieved. "Thank goodness. I don't want you to be disappointed if . . ."

She climbed out of the car, then leaned back in and gave him a smile and a wink. "Don't you worry about a thing, sugar dumplin'. Twice a day'll be plenty."

"Oh, good. You had me worried there."

She closed the car's door and watched as he backed out of the driveway and drove away. Feeling a little heart string tug when he disappeared, she wondered why. Thousands of times had she watched him drive away from her house over the years, and it had been just part of the old routine.

But a few months ago, the routine had been shattered.

They had rebuilt. Now, everything was different. And for the most part, it was pretty darned good, she decided, standing there next to her driveway, still feeling the warmth of his kiss on her lips.

When she started to walk up the path toward her front door, she felt the pain in her thigh, and another twinge in her abdomen, and that half-numb, half-tingling sensation just below her left breast. That was the shot that had nearly killed her.

And there were the nightmares.

So, everything that was new wasn't good. But, all in all, she felt terribly lucky to be alive.

And even though she had planned to be on her honeymoon tonight, it was still delicious to arrive home to this tiny, Spanish-style house with its gleaming white stucco walls, red clay tile roof, and elegant draping of thick, crimson bougainvillea.

Her mood lifted even more when she saw two beloved silhouettes outlined in her living room window. A pair of enormous black cats, Cleopatra and Diamante . . . watching and waiting patiently for Mom to come home. Ah, so sweet.

Then another pair of silhouettes . . . two curly-headed children.

The cats scrambled off their window perches and disappeared from view. One of the children, a boy, caught sight of Savannah. He pressed his face against the glass and stuck out his tongue.

"Jack! Jillian! You get away from that window this minute!" she heard her sister, Vidalia, scream from somewhere inside the house. "And you'd better keep your mitts off those cats! If your Aunt Savannah catches you pesterin' them, she'll have your hides stretched across the barn by mornin'!"

Savannah sighed. What Vidalia lacked in melodious tone, she more than made up for it in sheer ear-splitting volume. Especially when she was yelling at her twins. Either set of them.

As Savannah opened her front door and stepped into her foyer, the seven-year-old, curly-locked duo ran to her, arms outstretched.

"Aunt Savannah!" Jillian cried as she threw her arms around Savannah's waist. "I'm sooo sad that I didn't get to be your flower girl today! I practiced all day in your backyard with your roses. I got good at throwing them."

Okay, so much for entering those Mr. Lincolns in the fair this year, Savannah thought, imagining the devastation of her rose garden.

"I'm so sorry, snookums," Savannah told her. "You're just gonna have to be my flower girl on another day."

"When?"

"Soon. I promise."

Jack grinned up at Savannah, a dab of what looked like grape jelly and peanut butter on the tip of his freckled nose. "Are you really gonna stretch my hide on your barn tomorrow morning?" he said.

"I don't have a barn, but I reckon the garage will do just fine if you keep tormentin' my cats, young man." She ruffled his hair and marveled at its sweet, baby softness.

"I wasn't really hurting them," he said. "Just messin' around with them."

"Good. 'Cause in this family, we're very, very nice to animals."

"And people, too," Jillian added with a solemn nod.

"Eh, depends on who," Savannah muttered under her breath as she walked to the hall closet, removed her weapon from her purse, and secured it in a locked strongbox on the top shelf.

With this many people in the house, some of them children, you couldn't be too careful, she reminded herself.

And the moment she walked across the foyer and into the living room, she was instantly reminded of how many people she had in her dinky house.

As the oldest of nine children, Savannah had never known a moment of privacy during her upbringing. The tiny house in McGill, Georgia, had actually been smaller than this one, and only had one bath, instead of the one and a half that Savannah boasted.

But during those years, it had mostly just been the nine of them and Granny Reid, who filled the home with a nurturing mix of love and discipline. And now, the extended family included six extra children and one spouse, bringing the grand total to fifteen.

Most of whom were now under her roof.

Fortunately, no one was picky. If they had a horizontal surface, they could sleep. And as long as a stream of food and sweet iced tea continued to flow, the gang was a happy lot.

Usually.

"Boy! What a lousy day this was!"

"Honestly, Savannah! Nobody but you would have something like *that* go wrong on their wedding day! I reckon you're cursed or somethin'."

"Did the whole place burn to a crisp? Did they get our bridesmaids' dresses out? I worked overtime at the drugstore to pay for that dress, you know!"

"What are we gonna do now? We come all the way out here for a wedding and *this* happens! What a bite in the ass!"

Savannah drew a deep breath and addressed the complaints one by one. "Macon, there are children present, so please watch your language. A bite in the heinie will suffice. Cordele, I'm sorry about your bridesmaid's dress. I lost my wedding gown, too. We can probably find matching gunny sacks for you girls to wear, and I'll cut some holes in a white garbage bag for me. We'll make do somehow. Marietta, please turn off that dirty television show. What would Granny say if she walked in and caught you gawkin' at all that bare skin? And, Jesup, I may be low on luck in the wedding department, but Dirk and I caught the mangy dog who's been setting all the fires, so the day wasn't a complete train wreck."

She walked over to the windowsill and rescued Cleopatra, whose tail was being tugged by a miniature tyrant with freckles and a mischievous grin. "Vidalia, would you please corral your children? Better yet . . . it's getting late . . . put 'em to bed."

Comfortably positioned on the sofa, her feet on the coffee table, a dish of dessert in her hands, Vidalia nudged her husband, Butch, who was sitting next to her. "Would you stick the younguns in bed, sugar?" she asked him. "I've had a rough day. Gettin' all in a dither over the wedding and then the disappointment of it all going up in flames . . . I'm just plumb tuckered out."

Long-suffering Butch rose, brushed his long hair out of his eyes, adjusted his baggy jeans, and trudged upstairs to do his fatherly duty.

A happy Vidalia sprawled onto his recently vacated spot on the sofa, much to the dismay of Jesup, who needed the extra space while painting her toenails black. "Get over, you big cow," she said, elbowing her sister.

"*You* get over, and watch who you're callin' names, or you'll get your jaws boxed!" Vidalia deliberately jiggled her arm so that Jesup smudged her toe. "You already did your nails this morning. What're you doing them for again, twice in one day?"

"Knock it off, you two," Savannah said as she passed them, heading into the kitchen. "You get that ugly black polish on my couch, you'll both be paying the price in spilt blood."

As she entered her dining area, she breathed a soft sigh of relief. The troublemakers were all in the living room. Only the industrious and easier-going of her siblings ventured into a room, like the kitchen, where actual labor was to be performed.

At the sink stood quiet, gentle Alma, her arms in suds nearly to her elbows. And beside her was good ol' Waycross. Well over six feet tall, broad of shoulders, with bright red hair and pale blue eyes, he looked as manly a man as any son of Georgia. And that wasn't easy, as he applied a flowered dish towel to Savannah's rose-spangled dishes with as much gusto as any housemaid.

Lovely little Alma was a miniature version of Savannah. Not as curvaceous of figure, but the same dark curls and sapphire eyes. She had always been her big sister's favorite, and vice versa.

Savannah walked over to the sink, stood between them, and wrapped an arm around each of their waists. "Ah, my sweeties," she said, giving them a squeeze. "Leave it up to that gang o' rare-do-wells out there to leave you with all the work."

Waycross returned the affectionate squeeze. "Eh, we don't mind if it means getting a bit of peace and quiet for ourselves. I'd rather dry dishes with Alma than listen to all their hens squawking any day of the week and twice on a Sunday."

Savannah glanced around the cluttered kitchen counters and saw the remnants of a grand feast. Giant shrimps—though most of them had been reduced to nothing but tails—littered platters with exotic cheeses, fruit cut into interesting floral shapes, crackers, and miniature bread tidbits. There were still a few deviled eggs left and half a bowl of grits flavored with bits of bacon and browned onions.

She nearly burst into tears when she realized that the pile of crumbs, lemon filling, and white icing on that big silver platter was the earthly remains of her wedding cake. The bride and groom figurines were buried, face-first, in a mound of buttercream frosting.

"I don't suppose," she said with more than a little bitterness, "that the hounds of hell out there thought to leave me even one piece of that when they were chowing down."

"We grabbed two big pieces off the top layer for you and Dirk," Alma said, "and put 'em in that giant green Tupperware bowl of yours. It's in the ice box, down in the crisper. Figured they'd never think to look for it there."

"Smart. It's true that Marietta and Vidalia aren't likely to go foraging for lettuce and carrots where there's wedding reception grub to devour."

Savannah picked up a couple of shrimps and dredged them through the red cocktail sauce before popping them into her mouth. "What the heck," she said, reaching for an herb cheese biscuit with a smoked salmon filling, "this spread cost me a pretty penny. Might as well enjoy it. When we finally do get married, I'll do well to afford popcorn and peanut butter and grape jelly sandwiches."

"I'm sorry," Waycross said as he stacked plates into the cupboard. "I tried to talk some sense into that caterer. Told her what happened with the community center there. But she wouldn't have none of it. Said 'tweren't her fault, and since the stuff was all made up already . . ."

"I know you did your best," Savannah told him. "And it's only fair. Wasn't her fault that nitwit set that fire."

"What nitwit?" Alma brightened considerably. "You know who it was that done it?"

"Better yet. Caught him. Even pistol-whipped him with my purse. Unintentionally, of course."

Waycross grinned. "Of course."

"Hey, he laid hands on me. That ain't smart on any day, let alone on the day my wedding went up in flames."

Alma giggled and winked at Savannah. "My big sister don't take no guff off nobody."

"I seem to remember you beatin' the tar outta that Blalock boy for cutting off one of your braids in the second grade." Savannah turned to her brother. "And there was that time when you left a block of Limburger cheese on Jeb Patterson's manifold after he hit that bloodhound of yours with his pickup truck."

"I swear he hit my dog on purpose, 'cause Deputy

Stafford used it to sniff out Jeb's moonshine stile. The dog always did walk with a limp after that."

"I reckon a streak of vigilante justice just runs in our family," Alma observed.

"Now, now." Savannah shook her head. "We don't go espousing anything all that radical. We just have a strong sense of right and wrong and a serious commitment to making sure things come out right side up in a squabble."

"Yep." Waycross nodded. "Sounds like vigilante justice to me."

"There's a fine line. I'll give you that." Savannah poured herself a glass of sweet tea and nibbled on a piece of pecan-cherry fudge as the other two finished with their chores.

"You must be plum worn out," Alma said. "What with all the stress of the fire—"

"Not to mention the exertion of an old-fashioned Georgia purse whoopin'," Waycross added.

"I'm tuckered, I don't mind tellin' ya." Savannah pulled the tiny plastic bride and groom from the buttercream mess, rinsed them off under the faucet, and dried them with a paper towel. "I think I'm going to call it a night. Has Granny already gone up?" she said as she stuck the mini-couple into her pants pocket.

Alma nodded. "Retired half an hour ago to read her Bible. She's in your bed again, like last night."

"You'd better go stake out a claim on the guest bed," Savannah told her, "before Marietta and Jesup and Cordele hog it again." She gave Waycross a pat on the back. "Sorry about the army cot, big boy."

He shrugged and gave her a big grin. "No problem. It's the price you pay for being male in a family that's mostly womenfolk."

"That and never getting to use the bathroom and

having to change everybody's spark plugs and rotate their tires," Savannah said.

"And rousting 'coons and skunks out from under the back porch," Alma added.

Savannah gave them each a kiss on the cheek and left them to finish their labors of love.

As she passed through the living room, she said to those less labor-inclined, "Wouldn't hurt y'all to go give Waycross and Alma some help in the kitchen. There's a heap of dishes left to do, and everybody had a hand in dirtying them up."

"I did my do," Marietta said, staring at the television. "I set the table."

"I cut the cake," Jesup replied as she scrutinized the silver spiderweb she was painting on her black toenail.

"Butch heated up the biscuits," Vidalia added.

Macon continued to snore.

"Well, as long as everybody contributed." Savannah made her way to the staircase. "I'm going to bed."

"Good luck," Vidalia said. "Both sets of twins are already in it with Gran."

Savannah paused, one foot on the bottom step. "Whatever happened to the Kids-Sleep-on-Pallets rule we had?"

Vidalia chuckled. "Yeah, right. Like kids as smart as mine wouldn't figure out after one night that 'Camping Out' means sleeping on a hard floor."

"How hard could it be with plush carpeting and five quilts under 'em?"

With a shrug, Vidalia shoved another heaping spoonful of ice cream and cake into her mouth. "I don't know. But they pitched a fit about it, so I told Butch to put 'em in your bed with Gran."

"Gee. Thanks."

She trudged on up the stairs, meeting Butch halfway.

"Sorry about the sleeping arrangements, Sis," he said with a sheepish grin. "I know I spoil those young-guns somethin' fierce."

"My sister's the one you're spoilin' rotten, boy," she said as she gave him a slap on the back. "Put your foot down once in a while. It'd make it easier for all of us."

Savannah continued on upstairs and went into the bathroom, which was, surprisingly, empty for a change. Once inside, with the door locked behind her, she stared at the woman in the mirror. A tired woman. A disappointed woman. A blue-eyed, light-complexioned, dark-haired, forty-something woman who was wearing a lot more makeup than she usually did, so carefully applied that morning in the anticipation of wedding photos.

"Happy wedding day, Savannah," she whispered. "Yeah . . . right."

Suddenly, she missed Dirk with a vengeance. She took her cell phone from its belt holster and called him.

He answered after the first ring. "San Carmelita Sheraton. Honeymoon Suite."

"Ugh. Don't remind me."

"Where are you?"

"Hiding out in the bathroom."

"Solitude's a precious thing."

"Precious and rare around here." She reached over and lowered the toilet seats . . . both of them. Darned brothers anyway.

Sitting down, she looked around her bathroom; it looked like Sherman's army had performed its evening ablutions in the tiny room. The hamper overflowed with dirty towels and washcloths. Several glasses from her kitchen were lined up on the sink with copious toothbrushes of all sizes and colors sticking out of them. Her bathtub had several new occupants—a rubber ducky, some bath chalks, a happy-looking tugboat, and an assortment of pumice stones and callus removers. There were at least seven different tubes, vials, and bottles of bath gels.

Bubble baths were serious business among the Reid womenfolk, and there was constant disagreement as to whose soaps and gels smelled best.

"What do you want to do next?" Savannah said, taking the wedding cake figurines from her pocket and turning them over and over in her hand, gazing at them pensively.

"Let's run away to Vegas tonight . . . get hitched, stay a few days, and then come back. Maybe by then they'll all be gone."

Savannah laughed. "Don't tempt me. If it weren't for Granny, that's exactly what I'd do. But she's been waiting so long for you and me to 'come to our senses,' as she calls it, and do this. She'd be heartbroken if she couldn't see the big event with her own eyes."

"So, we'll take Gran with us."

"To Sin City? Get real. She wouldn't let us kids play with the dice in our Monopoly game."

"But how are we going to put another wedding together on the spot like this? Took us months to plan that one."

Savannah grinned, thinking how Dirk had slaved over the extravaganza. "Let's see now," she mused, "you picked out those little hot dog hors d'oeuvres and the ham loaf spread on crackers."

"And the M&M cups. And the matchbooks with our names and the Harley-Davidson logo on them."

"Ah, yes. How could we forget those?"

She heard him sigh. "I guess those burned especially good, along with everything else there at the center."

"I guess we have to be thankful that nobody was

hurt," she heard herself saying in a far more cheerful tone than she felt. "Could've been worse. Everybody we love could have been under that roof."

"True."

"We'll put something else together. Not as fancy . . . 'cause I can't afford it."

"Me either. Those matches weren't cheap, you know. Not even with *my* connections."

Savannah snickered. "Oh, yes, your connection . . . that old Hell's Angel you busted years ago who's your best buddy now."

"Naw . . . you're my best buddy."

Her heart did a little pit-a-pat. "I miss you."

He broke into a passable rendition of Elvis's classic: "Are you lonesome tonight? Do you miss me tonight?" It brought tears to her eyes.

"Yes, I do. I miss you something fierce. Come over for breakfast tomorrow morning, and we'll figure out what's next on the agenda."

"And eat with the hoards? Last time I tried that, I got hit in the head with a flying biscuit."

"That was because you were trying to take the last one."

"Suppose we could find a place to eat alone?"

"Sure. Here in the bathroom. You can sit on the john. I'll lie in the tub."

"Sounds like a plan. Good night, babe."

"Dream a little dream of me."

"Oh, I will." He gave a naughty little chuckle. "You can bet on that."

A few minutes later, she crept to her bedroom door and slowly, quietly opened it. But when she stepped inside, she found everyone wide awake.

Granny Reid was sitting up in bed, her Bible open on her lap, the reading lamp setting her beautiful white hair aglow with its golden light. In bed with her were Jack and Jillian as well as the youngest set of twins, Peter and Wendy, and Savannah's two black cats. All seven were bright-eyed and bushy-tailed.

And for Savannah, with her not-so-bright eyes and totally bush-free tail, their smiling faces and enthusiastic greetings were a mixed bag of blessing and curse.

"Hi, Auntie Savannah," Jillian piped up. "We're having a slumber party with Granny. Come join us!"

"Yeah!" Jack rolled to one side, vacating a one-foot-wide strip of bed for her. "You can lay right here by me."

"Auntie's a little wider than that, sweet cheeks," Savannah said, as she kicked off her slippers and tossed them into the closet. Then she squeezed inside the closet just enough to have a bit of privacy while pulling off her clothes and wriggling into her nightgown.

For a moment, she recalled that this was one of the reasons why she had arrived at the ripe old age of forty-plus without marrying. Having had no solitude at all as a child, she had been loath to give it up as an adult.

Though after this invasion, having only one man in her house would seem like a luxury. Even if that roommate was Dirk.

Savannah emerged from her closet just as Granny was scooping up one adorable seven-year-old in each arm and kissing them soundly on their cheeks. "We already talked about this," she was telling them. "I told you, when Auntie came to bed, you two were going onto the pallets, like we agreed."

"We don't wanna sleep on the floor," Jillian whined. "We wanna sleep with Auntie. She's warm and soft, like a big cushy pillow."

Granny set the oldest twins onto the floor first, then reached for the younger ones.

"No. Bogeyman bite me!" Wendy wailed as she lifted her pudgy baby feet high, avoiding the bedroom floor as if it were studded with red-hot spikes.

"No bogeyman is gonna bite anybody while *I'm* around," Gran said, setting the youngster on the pile of soft quilts and comforters. "If you see hide or hair of him, you just let me know. *I'll* bite *him*."

"On the heinie?" Jack wanted to know.

"I'll bite him on whatever's handy," Granny assured him. "Now you younguns cuddle down there and get quiet. I don't wanna hear nothin' more outta any of y'all, except some serious snoring."

Savannah marveled at how quickly they obeyed and how deliciously, deceptively angelic they looked as they snuggled close together, like a litter of puppies, under the tulip quilt that Gran had made so many years before.

Savannah could recall sleeping under that quilt herself when she had been about that age.

Some of the colors might have faded a bit, and a few of the ribbons had come untied, but it was all the more precious for the passing years. And it warmed her heart to see the next generation cuddling under it as she and her sisters and brothers had before.

"Can the kitties sleep with us?" Jillian asked.

Savannah lifted Diamante and Cleopatra off the bed and deposited them in the middle of the squirming brood. She could tell by the baleful looks the cats gave her that they wouldn't be lingering long. Hopefully, at least until the kiddos were snoozing.

Savannah tweaked one of Jack's curls. "If you mistreat those cats, boy, I'll jerk a knot in your tail. Maybe two knots. You hear?"

He nodded with a devilish grin.

It wasn't a "promise" that she put a lot of stock in.

As Granny turned out the nightstand lamp, Savannah carefully set the tiny wedding cake figurines, side by side, on her dresser, then climbed into bed next to her grandmother. And even though it was lovely to be able to sleep alone after so many years of sharing everything, including her bed, Savannah had to admit it was comforting to be enveloped in a loved one's warmth and their endearing scent.

Gran's had always been the fresh-scrubbed fragrance of bath soap, hand lotion, and rose-scented talcum powder. It was a smell that always made Savannah feel safe and loved.

"Tough day for you, huh, snookums?" Gran said as she reached over and grasped Savannah's hand, giving it a gentle squeeze.

"Not one of my best," Savannah admitted. "But I guess all's well that ends well. We caught the guy and, last I heard, the fire department's got the blaze eighty percent under control. Most importantly, nobody got hurt."

"Maybe nobody got burned, but you were hurt. And your Dirk, too."

Savannah fought back some tears that stung at the backs of her eyes. "I'm trying to be brave here, Gran. You aren't helping."

"There's bravery in honesty, too. A great harm was done to you today, Savannah girl. No point in denying or sugar-coating it."

Savannah allowed the tears to flow. "It's true. I was really looking forward to today. It took Dirk and me a long time to get to this day. I believed that by tonight, it'd all be done with, and we'd be starting our new lives together."

"Not exactly how you'd imagined your wedding day to be, back when you were a little tike, parading around the house with my white pillowcase on your head, holding a handful of dandelions, huh?"

Savannah laughed through her tears at the memory. "That's for sure." She sniffed and wiped the drops off her cheeks before they rolled into her ears. "And that may be what I'll wind up wearing . . . and carrying."

"It was pretty bad timing, that fire roaring over the hill just as we'd got everything delivered to the community center there."

"Thank heavens the caterer hadn't dropped off the food yet."

They both giggled. In the Reid clan, it always came down to the food.

"Did you get any of it?" Savannah asked.

"Of course I did. I might be old, but I haven't slowed down *that* much."

"I think we're gonna have Dirk's little hot dog hors d'oeurves for breakfast."

"With pancakes and maple syrup."

"Or maybe chocolate gravy on top."

Savannah shifted closer to her grandmother and laid her head on her shoulder, as she had so many times as a child. "What am I going to do now, Gran?" she asked her. "Where do we go from here?"

Gran stroked her hair and pressed a kiss to her forehead. "You get a good night's sleep, darlin'. And when you wake tomorrow, you'll know what to do. It'll come to you with the mornin' light."

With those words of comfort and sage advice, Savannah was able to drift off to sleep.

* * *

Two hours later, she woke with a start, her nightgown drenched with a cold night sweat, her breath ragged, her heart pounding.

She sat up in bed and tried to orient herself. Where was she? What had happened?

Slowly, reality dawned on her. She was safe in her own bedroom. She was alive. He hadn't killed her.

She's just had the nightmare. Again.

One more time, as he had many nights since the shooting, the intruder had pointed his gun at her and pulled the trigger, over and over again. In horrifying, helpless, slow motion, she had looked down and watched as the front of the white gown she was wearing exploded in red.

But this time, it wasn't her white nightgown, as it had been in all the previous dreams.

This time, she was wearing her wedding gown when he killed her.

"Savannah? Are you all right, sugar?" Gran asked, shaking her arm. "Honey, I think you had another bad dream."

"Yes, a dream," Savannah said, fighting down the fear that was making her nauseous, fighting the anger that poisoned her spirit.

He's gone, she told herself. *Gone forever. He'll never, never hurt me or anyone again.*

But he hurt her nearly every night. And no matter what she did, she couldn't seem to stop him.

"Post-traumatic stress," the shrink had told her. *"It's to be expected after such a near-death experience. It's perfectly normal."*

Well, it might be normal, she had decided, but knowing that didn't really help much at one or two in the morning when you awoke in terror . . . living the horror over again and again.

"I'm sorry, Gran," she said, trying to take deep breaths. "I didn't mean to wake you."

"Don't be silly. I been woke up plenty of times before. Your sister, Vidalia, used to wake me up every bloomin' time there was a thunderstorm. Remember?"

Savannah nodded and wiped her hand across her forehead, pushing the perspiration-wet hair away from her face. "It's a wonder you got any sleep at all, considering that outta nine kids, at least one of them had a nightmare every night."

"I didn't mind." Granny rubbed her back. "Are you okay?"

Savannah tried to banish the bloody, violent images from her mind. "Sure. I'm all right."

Then Savannah felt a tiny hand slip into hers as a munchkin climbed up onto the bed beside her.

"Did you have a bad dream, Aunt Savannah?" Jillian asked as she snuggled close to her.

Savannah considered denying it. But she believed it was best to tell children the truth as often as possible. Maybe not the whole truth, but . . .

"I did, babycakes," she told her little niece. "But I'm fine now. Don't you worry."

"I'll sleep here beside you," Jillian said, pulling Savannah down and making her lie next to her. "And then you won't have any more bad dreams. You know . . . like you did for me when I had the scary dream about the neighbor's mean old cat. You let me sleep with you and that made me feel all better."

Savannah vaguely remembered the deed that had meant so much to her niece. But the innocence and depth of the child's gratitude touched her heart.

She lay down on her side and pulled the little girl against her chest. The sweetness of the contact seemed to heal the wounds . . . the deepest ones that still ached.

And just as she had wrapped her arm around her niece, from behind her grandmother's arms slipped around her waist, holding her tight.

Surrounded by the warmth and comfort of her family members, old and young alike, Savannah drifted into sleep once again.

And this time it was a deep sleep.

No monsters, no bogeymen, and no armed intruders. Only love and peace.

Chapter 3

When Dirk arrived the next morning, Savannah was in her backyard garden, examining the damage done to her roses by her cherub of a flower girl niece. Fortunately, Jillian had picked as many dandelions as roses, so the benefits balanced the losses.

Savannah was kneeling beside the mangled Mr. Lincoln bush with its velvety crimson blossoms, debating whether to give him a serious pruning or just leave him to heal on his own. She'd just decided to leave it up to the resident rose expert, Granny, when she looked up and saw Dirk emerging from her back door.

He had a slightly desperate look on his face, like a fellow who had just run some sort of gauntlet and barely escaped with his hide intact.

He hurried over to her, pulled her to her feet, and gave her a brief hug and kiss. "Wow," he said, breathlessly, "I don't know how you take that bunch. The kids are bad enough, but the grown-ups! They're the scary ones!"

"Poor baby," she said, grinning up at him. "What did those mean, awful Reids do to you?"

"Vidalia asked me if I'd settle a fight between her and Butch by telling him that he shouldn't bring nudie magazines home, and Marietta asked me if I liked that purple leopard-print miniskirt of hers. I hate it when she asks me stuff like that. I never know what her intentions are."

"Where Mari's intentions are concerned, always expect the worst. You'll probably be right. And stay out of Vi's and Butch's fights."

"I remember you told me they're famous for their battles."

"Let's just say that, with them gone, McGill, Georgia, is enjoying the longest crime-free streak right now that they've had in years. Since those two went out on their first date."

"I'm afraid to ask."

"As you should be." Savannah drew a deep breath. "Supposedly, Butch checked out some other girl's butt there in the Dairy Queen while he was eating his banana split."

"Uh-oh."

"Yeah. What Vidalia did to him is still a popular story, told in hushed whispers around campfires. A cautionary tale to husbands and boyfriends with roving eyes."

"So, I shouldn't offer him a banana split in front of her?"

"Not if you value your life . . . or your gonads."

He winced. "I'll remember that. I'm rather attached to my gonads . . . as they are to me." He brushed a lock of her hair out of her eyes and looked down at her lovingly. "How are you today? Little Jillian told me that you had a bad dream last night."

"I did."

"Same one?"

"With a slight, wedding-theme variation, Jillian and Gran comforted me."

"Yes, Jillian told me that part, too. Said she made you feel better by keeping the bogeyman away."

"I'm sure her motives were totally altruistic and had nothing to do with sleeping in a comfy bed rather than on the floor with her siblings."

"I can't blame her. I'd rather have slept with you last night myself," he said, his voice deep and low.

She looked up into his eyes that were so filled with affection for her . . . along with a healthy helping of lust. And she wondered how she'd resisted him for so long. Now that they'd crossed the line into a romantic relationship, it seemed the most natural thing in the world.

"Are you hungry?" he said. "We could go wrangle some free donuts at Patty Cake. And the guy at the service station on Lester and Main, he's been giving me his leftover coffee if I get there before he throws it out."

Ah, yes . . . now she remembered how she'd resisted him.

"And you were doing so well," she said.

"What?"

"Never mind. Come inside and I'll make you some breakfast."

He hesitated. The haunted, frightened look returned to his eyes. "In there? With . . . all of them? With Vi and Butch? With Marietta's purple miniskirt?"

"I'll protect you."

"But I don't want you cooking for me. You need your rest."

"Stop with that protective crap. And don't worry. I wasn't going to cook. I was going to give you wienie hors d'oeurves and ham spread on crackers with wedding cake for dessert."

His face lit up. "Oh, cool."

"You're hopeless."

Half an hour later, they were sitting at the picnic table in the backyard, Dirk eating reception leftovers and Savannah enjoying a standard-issue eggs-and-bacon breakfast, when two of Savannah's favorite people came around the side of the house.

"Ryan! John!" she exclaimed as she jumped up from her seat and hurried over to them.

They folded her into warm embraces, each taking turns clucking over her, expressing their sympathies about the thwarted wedding ceremony.

"I have to tell you, I'm cursing Fate that something so rotten would happen to *you*, of all people! Talk about unfair!" Ryan Stone said, his handsome face registering the same degree of pain and outrage that most people would feel over mass puppycide.

"My darling, it's beastly!" said John Gibson in his aristocratic, British accent. "And when I heard that all of your wedding apparel and accoutrements were burned as well, I could hardly bear it!"

She reached up and tweaked John's thick silver mustache. "Eh, don't fret. What's done is done. Can't be helped now."

Ryan walked over to the table and shook Dirk's hand. "I'm sorry, man," he said. "We were really looking forward to seeing the two of you tie the knot. It's been a long time coming."

"Tell me about it," Dirk said. He held out a cracker with ham spread. "Want some?"

Ryan's upper lip curled only slightly. "Uh, no, thanks. We've already had breakfast."

"How about some wedding cake?" Dirk asked, pointing to the plateful of crumbs and assorted wads of frosting he'd scraped off the platter.

"No, really," John replied, raking his fingers through his mane of gleaming white hair and adjusting his ivory linen jacket. "We had crumpets with our morning tea. Much the same, you know."

"Oh, okay. Well, sit down." Dirk moved his leather bomber jacket from the bench beside him to make room for John as Ryan sat beside Savannah.

As always, Savannah tried not to think about the fact that Ryan was the most stunningly handsome man who had ever walked the earth. Or at least, in her presence. Out of respect for John, Ryan's partner for many years now, she tried to keep her lascivious thoughts to a minimum. And now that she was herself engaged, it seemed all the more important to censor the graphic nature of her daydreams that starred Ryan.

But it wasn't easy.

Tall, dark, and handsome beyond belief, Ryan stole the hearts of every female—and numerous males, as well—wherever he went. So, Savannah didn't spend a lot of time beating up on herself for her occasional wayward fleshly fantasies.

He sat close enough to her that she could smell his expensive cologne and almost feel the softness of the charcoal cashmere sweater he wore over his crisp white shirt. And cuff links. He wore silver Tiffany cuff links. Engaged or not, she couldn't help thinking how very classy it was to be wearing cuff links at 9:30 in the morning.

She worked at not sighing.

Dirk resumed his breakfast, and between bites, he

said, "I didn't get a chance to thank you guys yesterday for hauling all our guests out of that center, and helping Savannah's family get back home."

"That's right," Savannah added. "They were all in a dither and running around in circles, like chickens who'd just paid a visit to the chopping block. You two really took charge, and we sure appreciate it."

"Glad to do it," Ryan said, "but just sick that it happened."

"That's for sure." John reached across the table and covered Savannah's hand with his. "If you don't mind us asking, love, what are your plans now . . . in light of this catastrophe?"

"Actually, we were just kicking that around," Savannah said, feeling awfully weary for so early in the day. "Needless to say, like most engaged couples, we spent too much already on that wedding. We don't have a lot left to blow on another one so soon afterwards. And to be honest, I'm pretty tuckered out from it all. Planning the wedding, putting it together, the stress of yesterday . . . not to mention all this close familial contact . . ."

"That's what we figured," Ryan said. He and John exchanged a knowing glance. "That's why we thought we'd make you an offer."

"And we'd be so grateful if you'd accept," John added.

"What sort of offer?" Savannah wanted to know.

"Well . . ." Ryan cleared his throat. "Remember, our gift to you was going to be two days at that San Francisco spa to end your honeymoon in style?"

"Ugh. Don't remind me," Savannah said, feeling yet another pang of disappointment. No wedding. No San Francisco honeymoon. No two days of pure decadence at a world-renowned club. No couple's chocolate body-painting indulgence.

"As it happens," John said, "the spa was gracious enough to allow us to cancel that reservation. Which means, we're looking for another wedding present to give you . . . for the next wedding, that is."

"You don't have to give us anything," Dirk told them. "Your friendship's enough and—"

"You don't mean that," Ryan said with a grin.

Dirk laughed. "True. I mean, you don't have to, but if you want to, far be it from me to refuse . . . considering the kind of presents you two give!"

"Well, this one's a bit unusual, but we think you might like it," Ryan continued. "You see, we've been worried about you, Savannah. All the exertion and stress, and you trying to recuperate from your . . . um . . . you trying to heal and . . ."

Dirk raised one eyebrow and said to Savannah, "Now, see there. I'm not the only one who's protective. Why don't you yell at *them* when *they* tell you to take care of yourself?"

"Because *they* don't hover over me, night and day, like a giant, half-starved, Louisiana mosquito." She shot warning looks at Ryan and John. "But if *they* get carried away and get on my nerves, I'll yell at them, too."

"Now, love," John said, "we just want what's best for you. And that's why we thought you might benefit from the services of a top-notch wedding planner."

"A wedding planner?" Savannah shook her head, unable to even conceive of such a luxury.

"We've already spoken to one, an acquaintance of ours, and told her about your sad situation," Ryan explained. "She knows about the fire, about all your family being here from out of state, about your . . . well . . . how you're trying to get your strength back."

"My strength *is* back. Wanna arm wrestle?" Savannah

propped her elbow on the table beside him, fist in the air.

Ryan blinked a couple of times. "You're kidding, right?"

She took her arm down. "Of course, I am. But watch what you say."

She took a long drink of coffee and tried to choose her words carefully so that she would sound appropriately grateful and not bitter. "So, you told this wedding planner gal about my . . . uh . . . run of bad luck, and she took pity on me and is willing to take me on as some sort of charity case?"

Okay. So much for not sounding bitter.

"I'm sorry," she added, staring down into her coffee mug. "That didn't come out right."

For a long time, no one said anything. Then, just as the silence became unbearable, Ryan reached over and put his arm around her shoulders. "Savannah . . . honey," he said, "you're not even close to a 'charity case' of any kind. There's nothing in the world wrong with letting the people who love you lend a helping hand from time to time."

"And this is one of those times, dear," John said. "Madeline Aberson is one of the best at what she does. Her client list is most impressive! She's wonderfully creative and resourceful and has connections that you or I never dreamed of."

Savannah shook her head. "I'm sure that her clients' pocketbooks have a few more shekels than mine. If I can't afford her services myself, I'm sure I can't afford her sort of party."

She looked down at the plateful of crumbs. "Heck, I'm going to have to bake my own cake next time."

"Naw," Dirk said. "I figure I can go into Patty Cake

Bakery and flirt with Patty and get a deal. I'll wear those jeans that she likes so much."

Savannah gave him a baleful look across the table as she briefly contemplated the feasibility of cramming that little groom figurine up his left nostril.

John rolled his eyes and gouged Dirk in the ribs with his elbow. "Anyway, if you could just speak to her, Savannah. She's willing to meet with you and discuss it, and you can make up your mind then."

She thought it over.

She hated the idea, but when she looked into her friends' faces, so hopeful, so eager to please, so determined to help—whether she wanted them to or not—what could she do?

"All right," she said. "I'll talk to her. That's all. No promises."

Ryan and John were all smiles. Even Dirk had a big grin.

"And *you*," she told him, "you stay away from Patty, or I swear, I'll slap you neked and hide your clothes . . . especially those damned jeans that she . . . and I . . . are so fond of!"

Chapter 4

I hate her.

The simple sentence kept running through Savannah's brain as she sat in the stuffy little tearoom of Madeline Aberson's choosing and nibbled a dry, tasteless, pastry thingamajig that Madeline called a Belgian roulade.

At only fifteen dollars each, they were a real steal, and it was Madeline's sincere opinion that Savannah should serve them at her reception.

Oh, yes, Savannah thought. *Macon can put away at least a dozen of these. Twelve times fifteen. For a mere one hundred and eighty dollars, we can fill one Reid sweet tooth. Woohoo! What a bargain!*

"And what will you be wearing?" Madeline was asking her. "A tasteful silk suit, perhaps, or—"

"Some sort of white wedding gown," Savannah said. "Not as nice as the one that burned, obviously, but as close as I can come."

From what Savannah could tell, considering that Madeline was wearing extremely oversized designer sunglasses, the wedding planner looked appalled. "Really? White?"

She glanced quickly up and down Savannah's figure, which was without a doubt considerably more . . . ample . . . than her own teeny-tiny bod. "White isn't exactly . . . slenderizing. And a lot of women who are . . . you know . . . closer to our age, opt for something simpler, more chic, and leave the traditional gowns to the young girls."

Savannah flashed back to a day, two months ago, when she had mentioned to Dirk that she was considering buying a sapphire silk dress for the wedding. His face had fallen, but he had quickly covered his disappointment with a fake smile and said, "Oh . . . okay. Wear whatever you want, sweetheart. It's your day."

"Did you want me to wear a wedding gown?" she'd asked him.

"Well, I guess I thought you would. I sorta pictured you in one, walking toward me, but . . . you know, whatever you want is fine with me."

She had decided then and there to give herself permission to wear the gown that every little girl dreams of. For herself and for her groom. After all, didn't that poor child she had been in McGill, Georgia, who'd practiced walking down the aisle wearing her grandmother's pillowcase on her head, deserve to be a princess for a day?

"No. I choose to wear a wedding gown," Savannah told Madeline Aberson with a smile that didn't light her blue eyes.

"But, as I said—"

"No. I said, no. And that ends that particular topic of conversation. What's next?"

Madeline sat, stone still, for an uncomfortably long time as Savannah watched and tried to determine if she was even breathing. It seemed she'd suffered a shock to her system. Apparently, the word no wasn't uttered frequently in her presence.

At last, she patted her perfect ash-blond pageboy, adjusted her boucle tweed jacket, pursed her perfectly glossed lips, and said, "Oookay. Let's discuss flowers. Beautiful flowers, plenty of them, are the heart and soul of any great occasion. My personal favorites are lilies and cherry blossoms. Although orchids are always elegant."

"I can't afford orchids. My flower budget is gone. I'll be raiding my garden. I have roses and hydrangeas and the lilacs are in bloom. I've always loved lilacs. They're my grandmother's favorite."

"Okay."

Madeline reached into her quilted leather, designer handbag and pulled out a small notebook. She made quite a show of opening it and scanning a list. "Hmmm . . . let's see now. Attire—can't be swayed on that. Flowers— fresh from the backyard garden."

Her lips puckered even tighter, as though she were sucking on an under-ripe persimmon. "Candles . . . I can get you some delicious soy blend candles that are to die for."

"My sister, Alma, has that covered. She made some cute votives with tea lights in them. Tied a bow around them and hot glued a silk flower on each one. They burned in the fire, but we can afford to do them again. They didn't cost much."

"No, I don't suppose they did. Got them at the dollar store, did we?"

"Yes, as a matter of fact, we did."

Madeline glanced down at her list, drew a deep breath, and said, "Photographer?"

"We're passing out those disposable cameras. Get lots of candid shots that way."

"Oh, yes. Amateur photography. That's always the best way to go. How about food?"

"I'm going to bake a big carrot cake with lots of

cream cheese frosting and, as luck would have it, I've got a plastic bride and groom to stick on top."

"That's it?"

"Granny'll make up some of her famous punch, and I can probably get my sisters to put together some mint and nut cups. Maybe we'll crank up some homemade ice cream."

"How quaint."

"Well, we're just quaint sorta folks."

Madeline snapped her notebook closed. "Frankly, Ms. Reid, I'm not sure why you hired me. It appears to me that you've already made up your mind about every aspect of your . . . um . . . affair, so . . . ."

"Actually, Ms. Aberson, I didn't hire you. Two people whom I happen to adore hired you, as a loving gift to me and my groom-to-be. And that's why we're sitting here in this"—she glanced around, taking in the tea-room's gaudy, cherubim murals, bright pink chande-liers, clusters of fake grapes hanging from the ceiling, and overstuffed, diamond-tucked, brocade booths—"lovely establishment, eating this expensive rolled mar-malade."

"Roulade."

"Whatever." Savannah reached for her purse. "And for my friends' sakes, I'm going to tell them that this meeting went beautifully, that you and I love each other, and that your services are going to make all the difference in the world to me. Because, loving me as they do, that's what they'll want to hear."

To Savannah's surprise, Madeline ripped off her sun-glasses and tossed them onto the table. This gave Savan-nah her first real look at the woman's face, and she could instantly see the reason for the oversized shades.

Madeline had, apparently, had some "work done." And it hadn't gone well. One eye seemed unnaturally

wide open while the lid of the other drooped badly.
And no amount of concealer could cover the promi-
nent scars or diminish the heavy bags under the right
eye or the sunken, dark area below the left.

Savannah felt a wave of sympathy for the woman,
who had tried to improve her appearance, only to have
to hide behind sunglasses for the rest of her years.

Madeline couldn't be more than forty-five years old.
How bad could her natural aging have been that she
would feel the need for surgery?

"Savannah," she said, suddenly dropping the whole
hoity-toity persona and looking far more like a simple
woman in need of a job. "I'm sorry we're getting off on
the wrong foot here. I really do want to help you."

Savannah thought it over for a moment, then said,
"Okay. Let's try again."

"I have connections," Madeline said, toying with her
sunglasses. "I know people. I can get things done quickly
when my client needs it. And Ryan and John said that
you need a location right away. Let me arrange that for
you."

"I have to be able to afford it."

"Of course." She opened her notebook again and
flipped through the pages. "How many guests are you
expecting?"

"We had about fifty coming . . . to the other one, that
is. I reckon most of them could make it to the next
one."

"Okay. Maybe I could get you a nice room at the
country club. You could have the ceremony there by
the lake, the reception inside, and you two could spend
the night in the bridal suite. It's lovely since the redeco-
ration."

"Nice, but too expensive."

"How about the Stardust Pavilion down in McGivney Canyon? They have a large reception room and--"

"I tried to book it this morning, and the gal in charge said they had a fierce mudslide after last night's rain. Most of it's got a foot of mud in it."

"Hmm. Natural catastrophes just seem to be following you everywhere."

"Story of my life. I hear tell I was born on a dark and stormy night. Then my high school prom was canceled when a twister took out the gym. And I made sergeant on the police force the day of the Northridge quake."

"Yeah, well, my birthday is April fifteenth. Income tax day. The day the Titanic sank. The day Lincoln died."

"It's a wonder we're still alive and kickin'!"

Savannah laughed, noticing that when Madeline smiled, only one side of her face went up. Apparently, that surgery hadn't gone well either.

And that was a crying shame, because—when she wasn't being a bossy, snooty, pushy, pain in the hind end—she didn't seem like such a bad sort. Savannah almost liked her.

"Thank you for your help, Madeline," she said, taking a sip of her lukewarm tea. "Let's grab something chocolate off that tray over there and get down to the nitty-gritty with this wedding malarkey. Good Lord, girl . . . how do you do this stuff for a living?"

When Savannah came to and went from the police station, she always used the back door, rather than the front. Although the rear entrance was more convenient to the parking lot, the chief of police was known for using the front door for one simple reason: photo opportunities.

He never missed a chance to see his own mug on the evening news.

And since Savannah harbored a deep and enduring dislike for the guy, she avoided running into him when at all possible. Her "divorce" from the San Carmelita Police Department had been anything but amicable. The details had been gory, and both she and the department brass had excellent memories. So, they avoided each other whenever possible.

The other occupants of the building were another story.

From the moment she entered the station house, she was warmly greeted by the rank and file.

"Hey, Savannah! Lookin' good, gal!" Jake Murphy said as he passed her in the hallway.

"So sorry about what happened with the community center," Belinda from CSI told her as she bumped into her outside the ladies' room. "Mike and I had our party clothes on and were ready to leave the house when we heard."

"Yeah, it was a bite in the ass," Savannah said. "But don't put those fancy duds away. We'll be rescheduling soon. Very soon."

"Good," Belinda said. "It's about time you made an honest man outta that guy."

Savannah nodded toward the detectives'-room door. "He in there?"

"Yeah. And in a pretty good mood, considering he's doing paperwork."

Savannah hefted a bag from Dirk's favorite deli. "He'll be even happier in two minutes. That's about how long it takes a pastrami and rye to hit his bloodstream."

She said good-bye to Belinda and found Dirk at his desk, pecking with two fingers on the computer keyboard and squinting at the screen. He must have lost his glasses again.

Otherwise, the room was empty—not an unusual state, considering the budget cuts. The force was half what it had been when she'd joined years ago. And, thanks to the encroachment of Los Angeles and its gang and drug problems, crime had at least doubled.

Not a healthy equation.

His face lit up when he saw her in a way that warmed her heart every time she saw it.

She and Dirk had been close friends from almost the moment they had met, years ago. The cantankerous side of him, the side that put off a lot of people, hadn't bothered her. Dirk's bad moods weren't any worse than anyone else's; he was just more honest and outspoken about them.

She respected that.

And even if he wasn't the most polished guy around, he meant well—most of the time—and that was more important than knowing which fork to use and lifting one's pinky when sipping tea.

And he loved her. He loved her with all his heart and showed it in a hundred practical ways.

Like standing up and moving the chair he'd been sitting in—the comfortable one with the good back support—to the side for her and pulling up a hard, cold, metal chair for himself.

She sat in the one he provided and gave him a kiss on the cheek. Glancing at the screen, she saw he was working on an arrest report.

"Our twitch with the matches?" she asked.

He nodded.

No wonder he was so cheerful.

She offered him the sack with the sandwich inside.

The moment he saw the logo, he snatched it out of her hand. "Oh, whoa! Really? Babe, you rule!"

"I do. It's true."

He dove into the bag, then looked puzzled. "What? Just one? Where's yours?"

"I'm not hungry."

"Since when?"

"Since I filled up on Rolaid pastries and a big piece of chocolate cake there at the tearoom with Madeline."

"Oh, yeah, Ryan's and John's fancy-dandy wedding planner. How'd that go?"

"I had to set her straight about the generous budget I ain't got and that went over like a pregnant pole-vaulter."

He nodded and chewed thoughtfully. "That's what I figured. I think some of those wedding planners charge according to the size of the budget."

Reaching over and wiping a smear of mustard off the side of his mouth, she said, "Then I hope she's given some serious thought as to how to invest the five dollars and twenty-seven cents she's going to earn from this gig."

"She didn't help at all?"

"To give her credit, she tried. She suggested the pavilion. Hadn't heard about the mudslide yet. And the country club, but that's out of the question."

"The one there by the lake?"

"Yeah. She thought we could have the ceremony by the water, then go inside for the party and stay there that night in their bridal suite."

"How much does something like that cost?"

"I don't know, but it's a really nice place. Must be a king's ransom."

He licked the last remaining crumb from his finger,

wiped his hands on the paper napkin, then wadded the sack and wrapper into a ball and tossed it into a nearby waste can.

Then he reached into his back pocket and pulled out his wallet. Taking a debit card from inside, he said, "What the heck, Van. We're only going to do this once. Let's do it right."

He handed it to her.

She stared down at it. "Really?"

"Yes. You deserve it."

"But . . . but . . , I . . . you . . ."

He laughed. "You figure a dude who lives to score a free cup of coffee off somebody ain't the type to plunk down a king's ransom for a wedding?"

"Something like that."

"Well, that's how a guy like me operates. We save a nickel everywhere we can and only spend it on the important stuff."

Savannah felt tears welling up in her eyes for the umpteenth time in the past forty-eight hours. "Thank you, darlin'," she said.

"No problem." He turned his attention back to the computer screen. "By the way . . . the password for that card is Cleo."

"C-L-E-O? As in, my cat?"

"Soon to be *our* cat."

"How long has your password been Cleo?"

He thought for a moment. "How old is she?"

"She and Diamante are ten. I got them when they were six months old."

"Then my password's been C-L-E-O for nine and a half years." He gave her a quick sideways glance and saw that she was staring at him, love in her eyes,

He blushed and glanced around the empty room, as though wary of eavesdroppers. "When I first saw her, I thought she was really cute. Don't make a big deal outta it. Okay?"

She laughed. "Okay. Tough guy. I won't let it get around."

"Good. I got a reputation to maintain, you know. I'll catch a load of crap if it gets out that I like cats."

"It'll just be our little secret . . . that, and the fact that you watched William's and Kate's wedding with me. Twice."

"Shhh!"

Savannah was talking to Madeline on her cell phone as she walked into her house. Jack and Jillian nearly mowed her down as she passed them in the foyer—Jack chasing his sister through the entry and up the stairs.

"That's right," she was telling the wedding planner. "The groom says go ahead with the country club plans. But still, try to watch the outlay, okay? We don't need to go for broke here."

Madeline seemed vastly relieved, though eager to go, as she had another call coming through. She agreed to call once she had spoken to the club and gotten the earliest date possible.

They said good-bye. And as Savannah clicked off her phone and listened to the youngest set of Vidalia's twins wailing in the living room, she thought, *Whatever that date is, it won't be soon enough!*

She entered the room just in time to see Peter hurl his bottle across the room and take out one of her

African violets that had been sitting on a windowsill, minding its own business. Dirt flew everywhere, but as luck would have it, most of it landed on the seat of her favorite chair.

"Dadgummit, Peter!" Vidalia shouted from her position on the sofa, where she was stretched out, a tabloid magazine in one hand, a giant glass of sweet tea in the other. "If you keep throwing that bottle around like that, I'm gonna take it away from you!"

Marietta tore her eyes away from the R-rated movie on TV long enough to weigh in on the matter. "I always said, 'When they're old enough to run around with the nipple clenched between their teeth, the bottle swingin' back and forth, they're too big for it.'"

Savannah walked over to her chair to survey the damage. The violet was a goner. No doubt about that.

Fortunately, she'd been too busy to water it for several days, so the dirt on the chair wasn't too soggy.

For a moment she considered telling her sister to get up off her lazy hind end and clean up her kid's mess. But then she considered how little talent Vidalia had for housework. Vi's idea of cleaning would be wetting a handful of paper towels and grinding the dirt so deeply into the fabric that it would never come out.

As she walked into the kitchen to get a whisk broom and dustpan, Vidalia said, "Sorry about your plant, but it's sorta your own fault that Peter's upset."

Savannah stopped and turned back toward her sister, who had her nose back in her paper. "Oh? Do tell."

"He's bummed out 'cause he didn't get to see Mickey Mouse today."

"Mickey . . . what?"

"We'd promised the kids we'd take them to Disneyland today, once your wedding was over and done with. That's what he's bawlin' about."

As though to prove his mother's point, Peter toddled over to Savannah and gave her shin a hearty kick with his miniature sneaker. Not being that surefooted yet, he wobbled, then fell over, and started to cry again when he hit the carpet.

Savannah reached down and picked him up. When he tried to kick at her again, babbling something like, "Mick . . . ouse . . . wanna go," she gave him a kiss on the forehead.

"I'm sorry, puddin' cat, but you'll still get to see Mickey Mouse. Aunt Savannah promises. She also promises that if you kick her again, she'll swat your bee-hind for you. You don't get to kick people every time you want to.

"Obviously," she muttered under her breath as she set him on the floor, "or your momma'd have my foot-print on her backside right now."

Savannah left the still-squalling, mouse-deprived youngster and walked into the kitchen, where she found her brother Waycross sitting at her table. He was staring, goo-goo eyed, at the pretty blonde across the table from him.

"Tammy!" she said as she crossed the room to greet her friend. "I'm so glad to see you, sugar."

The young woman rose from the table and met her halfway. They hugged each other tightly for a long time. When they finally broke the embrace, Tammy kissed Savannah's cheek.

"I'm glad to see you, too, Savannah," she told her with downcast eyes and a look of sadness tinged with guilt on her lovely face.

Savannah's heart ached to see this same expression, day after day, week after week . . . for three months now. When was it going to end? When would they be like they were before? Ever?

Surely their friendship wouldn't turn out to be something else that bastard had taken from her . . . along with peaceful, nightmare-free nights.

"Can I get you something?" Tammy asked, far too eager to please. "Do you want me to make you a sandwich or get you a drink or—"

"No, honey, I just came in here to get a broom. We had a little accident in the living room. My African violet."

"Oh, no."

"Yep, he's toes up, I'm afraid. In my comfy chair."

Tammy ran to the pantry and snagged the whisk broom and dustpan before Savannah. "Let me do it. I've got it covered. You just sit down and rest."

With that, she hurried from the room.

Savannah sighed as she walked to the refrigerator and poured herself a glass of lemonade.

It seemed that since the shooting, everybody scurried around, doing things to please or help her. People were always rushing here and there to do things they thought she could no longer do for herself. And while it was endearing that they cared so much for her, it made her most uncomfortable.

She firmly believed that scrambling to do everything as quickly as possible was a waste of energy most of the time. And it was a downright sin when it was done to pacify impatient, controlling people.

She didn't want anyone to ever lump her into the category of someone who needed others to scurry around on their behalf. And certainly not someone as precious to her as her longtime friend and assistant, Tammy Hart.

Taking her lemonade to the table, she sat across from Waycross. He had a bowl of pretzels in front of him and was sipping from an ice-frosted bottle of beer.

"Don't let Granny catch you with that," she said. "You'll wind up wearing it instead of drinking it."

He chuckled. "Believe you me, I checked to make sure she was taking her nap before I popped the top. I wouldn't put it past her to take a switch to me."

"Demon rum."

"The only thing worse than rolling dice, playing cards—"

"Or chewin' tobaccy."

"Yep. Gran's death in drinking, gambling, and tobacco products. And fornication. Don't forget that one."

"Like I could forget it? She's been putting the evil eye on me every time I step out the door to go see Dirk now. She's just sure that he and I are already dancing the Grizzly Bear Hump."

Waycross's pale blue eyes probed hers with Reid intensity. "Well," he said, "are you?"

"How very ungentlemanly of you to ask."

"Sorry."

"No."

"No, what?"

"Not that it's any of your business. But, no, we aren't. We haven't. Figured if we've waited this long, might as well hold out and make the honeymoon night special."

He snickered into his beer. "I'd be afraid to roll the dice like that. Aren't you worried that maybe you'll wait and find out you don't like him? You know . . . what he does . . . and stuff."

Unbidden, Savannah's mind replayed some of Dirk's kisses, a few stolen caresses. No, she wasn't worried at all.

"What I'm worried about is having this conversation with my little brother. Change the subject and get that beer drunk before Granny comes downstairs."

Tammy reentered, carrying the broom and the dustpan filled with dirt. "Change what subject?" she asked. "Whatever you don't want Gran to hear . . . that's what I want to hear."

"We're talking about Savannah's and Dirk's sex life," Waycross said.

"Savannah and Dirko have a sex life? Ewwww!"

"We do not!" Savannah reached across the table and slapped his arm so hard that he nearly dropped his beer. "And you better stop spreading those nasty rumors, boy, or I'll be the one taking a switch to you."

Tammy emptied the dustpan in the garbage can, then put it and the broom away.

She hurried to the sink and began searching in the cupboard beneath it.

"What are you looking for?" Savannah asked her.

"That fabric stain removal spray you have. I got most of the dirt off your chair, but there's one little spot that I couldn't . . ."

She'd found the can and was already rushing back into the living room.

Savannah watched her sadly, then realized that Waycross was watching her watch Tammy.

"She feels guilty," he said softly. "She's trying to make it up to you. And she never will."

"She has nothing to feel guilty about," Savannah said, trying to control the sadness that felt like a squeezing tightness in her chest and her throat. "She didn't do anything wrong."

"But you'll never convince her of that."

"I know. Believe me, I know. And it breaks my heart."

Waycross finished his beer and set it on the table. His fingers were tight around the bottle. "Sometimes I wish I could kill that guy all over again."

Savannah closed her eyes, trying to blot out the image of her attacker's face. "Yes," she said. "I hear you. It's a good thing for all of us that we can't."

Chapter 5

Most brides don't hang out in their garages on their wedding days. Savannah was pretty sure of that. But then, most brides didn't have a house bursting with Georgia relatives to contend with either on that glorious, most important day of their lives.

"No, really," Dirk was saying as she cradled the cell phone between her ear and shoulder and applied mascara at the same time, "where are you?"

"I told you," she replied, "I'm sitting in my Mustang, putting on my makeup."

She squinted into the mirror clamped to her sun visor as she tried to de-clump her lashes.

The bright red, '65 Mustang was her baby, her home away from home, considering the many hours she had spent inside it while on stakeouts. And today, it was her refuge.

"You want me to come over there and throw them all out of the bathroom, so that you can get ready like a proper bride?"

"Naw. One of the first things you learn as a youngun with eight siblings is, 'Don't hog the toilet.'"

"How's about I come get you and bring you over here to my place? You can have the bathroom and bedroom all to yourself."

"Believe me, that's tempting. But there's the 'bad luck to see the bride on the wedding day' business. I figure, with the luck we've had, we'd better not tempt fate."

"True. So true."

She tried to screw the mascara wand back onto the tube with one hand and dropped it into her lap.

Looking down at the Midnight Black smear on the front of her tan linen skirt, she fought back the urge to cry. "Don't bawl, gal," she whispered to herself. "You'll have to redo your eyeliner, and you don't have time for that."

"What?" he asked. "Why are you about to cry? Are you having second thoughts about marrying an old coot like me?"

She laughed. "You aren't old."

There was a long pause on the other end. Then he said, "Well . . . I'm waiting for you to tell me I'm not a coot either."

"I prefer to think of you as a curmudgeon."

"Is that better?"

"In my mind, coots and curmudgeons are both cantankerous, but curmudgeons are better-looking."

"Oh. Okay. Thanks, I guess."

She pulled out her blush and began to add some "peaches" to her peaches and cream complexion. Lately, she hadn't gotten enough sleep to manage natural peaches on her own.

"How does your tux fit?" she asked.

"I'm sure it'll be fine."

She stopped in mid-blush. "Does that mean you haven't tried it on yet?"

Silence on the other end.

"Did you even open the bag to make sure they didn't give you the wrong one? For all you know, you could have a red and green checkered jacket with purple pants in there. And I have to tell you, I have my standards. I'm not marrying a guy in a plaid coat."

She could hear him frantically rushing around, then a rustling of plastic and zipper noise.

Then a sigh of relief.

"It's the one you told me to get. Black with a white shirt."

She smiled, gave the phone a smack. "You're so good."

"Just wait till tonight."

Savannah nearly ran headfirst into Madeline in the Hill Haven Country Club's lobby as she barreled through, her arms filled with a mountain of wedding gown that blocked her vision.

"I see you ignored my advice," Madeline said, eyeing the mass of satin and lace that was only half covered by the undersized plastic garment bag provided by the discount wedding apparel store.

"Don't you even start with me, gal," Savannah told her, shifting the weight of the gown to her other arm and nearly dropping it.

"Give me that." Deftly, Madeline took the massive garment out of her hands and held it expertly, the hanger in one hand, supporting the train with the other. "I'm going to go hang this in your bridal suite," she said with an authoritative tone that wasn't to be denied. "Now, where are your other things?"

Savannah turned and looked over her shoulder at the mob that was just entering the lobby. It was a riotous mass of humanity, laughing, shouting, stumbling all over themselves and each other, struggling to be first through the door.

Her family. Ah . . . you had to love 'em.

The women were all in blue dresses. Different styles, different shades—the discount store hadn't stocked that many plus sizes of any one dress—but all blue.

Waycross and Macon wore simple, but elegant, black tuxes, as did little Jack. Even the tiny toddler, Peter, was outfitted in one.

The only calm spot in the ocean of chaos was Granny. Dressed in a simple lavender suit, her best white Sunday-go-to-meetin' hat on her silver hair, she looked the picture of serenity and joy.

Alma was walking beside her, gently holding her arm while carrying an enormous white trash bag in the other.

"These are all yours?" Madeline asked, nodding toward the crowd with a strange combination of sarcasm and awe.

"All. Every last one of them."

Savannah hurried over to Alma and relieved her of the trash bag. She looked inside and did a mental check. Shoe box, makeup kit, stockings, lingerie bag, and a change of clothes for tomorrow.

She was set.

"Thank you, sugar," she said. "I wouldn't have trusted anybody in this crew but you with this bag."

Alma beamed, looking sweet and beautiful in her dress that was the same sapphire blue as her eyes. Unlike the other sisters, she was wearing her hair in her normal, simple to-the-shoulders bob. Everyone else had worked hard all morning, applying a cloud of spray to defy gravity and create the ultimate big-hair do.

"Granny, you're pretty as a patch of pansies and twice

as cheerful," Savannah told her, kissing her cheek that, for once, displayed a faint smudge of rouge.

Gran smiled. "Why shouldn't I be? My Savannah girl's getting married today. Finally!"

"Finally is right."

"Excuse me," Madeline Aberson said, interjecting herself into the conversation, "but the guests are going to start arriving pretty soon, and the bride has to come with me now . . . unless you want her walking down the aisle in a skirt with a big, black smear on the front of it."

Savannah glanced down at the forgotten mascara smudge. Then at Madeline, who was wearing a smug look that made Savannah want to laugh and smack her at the same time.

She kissed Gran and Alma quickly. Waved to the rest of the invading hoard. And followed the wedding planner down a hallway . . . toward the rest of her life.

Half an hour later, Savannah was standing in a reception room at the back of the club, before a pair of French doors that led to a lush, sweeping lawn. And on that stretch of verdure were rows of white chairs filled with the people she loved most.

Tammy sat in the front row with Granny. Behind them was Dr. Jennifer Liu, the county coroner, along with other members of the police department. Sprinklings of neighbors and other friends filled out the rest of the guest list.

Up front, Savannah's baby sister, Atlanta, was playing her guitar and singing. Savannah could hear her clear, strong voice even from so far away, and the sound touched her, filling her with pride and happiness.

But the one Savannah was watching, the only one in her heart and her mind at that moment, was the man who was standing in front of the minister, shifting nervously from one foot to the other, fidgeting in typical Dirk fashion.

Even on his wedding day, good ol' Dirk was still Dirk. And she wouldn't have wanted him any other way.

Next to him stood his best man, Ryan. Lined up beside Ryan were the rest of the groomsmen—John, Waycross, and Macon.

How strange, she thought. That this man would be her best friend for so many years and then, just a subtle shift in their relationship would change everything forever.

"Oh, the power of five little bullets," she whispered.

"What?"

Savannah turned around to see Madeline Aberson standing behind her. "Just talking to myself," she said. "Thinking about the events that led to this day."

"Yes, Ryan and John told me a little about your . . . incident. I'm sorry."

Savannah cleared her throat and lifted her chin. "I'm just fine now."

"Of course you are."

The constant pain below her breast where the bullet had torn through her body reminded Savannah that she was a liar. But she couldn't help thinking that if she kept telling the world how fine she was, eventually she would be.

"This is your day," Madeline said. "Don't let that son of a bitch take this from you, too. Don't invite him to your wedding. Don't let him hitch a ride, even in your own head."

Savannah allowed the woman's words to flow through her, all the way to her heart. Even to the painful spot in her chest. She smiled and said, "You're right. And thank you, for everything you've done."

Madeline shrugged. "Nothing special."

"Hey, I owe you . . . especially for pinning Marietta's gown in the back so that her pink paisley bra straps wouldn't show."

"Eh, no biggie. I always have spare safety pins. I've never been to a wedding yet where they didn't come in handy."

"And giving Macon the right socks."

"I always carry a pair of black dress socks in my bag, too. You'd be surprised how many guys show up in a tux, wearing white crew socks."

"I just want you to know that I appreciate it."

Madeline smiled, and it occurred to Savannah that she looked very tired. In fact, she looked far more exhausted than even Savannah, herself, felt.

"Just a few more minutes now," Madeline told her. "Are you ready to do this?"

"Very ready. My sister has a couple more songs to sing. She's been practicing for weeks. If I don't let her do the whole set, I'll never hear the end of it."

"She's quite good."

"Yes. She is. We're very proud of her."

The cell phone Madeline was holding in her hand rang with a cheerful little tune that sounded familiar to Savannah, but she couldn't place it at the moment.

When Madeline glanced down at the caller ID, a look crossed her face that Savannah could only describe as worried . . . maybe even frightened.

Quickly she switched the phone off, then shoved it into her purse. She glanced out at the congregation on the lawn. "As soon as your sister finishes, you can go. I think we've got your bridesmaids all corralled."

Savannah surveyed the long line of women standing behind her in their assorted blue dresses. The Reid girls. All of them, except Atlanta, the performer.

Marietta, Vidalia, Jesup, Cordele, and Alma. Each so similar to Savannah, yet unique in their own special way.

For the past few days, they had nearly driven her crazy, but she wouldn't have taken a million dollars for any of them.

"You have a nice family," Madeline said, as though reading her mind. "I don't have any sisters. You're lucky."

"Yes, I am."

"I don't think you need me anymore. I'm going to run back to the bridal suite and just tidy it up a bit. I don't want you and your groom going to a messy room afterward."

"I did leave my clothes thrown around and my rollers out," Savannah said.

Madeline gave her a sad, wan smile. "Don't worry. I'll take care of it and get back here in time to see you two kiss. Good luck."

As Savannah watched her walk away, she wondered why she had disliked the woman so much at first. But it didn't matter now. Some people just took some getting used to, and Savannah had decided that Madeline Aberson was one of them. Sorta like grits and liver without bacon and onions.

Two songs later, Savannah turned to her entourage. "Okay," she said, "it's about time. Are we all ready?"

There was a lot of nodding of big hair, some nervous grins.

Savannah did a quick check. "Bouquet, Granny's white Bible, Grandpa Reid's wedding band . . ." She turned to Marietta. "You have the ring, right?"

The blank look on Marietta's face struck terror in her heart.

"Oh, Lord, Mari! You *do* have the ring, don't you? You're the maid of honor, for heaven's sake!"

"I put it in the bag."

"What bag?"

"That big trash bag that had all your junk in it."

"You just tossed Grandpa's ring in there? Are you crazy? I'm supposed to be putting it on Dirk's finger in a couple of minutes!"

"I didn't know what to do with it! I was gonna put it in my bra for safekeeping, but it just felt . . . well . . . wrong . . . to stick our grandpa's ring in my bra with my boob. Yuck!"

"Marietta, I should brain you, you nitwit!"

Alma left her place near the back of the line and ran up to Savannah. "I'll go get it. Where is it?"

But Savannah was already on her way, running out of the room and racing down the hall toward the bridal suite.

She realized she was making quite a spectacle of herself, skirts hiked high, feet flying as she sped down the hall. People stared, open-mouthed, as she pushed past them, shouting, "Excuse me. Pardon me. Oops, sorry about that," as she stepped on a few toes.

Before she was even halfway there, the pain in her chest and her thigh warned her that running around like a maniac was not on the list of activities the doctors had recommended to aid in her recovery.

She forced herself to slow down as she neared the room. So what if she took a few seconds longer? She was the bride. Nobody was going to start the wedding without her.

With a shaking hand, she shoved the security card into the lock and opened the door to the suite.

She half expected to run into Madeline, but the rooms were silent and still as she passed through them, frantically looking for the plastic garbage bag.

"Oh, Lord, please help me find it," she muttered as she searched the sitting room, then the bedroom. "Please . . . they couldn't have thrown it out . . . please . . . please . . . please."

She was just about to burst into tears of full-blown hysteria when she saw the corner of the white bag sticking out of a small garbage can beneath the bathroom sink.

Yanking it out, she pulled it open and searched inside. At first she thought it was empty. But then she saw a small wad of tissue paper in the very bottom.

She pulled it out, unwrapped it, and found the precious band of gold that had adorned her grandfather's ring finger for so many years.

For just a moment, she clasped it gratefully to her heart, then turned to race back to the reception hall.

Then she heard it: the cheerful little song that Madeline Aberson's phone had played before. And in an instant she recognized it as "La Cucaracha." "The Cockroach," an old Mexican folksong.

The music sounded nearby . . . in the direction of the bedroom.

Savannah called out, "Madeline?"

But there was no response as the music got louder and louder.

She glanced toward the door. She really had to get back to the ceremony, and yet . . .

"Madeline?"

She hurried toward the bedroom and noticed, for the first time, that the French doors leading out onto a small, enclosed patio, were open. The music was coming from that direction.

"Madeline, are you there?" she said as she approached the doors. Just beyond them she could see the tiny, private pool . . . just big enough for the bridal couple to do a bit of skinny dipping, if they so desired.

The music stopped just as Savannah reached the doors.

From there, she could see the pool, adorned with floating white lilies and ivory candles. No doubt, thanks to Madeline. Savannah realized this was part of the "tidying up" she had been doing.

So romantic. Such a perfect setting for newlyweds.

At least, it should have been.

But for the body, floating facedown in the middle of it and the red blood staining the crystalline waters.

Chapter 6

Savannah tried to call Dirk, but, as any well-behaved bridegroom would do, he had turned his cell phone off.

Her hand was shaking so badly that she could hardly punch the buttons on her own phone, which she had stashed in her purse in the bridal suite closet.

She tried Tammy, Ryan, and John. But no one answered.

Get a hold on your nerves, gal, she told herself, as she drew some deep breaths. *You're not going to be any good to anybody if you don't get it together.*

She considered just running back the way she'd come to get help, but her knees felt like warm Jell-O, the pain in her chest made her wonder if she might be having a heart attack, and she wasn't sure she'd even make it.

Quickly, she ran down a mental list of her guests and wedding party. Who was the most likely to have their cell phone on . . . wedding or no wedding?

She punched in another number, and sure enough, there was an answer on the second ring.

"Hello?" drawled a syrupy sweet Southern voice.

"Marietta, it's me, Savannah."

"Savannah! Hightail it back here, girl! We're all waiting for you! Did you find Grandpa's ring?"

"Mari, listen to me. Go get Dirk. Right now."

"But . . . ? What are you talking about? Are you gonna . . . ?"

"Hush up. Don't argue with me, girl. Just do what I'm tellin' you. Walk out the door and down there where everybody's at and hand your phone to Dirk. Do it now!"

"Are you chickenin' out? Is that what this is all about? 'Cause if you dragged all of us all the way here from Georgia just so that you could—"

"MARIETTA! Damn your hide, girl! Make tracks! Now!"

"Okay! Sheez, Louise . . . you don't have to scream at me! I'm going! I'm going!"

Suddenly, every bit of strength in Savannah's legs disappeared, and she sank abruptly to the floor, there in the door frame, between the bedroom and the patio.

From where she sat, she could see, all too graphically, the face of the victim, whom she had pulled from the water.

She'd thought there might be a chance, even a slim one, that the body wasn't as dead as it looked.

But it was.

Madeline Aberson had definitely passed from life to death . . . and there would be no coming back.

Savannah wasn't sure what had happened to her. She didn't know if the woman had drowned, or worse. It wasn't clear where all that blood had come from.

The blood that was now all over the front of Savannah's white wedding gown.

For a moment, Savannah had a horrible sense of déjà vu. It was so similar to her recent nightmare.

Through the phone she could hear Marietta say to Dirk, "Yeah, it's her. She wants to talk to you. I don't know, but she's in a fettle about something. You'd better talk to her."

She heard a loud clatter and Marietta curse, "Damnation. I dropped it. Here."

"Savannah? Honey . . . what the hell?" Dirk sounded deeply concerned, and she couldn't blame him. It wasn't exactly standard wedding protocol for the bride to call her waiting groom on the phone. "Are you all right?"

"I'm fine. But you have to leave there and come to the bridal suite."

"What? Why? Aren't we supposed to be—"

"Yes, I'm sorry, sugar, but it ain't happening right now. We've got us a ten-fifty-five right here in our room."

"No way! You've got to be kidding."

"I wish I was. It's Madeline Aberson."

"Aw, man . . . this bites." He turned away from the phone and she heard him say, "No, Gran, she's all right. But there's a problem. A bad problem, back in our suite. I'm gonna have to go see about it. Atlanta, could you sing another song or two?"

She heard Atlanta begin a nice rendition of Paul Stookey's "Wedding Song."

Then Dirk said into the phone, "Is there any way in hell it's an accident or natural causes and not a ten-fifty-five?"

Savannah got up onto her knees and scooted closer to the body. The front showed no signs of trauma, so with considerable effort, she rolled Madeline onto her side and peered at the back.

She saw what appeared to be three small puncture wounds between the shoulder blades.

"No," she said. "It wasn't an accident, unless she fell on something and stabbed herself in the back three times."

"Damn."

"My feelings exactly. You might as well bring Dr. Liu along with you. And send everybody else home."

"Again." He sounded as sad and defeated as she felt.

"Yes, darlin'. Again."

"Who else has been in here?" Dr. Jennifer Liu asked as she looked around the luxury suite that was to have been Savannah and Dirk's private haven, but was now the scene of a gruesome crime.

Savannah stood on the opposite side of the corpse with Dirk, surveying the sad situation. Nothing looked out of the ordinary . . . except the dead woman sprawled on the tile between them.

"To my knowledge, just Madeline and myself," Savannah said. "Maybe a maid. The bed had been turned back since I saw it earlier . . . when I was in here, changing into my gown."

Savannah resisted the urge to look into the room, at the open closet, where her gown lay in a crumpled mess of satin, lace, pool water, and blood.

"And, of course," Dirk said, "the killer."

Dr. Liu stood, rising to well over six feet tall in her fashionable ultra-high pumps. She pulled a red silk scarf from around her neck and tied her long, silky black hair back into a ponytail. Her beautiful face registered the transformation from casual, carefree wedding guest to county coroner at the scene of a homicide.

"Those are stab wounds, no doubt about it," she said, pointing to the three wounds on Madeline Aberson's back. "Those are relatively small lacerations. Not large enough for a knife, even taking into account the skin gaping."

"An ice pick?" Savannah asked.

Dr. Liu nodded. "Something like that."

Dirk pointed to the pool with its water lilies, candles . . . and gruesome red staining. "It doesn't look like there's a whole lot of blood in the water there," he said. "Not enough for a person to have bled out, I wouldn't think."

"Me either," the doctor said. "But with that sort of a penetration wound, the fatal bleeding could be mostly internal. Depending on the trajectory, at least one of those looks like it could have pierced the heart itself. Wouldn't have taken long if that were the case."

"It couldn't have taken very long," Savannah told them as she sat on a nearby patio chair. She was feeling far more weak and shaky than she would have admitted to either of them. "She left me there in the reception room to come back here and tidy up a bit. It wasn't more than about six or seven minutes later when I came up here to get Grandpa Reid's ring."

"That's not much time for the killer to get his business done," Dirk said.

"And she was dead when you got here?" Dr. Liu asked Savannah.

"Absolutely. I pulled her out of the water, flipped her on her back, and did some CPR. But it was obvious to me right away that she was past helping."

"What are the odds she drowned?" Dirk asked. "After all, if she was facedown in the water . . ."

"It's possible," Dr. Liu said. "I'll know once I get her on the table and check the lungs."

Dirk left the patio and walked back inside. Savannah followed him.

She saw a look of sadness cross his face as he glanced over at the bed with its carefully turned-down covers and heart-shaped candies wrapped in pink and blue foil on the pillows, along with a card that read, "Congratulations to the Bride and Groom."

He turned toward her and caught sight of the bloodied gown she had left in the closet when she'd changed back into her street clothes.

She wished she'd thought to close the closet door.

He put his arm around her shoulders and drew her to his side. "Dammit, babe, I can't believe this happened to us again. The fire, the mud slide, and now this? What the hell's goin' on?"

She looked up at him and read her own thought there in his eyes. *Maybe it isn't meant to be.*

But just as quickly, she pushed the dark idea away.

"No," she told him. "Don't go there. We *are* meant to be together. We *are*! We've just got some world-class stink-o wedding luck."

He laughed, but there wasn't a lot of mirth in the sound. He kissed her on the forehead. "Fire, mud, and murder . . . You think?"

As Savannah stood on the sweeping lawn, watching her guests leave the country club premises—once again, not having viewed her nuptial vows—she couldn't help uttering a couple of unladylike curses under her breath.

Under her breath, because her grandmother was six feet away.

Then she added, a bit louder, "You'd think that with a couple dozen of San Carmelita's finest on the property, somebody would've seen something."

Faithful Tammy stood next to her, an equally mournful look on her face. "How about security cameras?"

"Dirk's with the club's manager checking them now," Savannah told her. "It doesn't look promising. Needless to say, they don't have any trained on the bridal suite's balcony. The whole idea for a honeymoon is to have some privacy."

Jesup walked up just in time to hear the end of the conversation. Looking far less mournful than Tammy. In fact, she looked quite chipper as she said, "Maybe it was random . . . some lunatic who's still roaming the halls, looking for another victim."

Savannah tried to overlook her enthusiasm. The kid had been born on Halloween, a fact she took deeply to heart. She couldn't help being a bit of a ghoul.

"Could be," Savannah said. "But I doubt it. Most people who get murdered know who killed 'em and why."

"Huh?" Jesup shook her head and walked away.

Marietta hurried up to them, a distressed look on her face. "Are we gonna eat anything?" she asked. "I mean, just 'cause the wedding's off doesn't mean we have to starve to death, does it?"

"There's cake and ice cream in the reception hall. Go chow down," Savannah said.

The thought of one more wedding cake that wasn't going to be ceremonially cut by herself and her bridegroom was Savannah's undoing.

She could take a dead body showing up in her bridal suite. She could even stand yet another ruined bridal gown.

But another cake . . . it was just too much.

Granny Reid detected the imminent breakdown and reached for her oldest grandchild, drawing her into her arms. "There, there, sugar pie . . . Don't you go tunin' up now! You've been such a brave girl so far and—"

"Shhhh, Granny!" Savannah said, gently pushing her away, "Do *not* be nice to me! Just don't! If you say anything sweet, I'm gonna lose it right here and now, and it won't be a pretty sight, I guarantee you, 'cause I've been saving it up for a long time now."

Granny smiled and nodded. "I understand. Save it up a little bit longer. But sooner or later, you're gonna have to let it out, or you're gonna pop!"

Savannah's cell phone rang. She answered it and heard a depressed Dirk on the other end. "Van, honey," he said, "I hate to even ask you this, but . . . do you want your wedding gown? CSI wants to take it with them, but I'll fight 'em for it, if you want me to."

She sighed. "Let them have it. I had up-close contact with the body, wearing it. They'll have to check it."

"All right," she heard him say, "you can take it."

Savannah closed her burning eyes for a moment and wondered if Zsa Zsa Gabor or Liz Taylor went through that many wedding gowns.

"They're asking me if you're gonna want it back," he said.

She thought about it only for a second, remembered her awful dream, and the real-life nightmare of dragging Madeline Aberson's dead body out of that pool.

"No," she said. "I'd rather just get married in my Minnie Mouse jammies next time."

As she was telling him good-bye, a wave of women in blue flowed toward her, an ocean of discontent wrapped in silk and satin.

"What was that call about?" Marietta demanded to know, hands on her ample hips. "What is it *this* time?"

"Yeah!" Vidalia held a toddler on each hip. Jack and Jillian were hanging on to her skirt. "What's going on?"

"Don't I get to be your flower girl," Jillian whined, "again?"

"It's not my fault!" Jack complained. "Marietta never put the rings on my pillow! I couldn't be the ring bearer if nobody gave me the rings!"

But Atlanta was the most indignant of all. "What the heck were you two doing? You left me standing up there in front of God and everybody, singing my heart out for half an hour! I was running out of songs! It would have served you right if I'd started doing Christmas carols! I'm plum hoarse now."

"Okay!" Granny held up one hand like a traffic cop. "That's enough! You bunch o' hyenas back off right now. Can't you see your sister's got way more problems right now than the likes of you? She needs your support, not your belly achin'."

As they had when they were children, the entire group instantly amended their ways. When Granny spoke, they didn't dare not listen.

Memories of a certain wooden paddle, hung on the back of the kitchen door, lasted a lifetime.

"That's better," Gran said. "The sad fact is: Somebody got themselves kilt in Savannah's fancy bridal suite, and Dirk's in there with the coroner, trying to figure out what happened."

"Yes, he is," Savannah told them, "and I need to get back in there with him. I just came out here to tell everybody how sorry I am that this sort of thing happened . . . again . . . and to tell you to eat whatever you want in there in the reception room and then get along home."

"But when are we gonna eat supper?" Marietta wanted to know. "Are you going to be home in time to cook us something fit to eat? We can't keep ordering pizza like we've been doing. It's expensive."

"Yeah," Atlanta agreed. "And that cake and ice cream's

only gonna last so long in our stomachs, you know. I worked up a powerful appetite with all that singing."

Granny spun Atlanta around and gave her a not so gentle shove toward the clubhouse. Then she turned and did the same to Marietta. "You girls oughta give some thought to something other than your bellies once in a while. You know, gluttony's a sin when carried to extremes."

Fortunately, at that moment, Ryan and John strolled by on their way to the clubhouse. When Marietta caught sight of Ryan, she wasted no time leaving her sisters behind and scurrying after him.

"Look at her following him," Granny remarked, "trailing after him like an orphaned pup."

"Eh, more like a bitch in heat," Savannah muttered under her breath.

"I heard that, Savannah girl." Granny gave her a disapproving look, tinged with a grin.

"And you disagree?"

They both watched as Marietta caught up with Ryan and grabbed him by the arm. She leaned into him, making sure that her voluptuous curves nestled into his side, whether he wanted to be nestled or not. All the while she was tittering like a teenybopper, instead of acting like the forty-plus woman she was.

"Do I disagree?" Gran said. "Only with your choice of words. Not with your evaluation of the situation."

Gran turned to Savannah, reached up, and tucked one of her dark curls back behind her ear, then laid her soft hand along her granddaughter's cheek. "You get back to your man, sweetie pie. Don't pay this bunch no never mind. I'll see to it they behave themselves and get back home all right."

"What about feeding them?"

"That's the least of your troubles. Every blamed one of them knows full well how to stack a bologna sandwich if it comes to that. They're not a bunch of helpless children anymore, even if they do act like it when you and me are around. We spoil that lot, Savannah. Always have."

"Is it okay, then, really, if I work this case with Dirk and leave you all to fend for yourselves?"

"It's more than okay. It's the right thing to do. Take care of your detective business. It's what you do best, and the only thing that'll take your mind off what you lost here today."

As Savannah walked away from her grandmother and crossed the lawn, heading back to the clubhouse and the crime scene, she knew that she wasn't going to be able to hold it together much longer. She felt like she had been through a rough cycle in a giant washing machine.

And she was about to fall apart at the seams.

Chapter 7

When Savannah arrived back at the bridal suite, she found the Crime Scene Investigation squad in full swing.

The once immaculate room now bore a dark coating of fingerprint powder on nearly every surface. And the print technician squatted beside the bedroom door, deftly swirling her long bristled brush over the knob.

Another tech was in the bathroom, swabbing the sink with cotton swabs, which he then stuck into vials and sealed them.

A third was on her hands and knees, shining a bright light onto the carpet. She stopped and used a pair of tweezers to pick up a wad of some sort of fuzz and put it into an envelope.

Dirk stood over her, watching, with a look of dark concern on his face. His hands were thrust deep into the pockets of his tuxedo. His head was down. Savannah could tell, just by his posture, that he was very unhappy.

He did seem to perk up slightly, though, when he saw her.

Leaving the technicians to their work, he walked
over to stand with her in the open doorway leading to
the hall.

"Anything yet?" she asked.

"No. You know how hard it is to process a suite like
this where multiple guests stay. It's as bad as a hotel
room. You never know what you've got or who it's from.
Could be anybody, with all the people that pass through
a place like this."

"Any good prints?"

"A few. But how much you wanna bet most of them
are yours?"

"True. Did Dr. Liu transport the body yet?"

"She just left with it. Said she'd get right on the autopsy."

"Good."

He nodded down the hallway. "How're the troops?"

"Hungry. I told them to eat cake."

"Suppose we'll get some this time?"

"About as much as we got before."

"That's what I was afraid of." He glanced at his
watch. "I called Ryan a minute ago, asked him and John
to come by here."

"Do they know yet?"

"They heard it was a dead body, not who it was."

"Damn. She's . . . er . . . she was . . . a friend of theirs."

"I know."

Savannah heard footsteps behind her, and when she
turned, she saw Ryan and John striding down the hallway toward them, worried looks on their faces.

"I'd rather have a root canal than do this," Dirk said.

"I'll do it," she told him. "It would be better coming
from me."

"What's that?" Ryan asked as they approached. "What's
better coming from you?"

"What's wrong, love?" John said, taking her arm and looking into her eyes with sweet concern.

She'd rather do anything than hurt these dear people. But . . .

"I'm sorry," she said. "You may have heard that we had a . . . fatality . . . here in the hotel. Right here in the bridal suite, as a matter of fact."

"We heard that somebody collapsed in a pool or something like that," Ryan replied.

"It's a little worse than that," Savannah told them. "And I hate to have to tell you . . . it was Madeline."

Both men gasped. "No!" Ryan said.

"Are you certain?" John asked when he'd regained some of his composure.

"Absolutely sure." Savannah replied. "I discovered her myself. I tried to revive her, but she was gone. I'm really sorry."

"That's terrible." Ryan wiped a hand over his face. "What happened? Did she fall? Hit her head?"

"She couldn't have just drowned," John added. "She was a very good swimmer."

When Savannah hesitated, Dirk supplied the answer. "She had wounds on her back," he said gently. "We think it's a homicide."

"Wounds? What kind of wounds?" Ryan wanted to know.

"Dr. Liu isn't certain, but she thinks they might be puncture wounds."

John's face went dark as he registered the news. "Are you telling us that Madeline was stabbed?"

"We're afraid so," Savannah said. "We'll know more once the autopsy's finished. Dr. Liu said she's getting right on it."

Dirk laid a hand on Ryan's shoulder. "Man, I'm so sorry. This is tough, I know."

Ryan nodded, looking dazed. "It is. I mean, Madeline had her flaws. She was far from a perfect person in many ways, but we've known her a long time. It's so hard to believe she's gone. And that way . . ." He shuddered.

"We need to inform the next of kin," Dirk said. "Who would that be? Her husband?"

Ryan shot a quick look at John. "Uh . . . that might be a bit complicated."

"Why?" Savannah wanted to know.

John cleared his throat. "As it happens, she and her husband are going through a divorce right now. A rather nasty one."

"Oh, really?" Savannah could feel her antenna rising out from under the big hairdo that Marietta had given her that morning. "How nasty?"

"Very," Ryan said, "especially the custody aspect. They have a daughter who's ten years old. It's getting, well, ugly."

Savannah glanced at her watch. "Where would her daughter be this time of the afternoon?"

"To my knowledge, Madeline doesn't have any family of her own. I think her mother-in-law watches the little girl when Madeline's working," Ryan said.

"That poor child." John shook his head sadly. "This is going to be dreadful for her. She loves her mother so."

Ryan nodded. "Most people didn't like Madeline. Quite a few even hated her. But say what you will about her . . . she seemed to be a devoted mother."

In deference to her friends' grief, Savannah didn't ask who hated Madeline Aberson or why. Not yet.

But sooner or later, she'd have to make it her business. Because one of those people on that long list apparently hated her enough to kill her.

* * *

Savannah was expecting something a bit more posh than the simple modular home on its tiny lot in a not-so-great part of town. Madeline had dressed so expensively and driven a large, luxury car. Somehow, Savannah had thought her in-laws would be more well-to-do than this.

The property was well tended, with a charming cottage garden in the front, surrounded by a white picket fence. There was even a cedar arbor over the front gate, bearing a cascade of pink, climbing roses.

A small, purple bicycle leaned against a tree that had a swing hanging from one of its largest limbs.

Savannah's heart ached at the thought of making this notification. All notifications were tough, but when there were children involved, it was pure hell.

"This bites," Dirk said as they walked up the sidewalk and under the arbor.

"Yeah. Really." Savannah could feel her jaw tightening, her spine stiffening. "We've gotta close this case . . . for so many reasons."

"Oh, yeah."

They knocked on the door and heard a small dog yipping ferociously inside.

"Watch out," Dirk said. "A barking rat."

"Yeah. Might rip out your Achilles tendon, if you're not careful."

Eventually, the door opened and a grandmother straight out of central casting appeared. Every wave of her silver hair was in place. She wore a simple house dress with pastel pink and lavender flowers. And Savannah was surprised to see that at least one woman in the world, other than Granny Reid, still wore a snowy white apron when cooking.

She even had a small smudge of flour on her chin.

At her feet, a small, fluffy white dog of questionable heritage scampered, still barking with impressive volume and endless enthusiasm. Savannah couldn't help thinking that she could quickly get tired of such an animal. It made her glad she had non-barking cats.

"Yes?" the woman said with a smile, wiping her hands on her apron. "May I help you?"

A little girl with big brown eyes and glittery butterfly barrettes holding back her long, chestnut hair peeked around her grandmother's skirt. She was holding a large chocolate chip cookie in her hand. Some of the chocolate was smeared around her mouth.

The scent of the cookies wafted through the door, smelling like heaven itself.

"Are you Mrs. Geraldine Aberson?" Savannah asked.

"Yes, I'm Gerri Aberson," she replied as she scooped the dog up and tucked it under her left arm. "Shhh, Snowflake. That's enough." It stopped barking immediately and began to lick her cheek.

Dirk pulled his badge from his pocket and showed it to the woman. "I'm Detective Sergeant Dirk Coulter. This is Savannah Reid. We need to talk to you." He glanced down at the child. "Is there anyone else here, other than the two of you?"

The woman looked confused, concerned. "Yes, my husband is here."

"Anyone else?"

"No, just the two of us and our granddaughter here, Elizabeth. Why?"

Dirk glanced down at his shoes, then at the girl. "Are you friendly with either of your neighbors?" he asked.

"Uh, yes. All of them. Why?" the grandmother wanted to know.

"Are any of them home now?"

She nodded and pointed to the house on the right. "Leslie's always at home this time of day."

"Could you send Elizabeth over there for a little while?"

"Yes, I suppose so." She bent down, eye level with the girl. "Lizzie, could you go to Mrs. Connell's house and knock on her door and ask her if you can stay with her for a few minutes?"

"Can I have more cookies when I get back?" the girl asked.

"Sure you can. And a glass of milk, too. Scoot along now."

Dirk and Savannah waited until the child had left the yard before Savannah said, "Could we please come inside? We really need to talk to you about something very important."

"Of course. Please come in." Geraldine took a few steps back into the house and beckoned to them.

They followed her inside to find that the home was as quaint and grandmotherly as the lady who lived there. With its Victorian-style furniture, assorted antique accessories, classic art in gilded frames, and stained glass windows, Savannah imagined that this would be the way Granny Reid would furnish her home . . . if only she could afford to.

"You should call your husband in here, too," Dirk told her.

"Oh. Okay. Just a moment, please." She set the dog on a hand-hooked rug and walked halfway down a hall. "Reuben!" she called out. "Reuben, come here! We've got company!"

"Who is it?" replied a male voice from the depths of the house.

"Leave that birdhouse alone and come out here now."

She walked back to Savannah and Dirk, shaking her head. "He's converted that back bedroom into a workshop, and I can't get him out of there. If he's not working on Lizzie's dollhouse, he's making feeders and houses for the birds."

Savannah thought of her own grandfather, forever tinkering in the shed behind his and Granny's house. And she felt a pang of sorrow for this couple, whose family had been visited by tragedy . . . and they didn't even know it yet.

Stealing a look at Dirk, she saw he was feeling as miserable as she was. Notifications were the pits; no way around it.

An older man came down the hall, looking mildly disgruntled to have been disturbed. With his shoulder-length, curly white hair, big white mustache and goatee, and a red and green plaid, flannel shirt, he reminded her a bit of Santa Claus.

"What's all this about?" he asked as he entered the room. "Who's this?" He nodded toward Dirk and Savannah.

Again Dirk took his badge from his pocket and introduced himself to the man.

Less friendly than his wife, he eyed them both with suspicion. "Well, what can we do for you two?" he asked gruffly.

"Honey, we should at least ask them if they want to sit down," Geraldine told her husband. Then she turned to them. "And would you like some cookies? They're fresh from the oven."

"No, ma'am," Dirk said. "We'd best get to what we came here for." He shot Savannah a helpless look. He often froze at this point in a difficult notification.

"I'm afraid we have some bad news for you," Savannah began.

"Our son, Ethan?" Mr. Aberson asked, his voice cracking.

"No. To the best of our knowledge, your son is all right. It's his wife, Madeline."

Geraldine gasped and sat down abruptly on the footstool of a winged-back chair.

Reuben placed his hand on her shoulder and drew a deep breath. "Well, I guess it's bad, or you wouldn't have come here in person to tell us about her."

"Yes, sir," Savannah said. "Earlier today, there was an incident at a country club where she was working. And I'm sorry to have to tell you that she . . . sustained some injuries. Those at the scene did all they could for her. But her injuries were fatal."

The elderly couple simply stared at them for the longest time. Savannah was beginning to think they hadn't heard her, or perhaps she hadn't been direct enough.

"Madeline has passed away," she said simply.

"She's dead?" Reuben asked.

"Yes," Dirk told him. "I'm sorry."

Geraldine clapped her hands over her face and she started to shake. She stared up at her husband, as though looking to him for direction on how to act.

But he was relatively impassive, considering the news he had just received.

"How did she die?" he asked, as though he were inquiring about the temperature outside.

"We won't know for sure until after the autopsy has been performed," Dirk told him, "but we're pretty sure she was murdered."

Geraldine started to cry softly into her hands. "This is terrible," she said. "Poor little Lizzie."

"Lizzie will be okay." Reuben Aberson tucked his shirt into his pants and adjusted his belt. "She still has her father . . . and us. She'll be fine without that stupid, heartless—"

"Reub! You mustn't speak ill of the dead," his wife said, grabbing his hand and pulling on it hard. "She's . . . well . . . she was . . . our granddaughter's mother."

"No matter what's happened to her, I'm not going to start pretending like she was a good person." Reuben pulled his hand away from his wife's and walked over to the door. "And if that's all you two have to tell us, I'll thank you for the news and tell you good-bye now."

"Mr. Aberson," Savannah said, "even if you weren't on good terms with your son's wife, you would still want her killer brought to justice, wouldn't you?"

He didn't reply, but he didn't open the door.

"Do you know anyone who would want to do her harm?" Dirk asked.

"Everyone who ever knew her," Reuben replied, stone-faced.

"That bad, huh?" Savannah said.

Geraldine rose and walked over to stand beside her husband. "You'll have to forgive us," she said, "even if you think we're hard-hearted. But Madeline and our son were in the middle of an awful divorce. And she's said some terrible things about our boy, horrible lies . . . to try to gain complete custody of our little granddaughter." She drew a deep, shaky breath. "We aren't bad people, but we can't help feeling the way we do about her."

Savannah studied the couple, appraising every word and gesture. They seemed surprised enough at the news, but the coldness in Reuben's eyes was disquieting, to say the least.

And as she tried to decide whether or not she considered him capable of murder, Dirk stepped closer to him, wearing a grim look on his face. It was the look that Dirk often wore when he thought someone might have done something horribly wrong.

"Do you mind telling me where you've been today?" Dirk asked him.

"Right here, building birdhouses," was the even, emotionless reply.

Dirk turned to Geraldine. "And can you vouch for him?"

She nodded vigorously. "He's been right here with me all day. Both of us have. Except for when I went to pick up Lizzie for Madeline. She'd had a sleepover at her little girlfriend's house."

"And what time was that?" Dirk wanted to know.

"About two thirty this afternoon."

"How long were you gone?"

"Well, I stopped and got gas, first, so . . . I guess I was out of the house forty-five minutes, give or take."

"And, Mr. Aberson, you were making birdhouses all day long?" Dirk asked.

"Except for when my wife was gone."

Dirk raised one eyebrow. "Oh?"

"Yes. That's when I called our son. We talked on the phone most of the time."

That would be easy enough to verify, Savannah thought, if they needed to. "Where is your son?" she asked.

"He's in Las Vegas on business," Geraldine replied. "A convention. He's an extremely successful businessman. We're very proud of him."

"I'm sure you are." Savannah gave Geraldine what she hoped was a kind, comforting smile.

It wasn't easy to appear kind and comforting when you were trying to weasel information out of somebody.

"And how long has Ethan been in Las Vegas on business?" Savannah asked.

"He's been there for the past three days," Reuben said, with a tone that suggested he was daring her to contradict him.

"Where is he staying?" Dirk interjected with an equally confrontational tone.

"He always stays at the Victoriana when he's in Las Vegas," Geraldine said. "It's a nice, quiet hotel."

Savannah glanced over at Dirk, who was reaching for his card. It was the end of the interview.

He handed it to Geraldine. "If you think of anything that might help us, would you please give me a ring there at that number?"

She took the card, looked at it, then tucked it into her apron pocket. Reaching down, she scooped up the dog again and held it close to her chest. "We will," she told him. "Good luck with solving your case."

"Thank you," Savannah said.

Silently, she added to herself: *We'll need it. It's hard to figure out who killed someone like Madeline.*

Because, if her father-in-law was right, she was somebody that nearly everybody wanted dead.

Chapter 8

Savannah had always considered herself a "house" kinda gal, rather than an apartment dweller. She couldn't vacuum or dust without loud rock and roll, couldn't cook without blasting her country tunes, and couldn't fully celebrate Christmas without at least once shaking the house on its foundations with the Mormon Tabernacle Choir's rendition of the "Hallelujah Chorus" at top volume.

She wouldn't have been popular in an apartment building.

But if she were ever forced to opt for communal living, her first choice would definitely be Ryan and John's complex.

Perched high, high, high on a hill overlooking San Carmelita and the ocean, the condos were the envy of everyone beneath them . . . which was everyone in town.

Whenever she strolled through the place, which was lushly landscaped with mature tropical plantings, she always felt like she had stepped into a South Pacific paradise. The giant pool with its rock waterfall and swim-up bar was deliciously inviting. And overhead, what seemed like a hundred giant palms danced, their graceful fronds swaying in the sea breeze.

"I always forget how nice this place is," Dirk said to her as they walked the stone pathway leading to the most exclusive of the buildings . . . the one in the far corner with the most privacy and the best ocean view. "Maybe you and me should've gone into the bodyguarding business."

"I tell myself the same thing every time we come over here," she replied. "I wouldn't mind keeping a few spoiled starlets safe if it meant I could pay the mortgage and maintenance fees on a joint like this."

"Probably doesn't hurt that they've got 'former FBI agents' on their resumes."

"Or that they look like movie stars themselves."

Dirk didn't reply to that. Dudes like himself couldn't afford to notice that another guy was attractive.

It was a manly man sorta thing.

When they reached the front door, with its sparkling beveled glass, Dirk rang the bell. It only took a few moments before John answered, wearing a dove gray, brocade smoking jacket and holding a briarwood pipe.

Dirk looked down at his own faded Harley tee-shirt and his frayed jeans. "I see I'm underdressed, as usual."

John laughed and beckoned them inside. "Ryan's pouring us a cognac. Would you like to join us?"

"Naw," Dirk said. "I never sip cognac without my fancy smoking jacket."

Inside the living room—which looked more like the library of a Tudor mansion, with its stone fireplace, heavy leather furniture, and bookshelves filled with antique leather-bound books—Ryan was pouring Remy Martin into a pair of snifters. He was still wearing the tux shirt and slacks he'd worn to their almost-wedding.

Savannah tried not to sigh.

It just wasn't appropriate with your fiancé in tow.

"I'll have one," she said. "I'm not driving, and I've had a rough day."

"No kidding." Ryan placed the Waterford crystal snifter in her hand. "In fact, I think after a day like the one you just had, you deserve a little something to go with that. . . ."

He walked to an intricately carved, drop-front desk, opened it, and took out a box of candy. "Here," he said. "You have to try one of these with it. Dark chocolate pralines from Lyon."

"Lord bless your pea-pickin' heart," she said, taking one of the glistening delicacies from the box. "I've moved up in the world. When I was a kid in McGill, I bought Hershey bars from a guy named Leon. He worked the counter at the little grocery shop by the railroad tracks."

She decided not to mention that, as delicious as Ryan's imported chocolates were, nothing surpassed the flavor or the joy of that rare candy treat she'd had as a girl.

Early in life, Savannah had realized there was one major advantage to being poor: Everything was a treat . . . be it a candy bar, a few hours with no backbreaking chores to do, a precious moment of solitude in a family of nine children, or a loving hug or a kind word from a grandmother, when none had been forthcoming from one's parents.

That hard-earned sense of gratitude had greatly enriched her years. And she would never take anything for granted.

"Have a seat over here, love," John said, ushering her to a soft, leather chair with a great view by the window. "Make yourself comfortable and relax." He turned to Dirk and pointed to the sofa. "You, too, old man."

"Can I get you a beer?" Ryan asked Dirk.

"No, thanks. I'm kinda working." He walked over to the sofa and sat down. For just a second he looked at the marble-topped coffee table, and Savannah knew what he was thinking.

Quickly, she shot him a don't-even-think-about-it scowl.

Since the day she'd met him, Savannah had been trying to teach him the difference between a coffee table and a footstool. Someday he'd learn. Probably about the same time as he got the hang of putting down the toilet seat and chewing potato chips more quietly.

She wasn't exactly holding her breath.

Ryan took a seat on the other end of the sofa from Dirk, while John stepped through the sliding doors, out onto the balcony. He placed his pipe in an antique, brass filigree ashtray.

John had always been conscientious about his tobacco smoke, but especially so since Dirk had given up cigarettes.

Everyone had been forced to endure Dirk's crankiness during his withdrawal stage—which had lasted about two years—and no one wanted to go through it again.

When John returned, he sat in a matching chair next to Savannah's.

"I'm so sorry," he said, "that our 'gift' to you has caused you far more stress than it relieved. Good intentions paving the road to hell and all that dreadful business."

"I'm sorry your friend is dead," Savannah told them. "We informed the in-laws."

"And how did that go?" Ryan wanted to know.

"They seemed surprised, but not particularly grief-stricken," Dirk said. "Pending divorce or not, you'd think they'd hate to hear that their granddaughter's mother had been killed."

"Especially the father-in-law, Reuben," Savannah said. "Have you two ever met him?"

"No." Ryan removed his cuff links and rolled up his sleeves. "We really didn't know Madeline all that well."

"Where did you meet her?" Savannah asked.

"We first made her acquaintance," John said, "at an enormously extravagant party at a Malibu yacht club. It was for Juliana Carvalho . . . to celebrate her Oscar win."

"We were security for the party," Ryan added. "And Madeline was the event coordinator. She did a wonderful job, and we felt free to recommend her after that. Soon afterward, she began to specialize in weddings."

"Did you know her husband?" Dirk asked.

John shook his head. "No. We never met him. But we did see her daughter, Elizabeth, at the singer Paula Berntzen's wedding. Paula didn't have a flower girl of her own, so the little lass stepped in. Did a lovely job, too. You could tell that Madeline positively doted on the child."

"Yeah, we saw the little girl, too, at her grandparents' house," Dirk said. "Cute kid. I feel bad for her."

"I'll feel even worse if we find out her daddy had anything to do with it." Savannah turned to look out at the ocean. She needed to borrow a bit of its tranquility. "His folks said he's at a convention in Vegas on business. Hopefully, for the child's sake, that's true."

Dirk turned to Ryan. "Do you two know anybody else who might have wanted her dead?"

"You might want to talk to her former business partner, Odelle Peters," Ryan told him. "I'm pretty sure that the two of them had a falling out recently. I overheard some gossip about it at the library system's spring fund-raiser."

Dirk took a pen and a pad from his pocket and scribbled down the name. "Do you happen to know where she is?"

"Last I heard, she was working out of her home in Spirit Hills," John said. "A lovely place. She designed and built it herself, I believe. She's quite proud of it."

Savannah took another sip of the exquisite amber liquid and felt its welcome warmth sliding down her throat and nestling deliciously in her belly. From there, the fire spread throughout her body.

And while it was a wonderful sensation, it reminded her of how very tired she was.

She glanced across the room and saw that Dirk was watching her, the omnipresent look of concern on his face.

She hated that look. Although she appreciated the love behind it, she didn't want him or anyone else to worry about her. Mostly, because it caused her to worry about herself. And she could do quite enough of that without anybody's help.

She hadn't been the same since the shooting. She wasn't as strong. She wasn't as stable. She always had the feeling that, at any moment, she could lose her balance and go tumbling . . . she wasn't sure where.

"Are you okay, love?" John asked, leaning toward her, the same anxious expression on his face.

"Eh, of course I am," she said, waving a dismissive hand. "Why does everybody keep asking me that? When haven't I been all right? You're talking to a mighty tough gal here."

"A tough gal who's been through a helluva lot," Ryan said softly.

Abruptly, Savannah stood and placed her half-finished

cognac on the marble coffee table. "I'm fine. And we should get going," she told Dirk. "We've got a murderer to catch, and we aren't going to nab him by sitting here, swigging brandy from Cognac and munching chocolates from Lyon . . . pleasant as that might be."

The three men jumped to their feet in unison.

She gave Ryan and John each a quick kiss on the cheek, then grabbed her purse. "You two take care, hear?" she said as she sailed for the front door, leaving a surprised Dirk in her wake.

As Dirk followed her to the door, Ryan caught him by the arm and whispered, "Take care of her for us, buddy. She's a lot more fragile than she thinks."

"I know," Dirk replied. "I'm trying. Believe me . . . with a gal like that one, it ain't easy."

Once Savannah and Dirk were back in his car, she felt that surge of energy she had experienced in Ryan and John's apartment—born of a high degree of annoyance—quickly waning.

A shot of adrenaline only took you so far.

She had to admit, even if it was only to herself, that she was exhausted.

"What's next?" she asked, glancing at her watch. It was six o'clock, and she'd been going since six in the morning. It had been a long twelve hours. "Are we going to talk to Odelle, the business partner, or check on the hubby to see if he was in Vegas, like he told his parents he was?"

Dirk hesitated before answering, his eyes on the road ahead as they wound their way down the hill toward Main Street. "Odelle can wait until tomorrow," he said. "Once Dr. Liu's done with the autopsy, we'll know just what we've got."

"True. But you don't really expect that with three stab wounds in her back, the doctor's going to rule it an accident, a suicide, or natural causes."

"Of course not, but I like knowing as much as I can about the crime before I go accusing people of committing it."

Savannah nodded and said nothing as she watched the scenery from her passenger's window. The sun was low on the ocean, spreading red and coral splendor on the waves. The peace of it soothed her spirit and gave her a moment to assess her own internal state.

She was angry. And, although sometimes a bit of fury served an investigator well, adding fuel to their determination, this time it was interfering with her thought processes.

Like Dirk, she knew that you needed to find out as much as you could about the crime before interviewing suspects. You never got a second chance to collect those precious first impressions, and you needed to know exactly the right questions to ask.

She was embarrassed that it was so obvious, to them both, that he was behaving more professionally than she was.

"So," she said in her most officious tone, "we can call the Victoriana in Vegas and see if he's checked in there. Find out what convention he's attending, with what company. See if he's made all the meetings, etcetera."

"Yes," Dirk said softly. "That's what I'm going to do. I'll go to the station, make the calls. See if his alibi holds."

"*You'll* go to the station? Just *you*?"

"I think that's best." He reached over and placed his hand on her knee. "I'll take you home, and you can get something to eat and rest. We'll start fresh tomorrow."

"Since when don't we work a case together?"

"It's just some phone calls, babe."

"Don't 'babe' me when we're having a fight."

"Are we having a fight?"

"Yeah . . . kinda."

"Well, *you* might be having a fight, but *I'm* not having a fight. In fact, I'm working hard at *not* having a fight."

Savannah bit her lower lip as tears rushed to her eyes. She could hear the kindness in his voice, but instead of making her feel better, it only made things worse. Now she could add "being mean to your fiancé" to her list of failings, along with "overly jumpy," "unprofessional," and "crying at the tip of a hat."

"I don't know what's wrong with me," she admitted. "I'm just not myself lately."

He gave her knee a squeeze. "You've been through a lot. It hasn't been all that long since . . . you know . . . It takes a while to spring back from something like that. And with all that's happened with our weddings. That would put anybody on edge."

The tears trickled down her cheeks. She quickly brushed them away. "But usually, I take things in stride, you know. Seems like I should be feeling better. A little bit better anyway. But it seems to be getting worse."

Dirk thought for a long time as they drove along in silence. Finally, he said, "Would you consider maybe . . . talking to somebody about it?"

She knew what he meant. And she couldn't pretend that it hadn't occurred to her, once or twice, to seek professional help with this problem. But she couldn't imagine herself sitting in a room with a total stranger, sharing the details of the darkest moment of her life.

"I *am* talking to somebody," she said. "I'm talking to my best friend about it."

He gave her a smile. "You're doing better than you think you are," he told her. "You're a strong woman. You're gonna get through this, babe."

She returned his smile. "Thank you."

"I can call you 'babe' now, right? I mean, the fight's over?"

She laughed and patted his hand that was on her knee. "Yes, my darlin' meadow muffin. The fight's over."

"Hey, aren't meadow muffins piles of cow sh—"

"Shhh."

Chapter 9

Savannah knew something was up the moment she set foot in her house.

It was quiet.

Oh, the television was on. Upstairs, Atlanta was playing her guitar and singing. And there were several low-key conversations going on in the living room and in the kitchen.

But for a Reid house, it was strangely peaceful.

When she walked into the living room, the thought raced through her head, *Somebody's died.* She couldn't think of any other reason why they would be so subdued.

Lined up on the sofa were Marietta, Vidalia, Butch, and Jesup. The children, Cordele, and Macon sat on the floor at their feet. Granny was resting comfortably in Savannah's overstuffed chair.

All eyes were trained on the TV, a show about the joys and attractions of the Disneyland resort.

The room was free of fast food wrappers, empty soda cans, pizza boxes, toys, tabloid reading materials, and discarded clothing.

On the coffee table sat an attractive tray of goodies: crackers and cheeses, all sorts of fresh fruit, and a batch of freshly baked chocolate cupcakes with pecan and coconut frosting. Iced tea glistened in her antique, cobalt blue pitcher.

"I want to go to Pixie Hollow," Jillian said in a voice that was barely above a whisper.

"We will, sugar," Vidalia told her. "Right after we take Jack on the teacups."

"Goody!" Jillian clapped her hands, then quickly settled down. "We're going to Disneyland tomorrow," she told Savannah, her eyes aglow.

"That is . . . if you aren't figuring on trying to get married . . . again," Marietta added with an unmistakable sarcastic tone. It occurred to Savannah that the expression on her face was that of a constipated bloodhound. But she decided to keep that observation to herself.

Blood had been shed in the Reid clan for verbal infractions less incendiary than that.

"That'll be enough lip outta you, Miss Marietta," Granny said as she shot her a warning look. "Seems you've already forgotten that little family discussion we had earlier."

"No, ma'am," Marietta said, donning a hangdog look. The same expression she and the rest of the Reid kids wore any time there was a threat of a trip to the woodshed hanging in the air.

Oh, Savannah thought, *mystery solved. They're all behaving themselves because Gran laid down the law.*

That wasn't quite as nice as self-imposed reform, but she'd take what she could get.

"We figured you'd be home about now," Gran told her. "So, Alma and Waycross are in there scrounging up some dinner for you. This troupe done ate already."

"I helped Aunt Alma put the cupcake papers in the pan," Jillian said proudly.

"And I stirred the frosting for Uncle Waycross!" Jack added with a big, chocolate-enhanced grin.

"Thank you, sweet cheeks." Savannah reached down and tweaked Jillian's pigtail and ruffled Jack's curls as she walked past them on the way to the kitchen. "And thanks to the rest of you, too," she added. "But you don't have to be quiet as church mice. I don't mind you talking to each other, for heaven's sake."

No sooner had the words left her mouth than bedlam erupted.

"You better not expect me to go on that Space Mountain. I'll toss my cookies for sure!" Marietta exclaimed.

"Don't be a spoil sport, Mari!" Vidalia said. "You're always such a drama queen when it comes to stuff like that. You ruin it for the rest of us."

"Yeah, Mar . . . you're such a wuss." Macon gave her a playful smack on the leg with the back of his hand.

"Owww! Dang you, Macon Elmer Reid, that hurt!"

She hit him on the head, and a flurry of slaps ensued.

"Stop it!" Gran shouted. "Or I swear, I'll land on you like a duck on a June bug and whoop the tar outta the bunch of ya!"

Savannah chuckled as she walked into the kitchen, where Alma stood at the stove, making what appeared to be a toasted cheese and bologna sandwich.

Waycross was washing a big, red tomato at the sink. Beside him, on the counter, sat a bowl of sliced cucumbers and onions floating in a bath of vinegar, salt, and sugar water with a sprinkling of fresh dill.

"Boy, howdy," Savannah said, walking over to them and giving each a kiss on the cheek. "That smells plum fit to eat!"

"It ain't nothin' fancy," Alma told her, "but we figured it'd keep the sides of your stomach from stickin' together."

"Yeah. You ain't ate nothin' all day." Waycross cut a thick slice off the tomato. "We can't be havin' that."

He walked over to Alma and handed her the tomato, which she slipped inside the sandwich.

"Set yourself down over there," Alma said, nodding toward the table. "Take a load off. We'll have this ready in a jiffy."

Savannah didn't have to be told twice. Now that she was home, the day was hitting her . . . like a Mack truck with a bed filled with gravel.

While Alma placed the sandwich on a plate and cut it in half, Waycross filled a glass with ice and tea.

"You doin' all right, hon?" he asked Savannah as he slid the drink in front of her, then brought her the bowl with the cucumbers and onions. "You're lookin' a mite peaked."

"I'm fine. Frickin' ducky, in fact," she barked. "Why does everybody keep asking me how I am?"

"Maybe," he replied, "because you're pale around the gills, got big circles under your eyes, and because you keep snapping people's heads off if they even look cross-eyed at you." He gave her a good-natured grin. "I don't know for sure now, but call it a hunch."

When Savannah closed her hand around the frosty glass, she noticed her fingers were shaking. "I'm sorry," she said. "I didn't mean to bite anybody's head off, and especially yours. You two are the jewels in this here family crown, I swear. And I love you both to pieces and back."

Alma set the plate, loaded down with the sandwich and an unhealthy helping of chips, in front of her. She kissed Savannah on the top of her head. "Don't worry about it. Everybody's entitled to get outta sorts every now and again. You're always sweet to the younguns, and the rest of us are old enough to take it in stride."

Waycross pulled out the chair across from her and sat down. "It ain't like you haven't put up with our nonsense for years now. Turnabout's fair play."

Savannah waded into the sandwich. It had been a while since she'd eaten bologna. A lot more bologna eating was done south of the Mason-Dixon Line than in California. And she had adapted, somewhat, to her surroundings.

But it tasted just as good as she remembered. And maybe even a bit more, considering that the major condiment on this particular sandwich was unconditional family love.

"Did you find out anything about that awful killing?" Alma said as she took a chair beside Savannah, her own glass of tea in hand. "If you don't mind talking about it, that is."

"No, I don't mind," Savannah said as she fished some of the cucumbers and onions out of their brine bath. "But we didn't really find out anything important."

"Any idea who might've done it?" Waycross asked.

Savannah shrugged. "When a woman turns up dead under suspicious circumstances, we most always look at the husband or boyfriend."

"Why?" Alma wanted to know.

" 'Cause more times than not, it's him." She took a sip of the tea. "But this time, it looks like he might have a good alibi."

"He could have hired it done," Waycross offered.

"Oh, believe me, that's already crossed our minds. Especially since he's out of town. That's the perfect time to have somebody hit . . . when you're away and can't be blamed for it."

"Have you heard if the two of them gets along okay?" Alma asked.

"Quite the contrary. They're going through a bitter divorce right now. Custody issues and all that ugly business."

Alma shook her head. "That's a bad time for a couple. Seems like that's when women get hurt the most often, when they're leaving some guy who doesn't wanna get left."

Waycross nodded. "You see it time and again, even in a little town like McGill. Never could understand it myself. If some gal don't want me around, I start lookin' elsewhere. There's always another guppy in the fishbowl, and probably a prettier one, too."

"Well, that's because you're a good guy with a strong sense of himself and a lot on the ball," Savannah told him. "You've got better things to do with your time than try to run some gal's life."

"And speaking of pretty women . . ." Waycross grinned self-consciously.

Savannah raised one eyebrow. "We were?"

Alma chuckled. "He didn't work that in there none too gracefully. He's itchin' to turn the conversation to your friend, Tammy. She's all he's been talking about since she dropped by earlier."

"Oh, really?" Savannah turned to Waycross. "Do tell. . . ."

Waycross's cheeks blushed nearly as red as his hair. "Ah, come on, Alma. I just said I think she's nice and—"

"And that she's got shiny blond hair, and a nice shape on her, and that she seems like such a sweet person, and she's so bubbly, and—"

"I said all that?"

"And more."

"Oh, well. She is nice and cute as a speckled pup." He hesitated, then gave her a threatening look. "And,

Alma Jean, if you tell her I said that, I'll get you back for it. I promise you."

"My lips are sealed." Alma closed her mouth and pantomimed locking them shut and throwing away the key.

"Yeah, right." He shook his head. "No female in this family has a mouth that stays shut for long. "Don't you tell her I like her, you hear? I mean it."

Alma rolled her eyes. "I promise I won't say a word. I'll just pass her a note in class."

Waycross gave her a dismissive wave and turned to Savannah, a serious look on his face. "She dropped by to see if we'd heard anything about the case . . . you know . . . that woman getting killed. I could tell she was real curious."

"Tammy's the quintessential sleuth," Savannah said, popping a chip into her mouth. "She's the only person I know who's nearly as nosy as I am. That's why she's so good at it."

"I could tell she really cares about the case and about you," Waycross told her. "She wants to help really bad, but she thinks you don't want her to . . . you know . . . because of what happened before."

Savannah thought of her gentle friend, a person so kind and filled with the sunlight of pure love that she would never cause a living being pain for any reason. She thought of all the sad and remorseful looks Tammy had sent her way for the past three months.

And it broke her heart.

Tammy had nothing in the world to feel sorry about. She had been blameless in the whole miserable mess.

For a hundred days, Savannah had tried to make her understand that. And so far, it was a losing battle.

"Thank you for telling me that," Savannah said. "I'll speak to her."

Savannah stood and started to gather up her empty dishes. But Waycross reached across the table and took them from her.

"We'll do that," he said. "Gran's given strict instructions that everybody vacate the bathroom upstairs and let you have a long, relaxing soak without interruptions. So, you'd best be gettin' to it."

Alma jumped up and rushed to pour something from a small pan on the stove into a large mug. "Here you go, a cup of cocoa to go with that bath."

Waycross rummaged a top shelf until he produced a bottle of Baileys. "And this," he said, adding a generous amount to the mug, "will help it go down smoother."

"Granny'll have our hides if she sees you adding that evil booze to my beverage," Savannah said with a grin as Alma squirted a dollop of whipped cream on top.

"So, don't walk too close to her," Waycross said. "You don't want her getting a whiff of Demon Rum, or it'll be a hickory switch to the butt for both of us."

When Savannah slipped into the rose-scented suds and felt the warm water washing over her body, she couldn't believe her good fortune.

Candlelit bubble baths, fortified with some form of chocolate, were her number-one pleasures in life. And it had been over a week since she'd been able to indulge in one.

She had surely been going through withdrawal.

With a house full of guests who seemed to have bladders the size of thimbles, she had been lucky to squeeze in a two-minute shower. So, this was sheer bliss.

The Victorian claw-foot bathtub was the main reason she had bought the house, all those years ago. She could still remember the first time she'd climbed into it and instantly felt like a fairy princess.

Ah, the sheer indulgence of it all.

With the candlelight flickering on the iridescent bubbles, the flavor of the glorified hot chocolate lingering on her taste buds, and the smell of a rose garden floating in the steam around her, she could truly forget the troubles of the past week.

Almost.

Try as she might, she couldn't banish the disappointment of three wedding attempts that had been thwarted by fire, mud, and murder. If it hadn't been for a psycho arsonist, Mother Nature raining on her parade, and a cold-blooded killer, she'd be a married woman right now. The relatives would all be gone, and with any luck, her new husband would be there in the bathtub with her, smiling from the other end.

It was a big tub. She was sure there'd be room for two . . . if she could convince him that rose-scented bubbles wouldn't have an adverse effect on his manly naughty bits.

She smiled, just thinking about him . . . until she remembered how badly and how often she'd been snapping at him lately. Her nerves were a tad frazzled around the edges, to be sure, but the past week or so hadn't exactly been a cakewalk for him either.

Not to mention the past three months.

The suds were beginning to fade, and through the few that remained, she could see her body . . . all too clearly.

She had always loved her body. Overly voluptuous though it was—according to the weight/height charts. What were a few pounds here and a few there?

This body was uniquely, wonderfully hers, and unlike

any other person or object on earth, it had been with her every single second of her life. In some ways she considered it to be her oldest, dearest, most faithful friend.

Who cared if the fashion models on magazine covers were thinner or younger, a different shape and size? She loved her curves, all of them, and the feminine softness and pretty, creamy color of her skin.

But now . . .

Her skin wasn't perfect anymore. Far from it, in fact.

Above her left breast was an ugly, red puckered scar—a miserable reminder of the bullet that had nearly killed her, the slug that had lodged in her lung and nearly caused her to drown in her own blood.

Below her breast was an even larger, nastier looking one. That one had caused her to lose her spleen.

On her abdomen, an inch to the right of her navel, was a third scar, and a fourth was high on her thigh.

Then, there was the one on her wrist that she saw every day, all day long. An ever-present, constant reminder.

So many souvenirs. Horrid mementos of the day that changed her life and scarred her spirit forever, as well as her body.

Sometimes it felt as though it had happened years ago, maybe even in another lifetime altogether. Then, other times, it felt as though it had happened yesterday or even today.

"It hasn't been that long, Savannah girl," she whispered to herself in a comforting voice that sounded a lot like her grandmother's. "It takes time. Healing doesn't just happen overnight."

She took a washcloth, wetted it, and wrung it out, then placed it over her face.

She knew why. She didn't want to see the scars. Didn't

want to think about how pretty and perfect her skin had been . . . before. Didn't want to think about how it would never be like that again. Those scars might fade over the years, but they would always be there, a reminder of the violence that had been done to her.

And what made her the saddest was that Dirk would never see her body the way it was before. This would be all he would know of her.

Every time they made love, he would see those ugly scars, and she would know he was seeing them, and they would both remember every moment of that terrible night.

Suddenly . . . with a jolt of unwanted self-awareness, she realized she was glad that tonight wasn't their honeymoon night, after all. In her heart of hearts, she was relieved to have one more night's reprieve.

Because, as much as she wanted to be with Dirk and was looking forward to the joys and pleasures their intimacies would bring, she was more afraid than eager.

That made her sad. It made her angry. And it made her hate the man who had ruined her body . . . along with her self-confidence and her sense of security.

She started to cry, holding the washcloth tightly over her face to muffle the sound. Then her sobs grew and grew, until they wracked her body. She could feel the wounds deep inside that hadn't healed yet, aching with each breath.

Would she ever truly heal, or would she be in pain for the rest of her life because of what he had done to her?

The torrent of tears continued with a ferocity that scared her. She had never cried like this before in her life, and she wasn't sure how much worse it was going to get.

It was as though she were another person, observing

herself from a distance and saying, "She's lost it now. The gal's cheese has done slipped off her cracker. She's gone completely off the deep end, and she may not be coming back."

Then, from far away she heard a voice. A soft, sweet, little voice. And a pounding.

Someone was knocking on the bathroom door.

"Auntie Savannah? Auntie Savannah? It's me, Jillian."

With a heroic effort, Savannah sucked in her sobs and forced herself to say, "Yes, Jilly. What is it, sweetie?"

"I need to go potty."

Savannah took a deep breath, steadied herself, and wiped her eyes with the washcloth. "Auntie Savannah's taking a bath, sweet pea. Can you maybe go use the bathroom downstairs?"

"No, I can't. Uncle Macon went in there, and he stayed for a long, long time. Now it smells really, really bad, and I can't stand it. Can I come in there? Pleeeezz?"

"Honey, I—"

"Pretty please with sugar on it?"

With a sigh, Savannah climbed out of her princess tub, blew her nose on some toilet paper, tossed it into the commode, and then wrapped a large, fluffy towel around her dripping body.

Oh, well, she thought, as she walked to the door and greeted her niece, who was standing there, doing a lively pee-pee dance. *Reckon I'll have to pencil in some cryin' time on my calendar for tomorrow or the next day. There's a time and a place for everything. Even a nervous breakdown. And, apparently, this ain't it.*

Chapter 10

On the way to the county morgue the next morning, Savannah was unusually quiet. As Dirk drove along, he kept shooting her anxious sideways glances, which she chose to ignore.

She knew it was just a matter of time until he asked her what was wrong. He always knew when something was "off" with her, big or small. And it was going to be a hassle, because he wasn't one to take "Eh . . . nothing" for an answer.

She just wasn't in the mood to go into a long explanation—or even a short one—about bathtub breakdowns, disfiguring scars, or nieces who were persnickety about where they used the toilet. Some unpleasantries were best left alone and not even thought about, let alone discussed, if at all possible.

This wasn't a concept that Dirk was familiar with. He was not a guy who ever, under any circumstances, suffered in silence. If he was unhappy, uncomfortable, inconvenienced, or had his nose dislocated in any way, he wanted the entire world to know about it . . . and do something about it as quickly as possible.

So, he didn't understand the "just let it go" mentality, and couldn't rest until he had ferreted out any and all causes of what he perceived as her moodiness.

Of course, she could lie to him. She wasn't above it, if the circumstance called for a bit of creative truth-telling. But he was good at sniffing out bull-pucky, too, and fibbing usually caused more problems than it solved.

"What's the matter with you?"

There it was. Right on schedule.

She sighed and turned her face away from him to stare at the passing scenery out the window. "Nothing much. Just had sorta a rough night. That's all. No big deal."

"Hmmm." He reached for the plastic zip bag that he kept on his dash and took out a cinnamon stick. He popped it into his mouth.

It was a strange habit, but it had gotten him through the worst of his Quit Smoking campaign. And she'd found the aroma of cinnamon an improvement over cigarette smoke.

She'd decided it was rather pleasant, kissing a guy who smelled and tasted like apple pie.

"I talked to Granny this morning when I came to pick you up," he said, "and she told me they tried to give you a nice, peaceful evening."

"They did. She laid the law down to the whole clan, and, as usual, they obeyed . . . albeit grudgingly. They kept the racket down and gave me some space. As much space as one can get in a two-bedroom, one-and-a-half-bath house with fifteen people in it."

"So, what was the 'rough' part?"

She winced. Of course, it couldn't be that easy. He had to sniff and dig. She debated whether to try to throw him off the scent entirely, or just redirect him.

"Thinking about the case," she said.

"Oh, yeah?"

She could tell by the suspicious look he shot her way that he didn't buy it. Maybe he would pretend to. One could always hope.

"Okay." He cleared his throat. "Me, too."

"Oh, yeah?"

"Yeah. What did you come up with?"

"Not much."

"Me either."

They had arrived at the morgue. And as he drove the Buick into the parking lot and pulled into his usual spot, he said, "Maybe Dr. Liu'll have something good for us."

"That'd be nice."

He cut the key, reached over, and put his hand under her chin, gently turning her to face him. He gave her a sweet, sad smile. "You know, honey, I'm looking forward to the day when we can put all this . . . this mess . . . behind us. When we can concentrate on what really matters—us, making a home together, our friends and family . . . good things like that."

Once again, tears flooded her eyes. But this time she didn't fight them back. Instead, she leaned over and gave him a quick kiss. "That's what I'm looking forward to, too," she said. "More than you know."

"Then let's get going."

As they entered the front door of the building, Savannah steeled herself for the inevitable run-in with the officer at the front desk. Good ol' Kenny Bates, the bane of her existence . . . or, at least, a major irritation when she had the misfortune of having to enter that unhappy place.

Very few good times were had inside a morgue. And being greeted by and having to deal with Bates wasn't one of them.

Although, things had been easier since she'd bludgeoned him with his own rolled-up porn magazine.

Since that violent attack, he hadn't hit on her any more. Mostly now, when he saw her, he just sulked. No more invitations to come over to his apartment and watch dirty movies. No more comparisons between her and the latest "hubba-hubba" centerfold.

It was an improvement.

When he glanced up and saw that it was the two of them entering the reception area, he looked disgruntled, but he reached up and self-consciously fiddled with his ill-fitting toupee. Then he brushed some nacho cheese chip dust off the front of his ill-fitting uniform. The hairpiece appeared to be too large and the uniform definitely too small to accommodate his overly cushy physique.

But, apparently, he still felt the need to look his best for her, even if she had pummeled him.

And the knowledge made her feel creepy . . . like she needed to go home and take a long, long bath in a strong, pine-scented disinfectant.

He shoved the clipboard with its sign-in sheet across the counter to Dirk, avoiding eye contact with Savannah.

"I haven't seen you two since you got engaged," he said with a pouting, mournful tone in his voice.

"Yeah, well," Savannah replied, "our luck was bound to run out sooner or later."

His face flushed with anger. "It's about time you got married," he said to Dirk. "Everybody knows that you've been slidin' her the salami for years now."

Dirk reached across the counter and grabbed a handful of Kenny's shirt front. Savannah heard fabric ripping. A button flew off and landed on the counter, where it spun a moment or two before rolling off onto the floor.

"As usual, Bates," Dirk said in a low and dangerous tone, "you don't know your ass from a gopher hole. And unless you want to have an unlucky, pissed-off gopher shoved, teeth-first, up yours, you'd better watch what you say about the lady I'm going to marry."

When Kenny didn't answer, Dirk shook him. Hard.

"Got that?"

Kenny's face was going from angry red to oxygen-deprived purple. He managed a feeble nod.

Dirk released him, and for a moment, Savannah thought he was going to faint as he clung to the edge of the counter and fought for breath. Finally, he recovered himself and slunk back to his desk, where he plopped down in his chair and pretended to stare at the half-finished game of solitaire on the computer.

Taking her arm, Dirk led her from the reception area and down the adjacent hallway, toward the autopsy suite at the back of the building.

"Next time that jerk mouths off like that, I'm gonna seriously hurt him," Dirk said.

Savannah giggled. "Worse than I did with that rolled-up magazine?"

He gave her a mortified look. "Hell no! Not *that* bad!" He sniffed and raised his chin a notch. "I couldn't live with myself if I were to unleash that level of violence on my fellow man . . . all the blood, the guts, the gore."

"Didn't bother me none. Went home right afterward and ate a plateful of spaghetti."

"You're a cold, heartless woman."

"And don't you forget it."

They reached the end of the hallway and the set of

double stainless steel doors. One had a sign that read: "Authorized Personnel Only Beyond This Point."

Often, Savannah had thought, when viewing that sign—and the soul-scarring sights beyond that door— that even authorized personnel would be better off not entering.

She had seen many sights inside Dr. Liu's autopsy suite that kept her awake at night and made her reluctant to go into a dark room alone. Even her own bedroom.

It was always horrifying to see, firsthand, what evil one human being could perpetrate upon another one.

But she had also learned many a valuable truth inside those doors. So, the journeys had always been worth giving up a portion of her naiveté with its accompanying sense of false safety.

And she hoped this trip would be equally helpful.

"When you talked to her earlier, did she say she was finished?" Savannah asked before pushing the door open.

"Not done, but just about."

Oh, well, she thought, *so much for the more pleasant alternative of sitting in the doctor's clinical little office and hearing about the autopsy, versus seeing it in person.*

After viewing so many over the years, Savannah had gotten more accustomed to it, but not if it was someone she knew. No amount of self-talk or attempts at attitude adjustment could prepare her for that.

Only yesterday Madeline Aberson had been coaching her on how to hold her wedding bouquet. And now she was gone, her body nothing more than a lifeless specimen on a coroner's table.

It didn't seem possible.

But it was true. It hit her like a hardball between the

eyes when she swung the right door open and stuck her head into the room.

There was Madeline. Lying on the stainless steel, naked except for a small white towel that Dr. Liu used to cover the private body parts of those she worked on.

It struck Savannah, as it always did, how vulnerable a person looked at that moment.

This was the first time she had entered this room since her own shooting. And the unwelcome thought rushed through her mind that, but for the grace of God and an inch this way or that, she would have been stretched out on this very table.

The mental image stopped her in her tracks. She stood there for a long, awkward moment as Dr. Liu, suited in surgical scrubs, stood on the opposite side of the table and waited for them to approach.

Dirk put his hand on Savannah's back, leaned his head down close to hers, and whispered, "You all right, Van?"

She nodded. And with a mighty effort, pulled her mind back to a better place.

If you could call investigating the murder of your wedding planner better, she told herself.

She forced herself to look at the body with impassive, professional determination.

The Y incision that extended length-wise down the center of Madeline Aberson's chest and branched out toward her shoulders had been closed with Dr. Liu's neat stitches. So had the cut from ear to ear and over the crown of the head.

The victim was ready to be bagged and transported to the funeral home.

Savannah was grateful, at least today, that she'd been spared the more graphic part of the examination.

"Did those three stab wounds do it?" Dirk asked the doctor.

She nodded. "One of them in particular. The penetrating trauma led to cardiac tamponade."

"What's cardiac tampon . . . whatever you said," Savannah asked.

"Our hearts are encased in an outer covering, a sac," Dr. Liu explained. "When blood builds up in the space between that sac and the heart muscle—in this case, because of the penetrating wound—it can compress the heart and interfere with its pumping. The victim loses consciousness because of the lack of blood supply to the brain."

"The stab marks themselves looked small," Dirk said. "The actual entrance wounds, that is."

Dr. Liu nodded. "They are. They were made by something very small and narrow. But long . . . eight inches at least."

"So, not a knife?" Savannah asked.

"Definitely not a knife."

"A screwdriver?" Dirk asked.

"No. More narrow than a screwdriver, and not flat on the end. Sharp and pointed."

Savannah thought it over for a moment. "An ice pick?"

Dr. Liu nodded. "Maybe."

"Would an ice pick cause that much bleeding, though," Dirk asked, "enough to press against the heart and interfere with its beating, like you said?"

"It doesn't take that much blood to cause tamponade. One hundred milliliters can do it."

When they both looked momentarily confused, she added, "That's less than half a cup . . . for you nonscientific, nonmetric-speaking types."

"Thanks." Savannah looked the body over, up and

down. "Were there any other signs of trauma . . . of struggle?"

Dr. Liu reached down and picked up one of Madeline's hands. "There are slight abrasions here, on the heels of her hands. As though she may have put her hands out to catch herself when falling forward."

The doctor moved to the lower end of the table and pointed to the body's right shin. "There's scraping there, too, consistent with that on the hands."

"She wouldn't have gotten those by falling inside the hotel room," Savannah said. "It has thick, plush carpeting. And the bathroom has smooth tile."

"The patio tiles are rough," Dirk added. "She might have been stabbed right where you found her, Savannah."

"And shoved right into the water." Savannah shuddered, thinking of how Madeline had looked when she discovered her. "Her feet were out of the water. She could have skinned her shins on the rock edge of the pool when she went in."

"Was she dead before or after she hit the water?" Dirk asked.

As Dr. Liu peeled off her surgical gloves and tossed them into a nearby waste can, she said, "She had some water in her lungs. Not as much as you would expect if the cause of death were simply drowning. I think she died quickly from the stab wounds, and the water was incidental."

"No defensive wounds?" Savannah asked.

"None." Dr. Liu removed her surgical cap and jacket and tossed them into a hamper. She looked tired, as she always did when she had finished an autopsy and ruled it a homicide.

Murder was hard on the spirit. Anyone's. Even a spirit as stalwart as Dr. Jennifer Liu's.

"Your lady there didn't fight back," she said. "Sadly, I don't think she got the chance to."

Savannah sighed and looked at Dirk. He seemed as tired and weighed down as the doctor. "And now it's up to us," she said, "to make sure that her killer doesn't have a fighting chance either."

Chapter 11

Savannah never passed up an opportunity to take a little sight-seeing trip into Spirit Hills, one of her favorite areas of San Carmelita.

Only rich people lived in Spirit Hills. Or, at least, people who had enough money to "put on the dog," as they said in McGill, Georgia.

Savannah had never figured out the logic behind that little Southernism, but as a daughter of Dixie, she knew that it had nothing to do with wearing anything canine related. It had to do with showing the rest of the world that you had more than they did . . . and, therefore, were a far more valuable human being than their sorry ass.

And Savannah would be the first to admit that anybody who could afford to live inside this gated, exclusive community in one of its Tudor mansions, Italian villas, contemporary wonders, or French chateaus, had to be better than she was.

They probably never had mussed-up hair, a bad night's sleep, a pimple on their nose, or a fight with their spouse.

Mundane problems like that simply wouldn't be allowed inside those giant wrought iron gates with the twenty-four-hour guard.

Of course, she knew better, because she had investigated murders and other horrors behind these gates, and knew firsthand that tragedy could strike anywhere. Life had an unpleasant and often unexpected way of circumventing the protective walls that wealth erected . . . twenty-four-hour guard or no.

"Who'd a'thunk that planning shindigs for rich folks would make enough money to buy a place in here?" Dirk said as they drove through the gates and into the community of enormous estates, sprawling grounds, gatehouses, and guest cottages.

"I guess it pays well if you're good enough at it," she replied. "And to hear Ryan and John tell it, Madeline and Odelle were the best at one time."

They turned onto a street called Whispering Wind Song, and Savannah thought how lovely that would look on one's stationery. She noticed that the numbers on the houses were single digits, too. Nice.

Ah, yes, Lady Savannah Reid at number seven Whispering Wind Song in Spirit Hills, she thought. *Has a nice ring to it.*

"I guess the people in here wouldn't be caught dead in my trailer court," Dirk said.

"You never know. There're plenty of rich folks who're down to earth and don't mind mingling with the riffraff."

Dirk chuckled. "That's me all right." Then he gave her an affectionate smile that went right to her heart. "I'm glad you don't mind mingling with the down-and-dirty . . . classy gal that you are."

"Yeah, I don't mind fraternizing with the rabble when it suits me. Adds color to life."

"Some say you're marrying beneath you. Quite a few say that, in fact."

She shrugged. "All women do."

They laughed together.

She reached over and placed her hand on his thigh. She could feel the well-rounded muscle, firm and warm, just beneath the denim, and she had to admit, it made her look forward to their eventual wedding night.

Or, at least, it would . . . if it hadn't been for her misgivings about her own perceived flaws.

She thought of the deep, red scar on her own thigh and moved her hand.

Fortunately, they had arrived at their destination, and she found it a welcome distraction.

Odelle Peters' house was one of the most beautiful examples of an Arts and Crafts home that Savannah had ever seen, either in person or on the pages of any of her architectural design magazines.

It looked like a quaint cottage that had drunk some of Alice's grow-larger potion and become a mansion.

With its brick walls, steep roof, deep porches, pointed window arches, and stained glass windows, it personified "cozy," while its massive proportions said, "grandeur."

"Wow!" Savannah said, taking in the elegant yet casual country garden-style grounds. "I wish Granny could see this! She'd love it! Lilacs and climbing roses and even hollyhocks . . . all her favorites."

"Didn't John say she designed this place herself?"

"Yes, and you can tell it's had a lot of love poured into it."

"Uh-oh," Dirk said.

"What is it?"

"Get a load of that. A 'For Sale' sign there by the mailbox."

She looked where he was pointing and, sure enough, there it was—a sign announcing that the property was listed with Golden Touch Realty.

"Ouch," she said. "That's gotta hurt, no matter what the circumstances."

Dirk pulled into the driveway and cut the key on the Buick. "Well, let's go find out what it's all about."

They walked through the fantasyland yard and up to the arched, Craftsman-style doorway with its colorful stained glass insert and hand-wrought hardware.

Savannah knocked and, only a moment later, they heard rapid, heavy footsteps coming their way.

The door swung open and a woman appeared, looking out of breath and highly annoyed. Her short, straight, salt-and-pepper hair was uncombed, sticking out like the back bristles on an angry dog.

At one time she had applied makeup, but now her mascara was smeared below her eyes and most of her purple eye shadow was gone from above her right eye but not her left.

Her simple cotton shirt and slacks looked like she had slept in them . . . for several nights in a row.

"What the hell!" she yelled at them. "Can't you people read? The sign says, 'Do Not Disturb Occupants!' Call the damned Realtor! Their number's right there, plain as day. Sheezzz!"

Before she could slam the door in their faces, Dirk stuck his foot across the threshold and simultaneously flashed his badge.

Savannah had always been impressed with that move. Dirk was a simple, straightforward sorta guy. It was his only multitasking skill.

"Not so fast!" he told her. "I'm Detective Sergeant Dirk Coulter of the San Carmelita Police Department, and if you're Odelle Peters, you and me's gotta talk."

Odelle froze for a moment and stared at him with blank eyes that were a strange shade of russet brown. It was almost red. And combined with her unusually pale skin, it gave her an unearthly appearance. On Halloween night, with very little costuming, she could pass for some sort of vampire or sorceress.

Jesup would love that look, Savannah thought. *A little fake blood running down her chin, a spiderweb painted on her forehead and she'd be ready for . . . oh . . . grocery shopping or a trip to the dentist to have her fake fangs readjusted.*

Savannah had always thought that some bat—not a stork—had left her sister under a cabbage plant.

"I don't want to talk to you!" Odelle said, kicking at Dirk's foot with the toe of her ballet slipper. "Get your foot out of my door before I slam it on you."

Dirk put his hand up to hold the door open and looked down on her with what Savannah called his "Clint Eastwood stare."

"I wouldn't recommend you do that, ma'am," he told her. "Because that would be assaulting an officer of the law, and getting hit with a charge like that is sure to ruin your day."

"My day is already ruined," Odelle exclaimed, looking like she was about to burst into tears at any moment. "In fact, my whole life is ruined, so you need to go threaten somebody who gives a damn what happens to them."

Savannah stepped forward and held one hand out to the woman. "I'm Savannah Reid," she said, "and it's obvious that you're very upset. I'm sorry about that. But it's important that we talk to you. And you need to understand that my friend here isn't going to leave until we do."

When Odelle didn't shake her offered hand, Savannah dropped it, but she took one step closer into the doorway. "Whatever's going wrong in your life right now . . . we can talk about that. Maybe we can even help. But if you shut the door on us, your problems are only gonna get worse, fast."

Odelle hesitated, obviously thinking things over. Then she raked her fingers through her mussed hair and glanced down at her wrinkled attire.

"I'm not exactly prepared to receive guests," she said, her voice shaky.

"That's okay, 'cause we're not anybody special," Savannah told her. "You don't have to get gussied up or dig out your crystal and china for us. Invite us in and give us some water in a Dixie cup, and we'll be happy."

"Yes, I've already heard about Madeline," Odelle said, as they sat with her in her gracious living room and watched the flames flicker in the massive stone fireplace.

"How did you find out?" Dirk wanted to know.

"Geraldine Aberson called me." Odelle fiddled with a crystal tumbler that contained the second shot of scotch that she'd consumed in less than five minutes.

The first she had bolted.

"You and Geraldine are friends?" Savannah asked, taking a sip of water from her own cut glass highball.

"I've known her and Reuben for years, through Madeline. I wouldn't say we're exactly friends."

"How long were you and Madeline business partners?" Dirk asked.

"Over twenty years. We started fresh out of college. We both knew exactly what we wanted to do, and we were good at it. You wouldn't believe some of the events we coordinated together in our heyday." Odelle looked sad as she stared down into her drink. "But that was before . . ."

"Before . . . ?" Savannah prompted.

The sad expression evaporated, replaced with one of

pure, raw anger. "Before Madeline went nuts and threw everything away for a guy who wasn't worth the bullet it would take to shoot him."

Savannah glanced at Dirk and saw his eyebrows go up a fraction of a notch. "And who was that . . . ? Ethan?"

"No. Ethan's a decent guy. And he deserved a lot better treatment than he got from his so-called loving and devoted wife."

"So, who's the dude?" Dirk asked.

"Arlo Di Napoli. He was Ethan's best friend—or so Ethan thought until he found Arlo and Madeline in his bed together. End of friendship, end of marriage."

"Yes, I can imagine so." Savannah jotted that one down in her mental notebook for much future consideration. "When did this happen?"

"About two years back."

"That long ago?" Dirk said.

"Oh, Ethan kicked her out that day and filed for a legal separation. But they were still haggling over the terms of the divorce. Mostly over Elizabeth. They both wanted primary custody of her."

"Sounds like a barrel of laughs," Savannah said dryly.

"Oh, you've no idea. And it's lovely for me." Odelle tossed back the rest of her scotch. "Madeline just stopped even trying where our business was concerned. She didn't give a hoot about anything but Arlo anymore. Showed up late or not at all for our bookings. Wasn't worth anything when she *did* appear. I've lost a fortune because of her. And now I'm financially destitute."

She glanced around the beautiful room with its handcrafted furniture that was an opulent mix of Mission and Art Deco with the occasional Asian accent.

Even Savannah's untrained eye knew the value of the intricate red oak woodwork and thick, silk, embroidered coverings.

"And now I'm going to lose all of this," she said, waving a hand. "My home. Everything I own. Because Madeline was too stupid to know that she had a good life—a loving husband, a thriving business, a beautiful little girl. And she threw it all away for a piece of trash like Arlo Di Napoli, because he was a bit more exciting in bed. Big deal."

She shook her head in disgust. Savannah could tell by the glassy look in her eyes that the booze was hitting her. She wondered how much Odelle was drinking these days.

"And the funny part is," Odelle continued, slurring a word here and there, "Arlo broke up with her! She gave him an ultimatum . . . 'Leave your wife or I'll tell her about us.' He told Madeline to go to hell, that she'd been nothing but an easy piece for him. So, what did stupid Maddy do? She made a beeline for his wife and told her all the sordid details. She thought that once Francie dumped Arlo, he'd come running back to her."

"Let me guess," Savannah said, "that didn't happen."

"Of course not. Madeline cost Arlo his marriage, his life. No way was he going to take her back. She's lucky he didn't kill her."

No sooner had the words left her mouth than she gave a little gasp and looked at Savannah, then Dirk . . . who looked at each other.

After a long, heavy silence, she said, "Or maybe he did."

"Maybe," Savannah replied. "I reckon we're just gonna have to make it our business to find out."

*   *   *

By the time Savannah and Dirk had finished with Odelle Peters, it was dinnertime, and Savannah had to admit, she was feeling pretty tired.

"A mite tuckered out," was the way she'd described it to Dirk when agreeing to let him drop her at her home for the evening.

But if she'd been honest, she'd have said, "So pooped I have to take a deep breath to get the energy to breathe."

She hated being so fatigued all the time. And couldn't help but think that her assailant had a lot to do with that.

Before the attack, she'd been tired after a long day's work. But now she even woke up tired in the morning after eight or nine hours of sleep. And that was something new and most unwelcome in her life.

Worst of all, she was deeply afraid that she'd never get past it, never be her "old self" again. And that bothered her as much as the scars on her body . . . wondering what damage had been done inside and whether it would ever heal.

"You want to come in and have some supper?" she asked him when he pulled into her driveway. "The gang's at Disneyland. We'll have a quiet house all to ourselves."

He hesitated, and she could tell he was really torn. There were few things he loved more than free food, and especially if it was her cooking.

"No, thanks," he said at last. "I need to get back to the station. I've gotta get that nitwit new gal at the desk to run checks on Arlo Di Napoli and his old lady. I'm gonna run one on our girlfriend, Odelle, too. Looks like to me she's got some major motive there, losing her house and all because of Madeline."

Savannah nodded. "It was hard to miss the hatred in her eyes when she talked about her."

He leaned over and gave her a kiss. "You go get some rest and enjoy your solitude. You can use a bit of peace and quiet."

"That's for danged sure."

She got out of the car, waved good-bye to him, and went into her house, expecting to find only Diamante and Cleopatra.

But instead, she saw her grandmother sitting in her big, comfy chair, reading her favorite tabloid newspaper.

"Gran!" Savannah said as she tossed her purse and keys onto the entry hall table. "What are _you_ doing here? I thought you were going to Disneyland with the rest of the hoodlums."

Granny folded her paper and got up from the chair. She walked over and sat on the sofa. "I wasn't up to all that running all over God's creation with that bunch," she said.

"But you love Disneyland! You're a Mickey Mouse Club fan from way back!"

"I do love the Mouse, it's true. But I like going there with you. I know them brothers and sisters of yours and their younguns. There's gonna be a whole lot of belly-achin' about standing in lines and fightin' up a storm over what ride they're gonna go on next, and gripin' if they don't get exactly the food they want when they want it. Lord have mercy, it wears me out just thinking about it."

Savannah walked over to her grandmother and gave her a kiss on the forehead. "Go park yourself back in that comfortable chair," she told her with pseudo sternness.

"But that's _your_ chair."

"Not when _you're_ here, it ain't."

"I'm done settled here."

"Resettle over there. I need to lay down on the couch."

Reluctantly, Granny did as she was told. Once she was nestled back in the winged-back chair with its rose spangled chintz covering and Savannah was stretched out on the sofa, she said, "You know, you'd have to get up mighty early of a morning to fool me, girlie. I know that you'd be sitting here if you was home alone. Lay on the couch, my foot."

Savannah grinned at her as she tucked a cushion under her head. "Maybe. And you'd have to stay up all night long if you wanted to get one over on *me*. You didn't stay home from Disneyland today because of no long lines or kids bellyachin'. You'd live every day of your life in Disneyland and be buried there if you could think of a way to pull it off."

Granny smiled back, but said nothing.

"You stayed behind because you were afraid I'd get all down in the dumps over all that's happened if you left me alone. Let's face it, you're here to babysit me."

"Am not."

"Are, too. And don't lie. What's that you used to always tell me? 'The good Lord's watchin', and if He hears you tell a lie, your tongue'll turn black and fall right outta your head.'"

Granny sighed. "Yeah, I shouldn't have told you kids that. It ain't true. I know a whole bunch of sorry jack-asses who've lied like rugs their whole lives, and they've still got their tongues . . . unfortunately."

"I didn't believe it past the age of five. That's when I stopped checking it in the bathroom mirror after I told a whopper. So, I don't reckon it scarred me for life."

She felt her breath catch in her throat as soon as she said the words, "scarred for life." Funny, how a simple phrase that you'd used since you were a child could suddenly take on new meaning.

Glancing over at Granny, she could see that Gran had caught it, too. Those eyes, as startlingly blue as her own, were searching her face with an intensity that made Savannah most uncomfortable.

It was hard to hide things from Dirk.

It was impossible to hide them from Granny Reid.

There was a long silence, then Gran said softly, "Life's hard. Everybody picks up scars along the way, Savannah girl. Some on the inside. Some on the outside."

Savannah put her head back and stared up at the ceiling. "These aren't like the one on my finger that I got opening that can of beans, Gran."

"I know."

"Or the one on my foot where Cleo scratched me when Di bit her on the butt."

"I know. And it ain't like the scar I got when they took out my gall bladder. Those were all got innocent-like. Not the way you got yours . . . through evil means."

"Exactly. That makes it harder."

"I'm sure it does, sweetie pie. I'm sure it does."

Savannah felt another, even deeper wash of fatigue sweep through her, robbing her of even the small amount of energy she'd had. The very thought of that guy seemed to drain the very life out of her.

"Are you gonna be all right, Granddaughter?" Gran asked with a tremble in her voice that Savannah hadn't heard in years.

A false, cheery, reassuring lie sprang to Savannah's lips, but she swallowed it and spoke the awful truth instead.

"I don't know."

"Well . . . that's gotta be a powerful burden to carry."

"It is."

Granny thought awhile, then asked, "What do you reckon it'd take for you to get better?"

"I don't know. Time, I guess."

"I don't put a lot of stock in time's healing properties. I've seen too many people spend too many years trying to get over bad injuries. Seems like a lot of those wounds fester instead of heal."

"That's what it feels like," Savannah admitted. "It feels like the hurt is going deeper and deeper. I find that, instead of getting past it, I hate him more every day."

"I can sure understand that. I ain't none too fond of him myself. I've had more than a few daydreams of how I'd do away with him . . . if he wasn't already done away with, that is."

Granny cleared her throat and took her time choosing her next words. "But one of these days, when you're ready, you're gonna have to start giving some thought to forgiving that lowdown skunk."

The very thought made Savannah feel nauseous. "How? Granny, how on earth does a body forgive someone for something like that? How am I supposed to love someone who tried to kill me? To understand what he did and say it was all right? I can't do that."

"You don't have to do that, darlin'. That ain't what forgiveness is all about. I mean, sometimes it is, when somebody who loves you accidentally hurts you. Then you can say to yourself and to them, 'I know you didn't mean to do it, and all's forgiven.' But this is different."

"You're darned tootin' it's different! He knew exactly what he was doing. He was trying to kill me, and I could see in his eyes when he was doing it that some part of him was enjoying it. I can't pretend to believe that he didn't understand what he was doing."

Granny got up from the chair and walked over to the

sofa. She sat on the edge of it and began to stroke Savannah's hair, as she had so many times when Savannah was a child. "Darlin'," she said. "You don't have to lie and say that he didn't mean to do what he did. It was a deliberate, evil act. There's no getting around that. You should never lie to yourself about that."

"Then how can I forgive him? How can I love him and feel all warm and fuzzy when I think about him?"

"That's not what forgiveness is, child. It's not some warm, fuzzy emotion. You can get a good feeling like that just eating a nice piece of chocolate or a perfect biscuit with peach preserves. Emotions come and go with the tides. They ain't worth spit."

Savannah reached for her grandmother's hand. "Then what is forgiveness?"

"Well . . . different people have different takes on it. And I don't claim to know what it is for sure. But I know a few things it ain't. It ain't pretending nothing happened to you when it did. It ain't saying that what happened wasn't no big deal and didn't matter. It ain't saying the person didn't know what they were up to, if they did. And it ain't deciding that the rattlesnake that bit you is now gonna be your best friend forever. That's just foolishness that'll get you bit again."

"Good. 'Cause if it was any of those things, I'd be up the creek without a paddle."

"I think forgiveness is a sacred thing, and it's so hard to get the job done proper."

She continued to stroke Savannah's hair, and the comfort of the simple gesture went deep into those areas of Savannah's soul that she was afraid would never find peace again.

"I think," Granny continued, "that it's more like just letting it all go. Letting go of the anger and the pain. Letting go of the daydreaming about how you'd like to get even with 'em, or at least make them understand what damage they've done to you. Letting go of the wish that you could change what happened, 'cause you can't."

"I do feel all those things. I wish I could go back and do things differently so that it wouldn't happen. I wish he was here so I could tell him how much he hurt me, what he took from me."

"Of course you want to. But you can't. And the anger and the pain are just going to hurt you. In the long run, maybe even more than *he* hurt you. You can't get even or change the past. And chances are, even if you could make him understand what he put you through, he wouldn't give a hoot. If he was the kind of person who felt compassion for others and remorse for his bad deeds, he never could've done such a wicked thing to you in the first place."

Savannah thought it over, long and hard.

Finally, she reached for her grandmother's hand and kissed it, thinking that for all its wrinkles, it was the dearest hand on earth.

"Just put it away?"

"Let 'er go."

"Easy to say, and hard to do."

"You're probably going to have to do it over and over again, a thousand times or ten thousand, till it's a habit."

Savannah smiled. "Like brushing your teeth and making your bed and feeding the hound dog."

"Yep. Only a whole heap harder."

Chapter 12

Savannah and Dirk got an early start the next morning, even foregoing the usual full Reid breakfast by opting for coffee and donuts.

But even though they were on the road by eight o'clock, it was after noon before they finally laid eyes on Francie Di Napoli.

And when they did, they got an eyeful.

When Francie was on the job, she was quite something to behold—a stripper better known professionally as "Candie Kisses" in a dive just outside San Carmelita's city limits.

Willy's Rendezvous was open twenty-four hours a day and seven days a week, catering to all sorts of guys— from run-of-the-mill blue-collar workers to motorcycle gang members to oil-field laborers to doctors and lawyers who decided to go slumming on their lunch hours away from their posh, seaside offices.

"You don't have to go in here," Dirk had told her when they arrived at Willy's with its flashing neon sign that said, "Girls, Girls, Girls!!!"

"I'll go in with you," Savannah told him. "But I'm not

going to sit on any bar stool or touch the doorknob if I can help it. I swear, the last time we had to take a perp out of here, I caught something creepy and had to use a prescription cream to get rid of it."

"Oookay," Dirk replied. "More than I wanted to know."

Once inside the establishment, Savannah's fears were not allayed. Willy's was just as clean and luxurious as she remembered, with spit- and beer-saturated sawdust on the floor, torn leatherette booths that had once been red but were now a suspicious shade of dirty maroon, and a bar that looked like it was cleaned every ten years whether it needed it or not.

Even the strippers' pole on a small stage in the center of the room looked grimy and sticky.

Savannah didn't dare give that too much consideration.

Francie Di Napoli was clinging to that pole in all of her sequined-string-bikini splendor. Her long hair was in serious need of a washing, she had a bit of a paunch in the belly area, and her makeup looked like she had applied it in the dark without a mirror. But she was a blonde, and she was taking her top off. And apparently that was enough for Willy and his faithful customers, who were hooting and hollering like a bunch of coyotes high on mescaline.

"I told you that you didn't have to come in," Dirk told Savannah when Francie whipped off her bottom as well.

"Eh, whatever," Savannah said, giving the dancer a quick once-over. "She ain't got nothin' I ain't got . . . and more of it."

Having completed her display, Francie pranced off the makeshift stage and donned a negligee that did little to cover what she had already exposed. Then she sidled up to the bar and downed a drink that Willy had waiting for her. Willy flashed her a big, flirty smile that was missing two front teeth. Francie returned the grin, gazing up at him as though he were the sexiest, most devastatingly handsome male walking the planet.

Savannah wasn't sure which appealed to her more, Sir William's hit-and-miss smile or his black leather vest that showed off his fat, pasty chest and gut. Both were covered with tattoos of more "Girls, Girls, Girls!!!"

The dirty, thin, gray ponytail trailing down his back and tied with a bunch of greasy-looking feathers and leather strips was a nice touch, too.

Yeah, Willy's a hottie, she thought to herself, trying not to gag.

"Reckon that's our girl?" Savannah said, nodding in the woman's direction.

Dirk gave her a quick head-to-toe appraisal. "The neighbor said she was short with long, frizzy blond hair, too much makeup, and an overdone boob job. Looks like she fits the description."

"Plus she's the only floozy in the place," Savannah said, looking around. Only males as far as the eye could see.

And that wasn't far, because the patrons at Willy's Rendezvous weren't observing the smoke-free work environment laws of the State of California.

"Miss Francie there could get cancer or emphysema from all the smoke in this place," Dirk said. "I should bust 'em all right here and now."

Savannah smiled, amused by what an antismoking crusader he had become . . . of course, only after he had quit. Former smokers were always the most zealous when it came to enforcing the antismoking rules.

"Don't worry about her," Savannah said, leading the way across the room to the dancer at the bar. "She's more likely to come down with pneumonia, wearing a get-up like that one."

"Are you Francie Di Napoli?" Dirk asked when they reached the dancer.

She put her empty shot glass down on the bar and turned to him, a look that was, undoubtedly, intended to be lusty on her face.

The look might have worked better if she had cleaned last night's mascara off first.

A hair brushing might have helped, too, Savannah thought.

"Actually," she said, "I'm Candie Kisses when I'm working." She leaned closer to Dirk, her nose only a few inches from his. "I'm very sweet . . . and yummy."

Dirk leaned back. "Yeah, well . . . I'm on a low-carb diet." He pulled his badge out of his pocket and stuck it between their noses. "You and us gotta talk."

"Oh, she's with you?" Francie tossed her blond hair in Savannah's direction.

"He's so *with me* that it ain't even funny," Savannah told her.

"That explains a lot." Francie shot Dirk an ah-okay-gotcha look.

"No, it doesn't," he told her. He reached across the bar and grabbed a dirty bartender's apron. "There," he said, tossing it to her. "Put that on."

"Why?" She struck a chest-expanding pose. "Are you uncomfortable around exotic dancers?"

"Nope. I was fascinated by strippers until I turned twenty-one and could go see them any time I wanted to. After that, it took me about two weeks to get over my adolescent obsession."

"Good thing all guys aren't like you," Francie muttered as she tied the beer-stained apron around her assets. "Come on, we can go talk in Willy's office.

*   *   *

Willy's office was wallpapered with centerfolds, littered with empty booze bottles, and smelled like stale cigarette smoke, beer, and dog.

Yes, Savannah thought, *this is the heart of Willy's world, the hub of his empire, the soul of his enterprise.*

Ah, the glamour of being a self-made entrepreneur.

The canine scent was explained when they saw an enormous pit bull, who was curled up on a folded blanket in the corner of the room. He was snoring loudly, and only opened one eye when they entered. He peered up at them with only mild curiosity, then closed it again.

"What's this all about?" Francie asked as she plopped herself down on the worn sofa in the corner next to the dog. She leaned over and patted him on the head.

When she saw Savannah staring at the animal, she said, "Oh, don't worry about Hercules here. He's a big pussy cat. Willy just keeps him around to protect the cash. One look at him and nobody even thinks of robbing us."

"And I'll bet that works quite well," Savannah said. She harbored a healthy respect for pit bulls. Maybe even a prejudice, if she were honest.

A pit bull had chased her over a fence one night when she had been running through someone's backyard, trying to apprehend a burglar. Since then she hadn't liked the breed.

But she did have to admit that Hercules was a pretty handsome, easygoing guy. He gazed up at Francie with big, brown doe eyes, gave her hand a grateful lick, then went back to snoring.

"You wanna pet him?" Francie asked.

"I'm sure he's very nice, but, no, thank you," Savannah replied.

"You wanna sit down?"

Savannah opted to stand, and so did Dirk.

"So, like I asked you before, what's all this about?" Francie asked.

"You don't know?" Dirk asked her.

"Nope." She glanced up at the large, school room–style clock on the wall and said, "But whatever it is, you'd better get at it because I'm on again in five minutes."

"You'll be on again in five minutes if you've answered all my questions," Dirk told her, clearly annoyed.

Francie looked a little flustered, as though she wasn't accustomed to males getting annoyed with her . . . or at least, showing it.

"Okay," she said. "What do you want to ask me?"

"Where were you the day before yesterday, in the afternoon?" Savannah asked.

"Why?"

"Please answer the question," Dirk said, sounding far less polite than his words.

"I was here all day."

"Doing what?" Savannah asked.

"Dancing." She hesitated a moment, thinking. Then added, "And taking a nap."

"You took a nap?" Dirk asked.

"Yeah. I take a nap most days. Is that against the law?"

"Where exactly did you take this snooze of yours?"

"Right here. I came in here and conked out on this sofa. Willy doesn't care." A sweet, sappy grin crossed her face. "Willy's nice to me."

Yeah, I'll bet he is, Savannah thought. *And in return, you're probably very nice to Willy's willy.*

But she didn't say it. Long ago, she'd learned that the key to being a good private detective was not mentioning out loud 99.9 percent of what crossed your mind.

That worked in one's nonprofessional life, as well.

Though she had a little more trouble implementing the rule there.

"How long was your nap?" Dirk was asking her.

"I don't know. It was two days ago. An hour or two, I guess. I get really tired. I work late every night. And it's hard work . . . harder than you might think."

"I'm sure you work your fingers to the bone," Savannah said. "Even when you aren't dancing."

Dirk snickered. Then quickly donned his poker face again. "Did anybody come in here while you were taking your nap?"

"No. Willy told everybody to leave me alone and let me rest. He takes good care of me."

"I'm sure he does." Dirk gave Savannah a quick look. "And where's the back door to this place?"

"Right out that door and to the left."

"That's what I thought." Dirk took a step closer to her. "Ms. Di Napoli, I want you to tell me about Madeline Aberson."

In less than two seconds, Francie's face turned a shockingly bright shade of red. "That rotten, lousy bitch. I hate her! What did she tell you this time?"

"What do you think she told me?" Dirk asked evenly.

"Did she complain that I was threatening her life again?"

When Dirk didn't reply, she said, "That's what I thought. I make a couple of stinking phone calls, and she runs to the police about it."

"When did you make these calls?" Dirk asked.

"Oh, I don't know. I guess a couple of days ago."

Savannah flashed back on Madeline's cell phone playing "La Cucaracha," and she smiled. *How much do you wanna bet,* she thought, *when Dirk gets the phone records, it'll have been her?*

"What a pathetic loser that Madeline is," Francie

kept spewing. "And while she was being a busybody tattle-tale, did she happen to mention *why* I threatened her?"

"We'd like to hear *your* side of the story," Savannah said. "We'd like for *you* to tell us why."

"Because she won't leave Arlo alone! He told her it was over, that he never wanted to see her ugly old face again." She turned to Savannah. "Did you get a load of that eye job. Oh my gawd, did that doctor butcher her or what?"

Savannah resisted the urge to meow and claw the air. Even Diamante and Cleo weren't catty enough to mention a botched plastic surgery.

Although, maybe it wasn't a fair comparison, since Madeline Aberson hadn't slept with either of their husbands.

"Why do you care if she calls Arlo?" Dirk asked. "Aren't you and him broke up now?"

"Well, yes. But we would be anyway, no matter what happened between her and him."

"Why's that?" Savannah asked.

" 'Cause he's in jail for hitting me again. And that's a real bummer."

"I'll bet it is."

"Yeah, when he's in jail, he can't work and there's no money. That's why I have to dance in a place like this. But we might get back together when he gets out . . . if she'll just stay away from him. That's why I called her and threatened to hurt her, to get her to leave him alone. I didn't mean what I said about shooting her in the back in a dark alley. I wouldn't do a thing like that."

She shrugged. "Hell, I don't even own a gun."

Savannah and Dirk exchanged glances.

"Shoot her in the back in a dark alley. Hmm," Savannah said. "How do you feel about well-lit bridal suite terraces?"

"What?" Francie looked genuinely confused, but Savannah wasn't sure.

"And how about ice picks?" Dirk asked. "Where do you stand on those?"

"I don't know what you're talking about. Yeah, I have an ice pick. But I hardly ever use it. Once in a while I do, when I have girlfriends over for margaritas. I have to break up the ice that comes in those plastic bags that you get at the liquor store. Why?"

Dirk stood there, looking at her, studying her face closely for a long time. Then he said, "Do you know why we're here, Ms. Di Napoli?"

"I figure it's because she called you and complained about me calling her, telling her I'd hurt her if she didn't leave my man alone." She reached back and nervously twisted her long hair into the facsimile of a ponytail. "You're here to tell me not to have any contact with her, or I'll get in trouble. Right?"

"No," Savannah said. "We didn't drive all the way out to a dive like Willy's—vacation hotspot that it is—just to soak in the atmosphere and referee a fight between an ex-wife and the 'other woman.'"

"Then why did you come?" Francie had been sprawled on the sofa, but she snapped to attention . . . even moved to the edge of the cushion. "What's up? Nothing's wrong with Arlo, right?"

"To the best of our knowledge, Arlo's okay," Dirk told her. "Madeline Aberson isn't."

"What's wrong with her . . . besides being a witch on wheels, that is?"

"If she's a witch, she's a dead one," Savannah said.

Francie gasped and clapped her hand over her mouth. Her eyes nearly bugged out of her head, reminding Savannah of a cartoon critter. "Are you kidding me?" she finally squeaked out.

"I wouldn't kid about a thing like murder," Savannah replied.

"Murder? Murder? Are you telling me that somebody actually killed that stupid bitch . . . someone besides me, that is?"

"Actually, that's what we're trying to figure out right now," Dirk said.

She jumped up from the sofa so fast that she nearly lost her apron. "Hey, wait a damned minute here. I didn't kill anybody! Not even *her*!"

"Sounds like you had a better reason than most," Dirk returned. "And you just admitted that you threatened to."

"Threatening to and doing it are two *way* different things! I'll admit that if I was gonna kill somebody, it would've been her, but it wasn't me!"

"Then do you have any idea who it might have been?" Savannah asked. "Give us somebody else to look at, and we might not look at you so hard."

"Yeah," Dirk added, "at the moment you're number one on our suspect list."

Francie appeared to be thinking hard, her forehead scrunched up, her eyes narrowed. Finally, she shrugged and said, "I don't know, but if I had to guess, I'd say her husband. He was even madder than I was when he found out what her and Arlo had been up to."

"It wasn't her husband," Dirk said.

"Then it must be Arlo." Francie nodded vigorously and looked momentarily relieved. "Yeah, he probably had it done. He knows a lot of people who'd do it for a six-pack of beer. And before he went to jail, she was driving him crazy with all the phone calls, trying to get back together with him. Arlo's got a temper on him. If she rubbed him the wrong way one too many times . . . Pow! He'd either do it or have it done."

"Pow?" Savannah raised one eyebrow. "Does Arlo have a habit of going . . . pow?"

"Oh, yeah. He beat the crap out of me at least once a week."

Savannah looked at the woman and shook her head. "He beat you once a week, fooled around on you, and you think he's capable of murdering another woman . . . but you want him back as soon as he gets out of jail?"

Francie got a sappy look on her face that made Savannah want to go . . . pow . . . herself, to try and knock some sense into her.

"You don't know what he's like when he's in a good mood and everything's going right. He can be so sweet, too."

"Uh-huh."

"No, he can! And he's sooo good in bed, too. Way better than even Willy is."

Suddenly, Savannah's ankles started to itch. And then her shins, and on up to her knees. The sensation wormed its way up her body, until she had a sneaking suspicion she was going to have to refill that cream prescription again.

An old proverb about "going to bed with dogs and getting up with fleas" ran through her mind.

Fortunately, Dirk was fishing a business card out of his pocket and handing it to Francie.

"If you think of anything that might help us, please give me a call at that number," he said.

She shot him a flirty grin as she tucked the card safely between her generous breasts.

"Maybe I'll give you a call whether I can think of anything helpful or not," she breathed up at him, batting her spidery eyelashes.

"No," he said. "Don't do that. Business calls only."

She giggled. "Sure. Whatever you say."

* * *

"You know she's gonna call you," Savannah told him as they walked out of Willy's and across the parking lot to his car. "And it's gonna be a booty call, for sure."

"I know," he said with a sigh.

They reached the Buick, and he opened the door for her. "Maybe she'll lose the card."

"Naw. That's just wishful thinking. She's got it tucked nice and safe, right next to her heart. Sooo sweet."

He snorted. "Hell, she could shove a typewriter in there and not be able to find it later."

Chapter 13

When Savannah and Dirk dropped by her house an hour later to refuel on whatever the invading hoards might have left unmolested in her refrigerator, they apparently didn't make enough noise coming through the front door. Because Savannah hadn't had time to put her purse on the foyer table before they overheard a lively conversation going on in the living room.

And it was all about them.

"I don't think they're even going to get married," said a voice that sounded a lot like Marietta's to Savannah's trained ear. "That Savannah's gonna mess this up and wind up an old maid, you mark my words."

Another voice—Savannah was pretty sure it was Cordele—replied, "If you'd ever picked up a psychology book instead of that crap you're always reading, you'd know that Savannah has major abandonment issues, brought on by an absentee father figure and an alcoholic mother."

"Naw, she's just too set in her ways to ever be able to live with anybody. You wait and see. She's gonna die alone here in this house with nothing but her cats, like those old cat ladies you read about in the papers. They might even eat 'er dead body if she's not careful."

"That ain't gonna happen!" someone shouted from the kitchen. "You gossiping hens stop your cackling in there and mind what you say about my big sister! I won't abide anybody talking dirt about her!"

"We're your big sisters, too," was the yelled reply. "You get your bloomers all up your crack over somethin' that's said about your precious Savannah. But you don't care what people say about *us*! I've never heard you utter one single solitary cotton-pickin' word in *our* defense!"

"That's because the two of you have mostly done whatever you're being accused of . . . usually worse. Savannah's never done a mean thing to anybody in her life!"

Dirk grinned at Savannah and nudged her with his elbow. "Is that Alma defending your case in there?"

"Yeah. She loves me."

"And obviously doesn't know you."

She elbowed him back.

As they walked into the living room, which was littered with her sunburned relatives and Disneyland memorabilia galore, she heard another voice join the argument, one without the thick-as-molasses Southern accent. "I agree with Alma. Savannah is a wonderful person, and I think she and Dirk are very brave to keep trying like this. If at first you don't succeed, try, try again."

Marietta gave a derisive sniff. "If you don't succeed, try, try again. And if you still can't pull it off, just give up. There's no point in being a damned fool about it. That's what I always say."

"I suppose you read that bit of wisdom on a fortune

cookie at the Chinese joint back home, huh?" Macon said.

As usual, Marietta and Macon were parked in front of the television set. Marietta was wearing a Tigger and Pooh tee-shirt that was a couple of sizes too small. Tigger had never looked more obscene.

Macon had a pair of Mickey Mouse ears on his head, which looked a bit odd on a man of his considerable height and girth. But Savannah reminded herself that Mickey wouldn't mind. He loved all his fans, whatever their size.

Vidalia was stretched out on the sofa, one leg thrown up on the back of it. On her feet was a pair of bright green ballet slippers with large, fluffy pom-poms on the toes. Savannah wondered if she'd actually had to mug Tinkerbell to get those off the pixie's feet.

This time Vidalia's literature selection was a movie world tell-all. According to the cover, the number-one male box office draw had sired a child with a female alien.

Jesup was reading, too. Hers was a Goth magazine that promised to reveal the best-kept makeup secrets from classic horror movies. She was wearing a black hoodie with a pirate logo, enhanced with a skull and crossbones . . . of course.

Savannah sighed.

They were a most literate and well-dressed family.

"All right, stop talking about me," Savannah said. "My ears are already burning like somebody poured Tabasco sauce in them."

Instantly, everyone became fascinated by their reading materials and the television show. A heavy, awkward silence reigned.

Savannah was thankful for the peace and quiet, even if it was guilt induced.

In the corner of the room at the rolltop desk, which constituted the office of the Moonlight Magnolia Detective Agency, sat Tammy. She was the only one not wearing an embarrassed look on her face . . . or fantasy-resort wear.

But she did look guilty.

To Savannah's deep sorrow, Tammy always looked guilt-ridden these days.

If Savannah had the choice, she would have kept her scars forever if she could only remove that look from her dear friend's face. In some ways, Tammy's wounds seemed to be more grievous than her own.

She walked over to the desk, tripping over some half-deflated balloons, a fairy wand, and a pirate's sword on the way. She leaned down and kissed the top of her friend's glossy, blond hair. "Hey, darlin'," she said. "Good to see you with your nose back to the grind-stone."

Tammy gave her a half smile. "I just thought I should come in and pay some bills. I know you feel strongly about having electricity and water."

"It comes in handy from time to time." She lowered her voice. "Especially when you've been invaded by Sherman's army. Can you imagine these troops without television?"

Dirk joined them and gave Tammy the closest thing to a physical display of affection that they ever exchanged. He put a hand on her shoulder and shook her like a bulldog would maul its favorite toy.

"We haven't seen enough of your mug around here," he told her. "And we've got a case to work now, too."

"Yeah," Savannah said. "Are you trying to avoid work or what?"

Tammy looked up, her eyes gleaming with rabid interest.

And seeing that light brought sunshine to Savannah's heart, too. Tammy was the most devout detective Savannah had ever known. She absolutely lived to "sleuth," as she called it.

"No!" Tammy said, jumping to her feet. "I mean . . . I'm not trying to avoid work. Is there something I can do to help you? I've got the bills paid and there's nothing else going on so—"

Savannah took her arm and pulled her toward the kitchen. "You can start by helping me scare us up some bologna sandwiches and potato chips. Then you can go out back and have a late lunch with us while we fill you in on the gory details."

Tammy hesitated. "Um . . . I've already eaten, and . . . uh . . . bologna, I couldn't. . . ."

"Oh, I know. We'll make you a refreshing drink. Organic water with a sprig of hydroponically grown celery."

"Hydroponic celery? Really?" Her eyes were so wide and filled with innocence.

It made Savannah want to lift the top of that pretty head and pour in a healthy dose of cynicism mixed with pessimism and a portion of old-fashioned meanness. It was a cocktail that every woman needed to avoid predators and to enhance self-preservation in general.

But those were gifts that Life itself bestowed on her daughters, and even though Tammy had recently experienced a pretty hard knock, it seemed she had more to learn.

"You're kidding me about the celery, right?" she said.

"Well, yeah. Duh."

Okay, maybe there's hope for her after all, Savannah thought. Trusting one's natural instincts had to start somewhere.

* * *

Half an hour later, Savannah and Dirk were sitting on Savannah's chaise lounges with their extra-thick cushions, stuffing their faces with peanut butter and peach preserve sandwiches.

The bologna had been previously devoured by her houseguests, along with the grape jelly and strawberry jam.

The hoped-for potato chips were history, as well. The only thing left in the way of munchies was some nacho cheese chip dust.

It didn't go particularly well with peanut butter and peach preserves.

"Next time we eat at my place," Dirk said, licking his finger and trying to mop up the last bit of crumbs from the bottom of the bag. "At least until all your company goes home. You haven't had anything good around here to eat since they arrived."

"Eat at your house? Really?" Savannah was surprised. It was so unlike Dirk to offer to cook. "You're gonna cook for me? Maybe breakfast for dinner . . . some of those amazing mandarin orange pancakes, you made for me that time?"

"Get real. I was gonna order a pizza. Wednesday nights you get two for the price of one, if you don't order any toppings."

Savannah stared at him. "Oh, of course not. I mean . . . who'd want those pesky toppings?"

"Exactly." He licked the orange chip powder off the end of his finger. "I just get a couple of regular cheese pies and throw some sliced lunch meat on it. Whatever I've got in the fridge . . . ham . . . turkey . . . liverwurst."

"Liverwurst?" Tammy nearly gagged on her organic water.

"Yeah." He gave her a blank look. Then he turned to Savannah, who was also staring at him in horror. He shrugged. "What?"

Tammy turned to Savannah. "I've got to ask: Are you seriously going to marry this guy?"

"That's the plan . . . eventually," Savannah said with a sigh. "It's been a little hard to fit it in, between the mournful notifications and the trips to flea-infested strip clubs."

"Fleas?" Tammy asked.

Savannah reached down and scratched her ankle. "For my own peace of mind, that's what I've decided it was. It's better than the alternatives."

"Yuck."

"Yes. Very."

"Hey," Dirk said, nodding toward the back door. "Get a load of them."

Savannah turned and saw Waycross coming out the back door, Jack and Jillian in tow. He was wearing a new, bright red Space Mountain tee-shirt. Jack was dressed in a pirate hat with an eye patch and a plastic hook over his hand. Jillian was in a long, pink Sleeping Beauty dress.

Waycross was carrying Savannah's mop bucket, a couple of washcloths, a bottle of car wash detergent, and a couple of her oldest towels.

"We're going to wash your 'Stang for you, Auntie!" Jack called across the yard as they headed for Savannah's Mustang, which was sitting in her driveway next to the garage.

"Yeah," Jillian piped up. "Uncle Waycross is going to pay us five dollars each if we help him."

"Well, that's mighty generous of Uncle Waycross, now, ain't it?" Savannah said, smiling at this obvious ploy.

Not that Waycross wasn't a sweetie who would have gladly washed her car for her anyway. He was a hard-working guy, and he loved the Mustang obsessively. But Savannah felt this strategic move had more to do with his attraction to a pretty blonde than a red, vintage Mustang.

"I don't think I've ever seen a princess or a pirate wash a car before," Tammy said, keeping an eye on Waycross as he unwound the garden hose from its hook on the side of the house and pulled it toward the car.

"First you gotta get it all nice and wet," he was telling the children. "Who wants to squirt it first?"

"I do! I do!" Both kids screamed, dancing in place, their hands in the air.

"Ladies first," he said, handing the nozzle to Princess Jillian.

She gave the trigger a test squeeze, and a moment later, the front of Waycross's shirt was soaking wet.

"Whoa, Bessie!" Waycross yelled. "You ain't nearly as accurate with a pistol as your Aunt Savannah. Hand that weapon to your brother before you put out an eye with it."

Jack wasn't much better, especially considering the challenge of a hooked hand. But at least he aimed the jet of water in the general vicinity of the car.

"Not too bad," Dirk commented, "for a one-handed guy wearing an eye patch."

Savannah couldn't help noticing that Waycross kept cutting glances their way—more specifically, *Tammy's* way—as he instructed the children on the proper way to scrub the rear chrome bumper.

And to Savannah's surprise and delight, she noticed that Tammy was sending just as many looks his way.

"He's really good with those kids," Tammy said, watching him squat by one wheel and show Jack how to scrub the whitewall.

"Waycross is a treasure," Savannah replied. "Always has been one of the best in the batch."

"He's tall, too," Tammy observed.

"Six-three, last time we measured." Savannah caught Dirk's eye and gave him a wink. But he had already tuned in to the situation and was wearing a little grin of his own.

"He has a nice physique," Tammy continued. "Does he work out?"

"He doesn't do a lot of deliberate exercise, the way you do. But he works hard there in Butch's garage and that keeps him pretty fit," Savannah told her. "Besides their usual mechanic stuff, they also restore cars and trucks. Waycross is a real artist when it comes to interiors. He did a beautiful job with the pleating on my bucket seats."

Tammy seemed sufficiently impressed by Savannah's sales pitch. "Really? I didn't know that you restored your Mustang yourself."

"With a lot of help from Butch and Waycross. They felt sorry for me after I wrecked my other car. Waycross found the 'Stang in bad need of a lot of work, and it helped me get over wrecking the Camaro."

"I think it's wonderful, restoring things. It's so . . . you know . . . green."

Yes, Savannah decided that Tammy's eyes were definitely sparkling as she watched Waycross wash a fender. Though it might have had something to do with the fact that her little brother filled out the back side of a pair of jeans quite nicely.

"Hey, kiddo," Dirk said, nudging Tammy's foot with his own. "Are you going to help us with this case or not?"

"What?" She seemed to take a few seconds to reorient herself. "Oh, the case. Sure! What do you want me to do? Just name it."

"The husband, Ethan Aberson, has an alibi . . . been in Vegas for days now on some sort of business trip," Dirk told her. "He's been staying at the Victoriana. I called the hotel and confirmed that he's checked in there. But, as you know, it's only an hour flight from LA to Vegas. And you can drive from San Carmelita to Vegas in five and a half hours."

Tammy was already on it. "So, you want me to do some more digging and make sure that he didn't slip back home on the day his wife was murdered?"

"That's right," Savannah said. "Find out what conference he's at and see if you can verify that he attended all the meetings, was seen at mealtimes, maybe hung out with his coworkers, stuff like that."

"We want every hour of that day accounted for, if at all possible," Dirk said.

"I can do that!" she said. "I'll get the names of his coworkers, and I'll call them, and I'll tell them that I'm his little sister and that I'm pregnant, and he was supposed to be my natural childbirth coach, but he didn't show up for the class like he was supposed to, and I'm just checking to make sure that he really did have to be out of town at a convention, so that I won't hold it against him for the rest of our lives. . . ." She stopped to draw a breath. "Stuff like that."

Savannah stared at her. "Considering that you're the most virtuous, totally honest person I've ever known, you're scary good at that."

Tammy lifted her chin and tossed her long hair back over her shoulder. "I do what I have to do for 'the cause.' It's not lying if the end justifies the means. You taught me that, Savannah. And how to pick locks. And how to make fake business cards in two minutes. And how to use my feminine wiles to get past male security guards. And—"

"Okay, okay." Savannah held up one hand. "As long as I've enriched your life in practical ways."

But Tammy wasn't listening anymore.

Brother Waycross had removed his soaking-wet tee-shirt and hung it on the fence, and now he was vigorously scrubbing bug debris off the Mustang's headlights. Muscles flexing, straining with every stroke of the cloth.

And, apparently, at least for the moment, Miss Tammy Hart had other things on her mind.

Chapter 14

Savannah didn't like going to jail. Never had. She didn't like going to county lockup, state prisons, or high-security mental hospitals for the criminally insane.

They all had bars. And she hated seeing steel bars. They gave her a creepy sense of claustrophobia.

What would be worse than living in a cage for the rest of your life? Nothing she could think of. And even though she knew that many of the people inside those places had done terrible things to land themselves behind those bars, she couldn't help feeling bad that they were there.

At least for the time she was in jail with them. And as long as she didn't think too much about their crimes or their victims' miseries.

But when it came to a guy like Arlo Di Napoli, those feelings of sympathy were hard to scrounge up. Cold, hard, ugly bars notwithstanding.

Savannah didn't like batterers. In fact, she had a hard time not bitterly hating them, having seen the damage they did to their partners, their children, society, and even to themselves.

So much suffering. And all because one person decided it was fine and dandy for them to use violence to get their way, to manipulate those around them into doing whatever they wanted, when they wanted it, the way they wanted it.

It was a pretty simple, self-serving philosophy: Do what I tell you or I'll hurt you.

And she bore the scars of such a mindset on her body and would for the rest of her life.

No. She didn't like batterers.

So, when she and Dirk visited Arlo Di Napoli in the county jail, she was prepared to loathe him on sight. And the sight of him didn't exactly change her mind.

Several words sprang to her mind when he walked into the tiny, grim, visiting room, wearing his bright orange prison suit, his dark hair slicked close to his scalp, a weird, wispy little goatee dangling from his chin.

The words that flashed across her intuition's radar screen were "slick" and "slimy."

He reminded her of the strippers' pole at Willy's Rendezvous.

She remembered what Francie had said about how good he was in bed, and the peanut butter sandwich in her belly did a flip-flop.

"What's this about?" Arlo said without preamble as he pulled out a metal chair and sat down at the metal table . . . metal handcuffs around his wrists.

That was another thing about jails that Savannah didn't like. All the metal. She didn't know how people could stand to live with all that cold, hard metal.

But under the circumstances, she was fine with the idea that this was Arlo's new lifestyle . . . and would be for a while.

"It's about one of your women, Arlo," Dirk told him, taking a chair across the table from him.

Arlo gave him a sarcastic little sneer. "I'm afraid you're gonna have to be more specific. I got lotsa girl-friends."

"Really? I thought this was an all-men's jail," Savan-nah said, unable to resist needling him just a bit. "But I guess you can call your honeys in here girls or bitches or cell mate bed warmers or anything you want to."

"I mean on the *outside*," he said, rising for the bait. "Real women!"

As she could have predicted, ol' Arlo didn't like women with sass. And that was fine, because she and every other sassified gal she could imagine wouldn't have given a jerk like Arlo a second glance.

Or a first one either, for that matter.

"You been in here how long now?" Dirk asked.

Savannah knew that Dirk was well aware of the de-tails of Arlo's little vacation on the county. But then, Dirk seldom asked questions that he didn't already know the answer to.

"Two weeks," Arlo replied. "And what's the matter with one of my girls?"

"Well," Dirk said, "I thought you'd want to know, dear little Francie's shaking her bare buzzungas and her naked butt, too, down at that scumbucket bar . . . Willy's."

Dirk waited for his information to sink in.

It looked to Savannah that Arlo hadn't been aware of that and didn't approve. At all.

Arlo, who didn't mind jumping his best friend's wife, didn't like other men looking at his woman's junk.

That was no surprise. Long ago, Savannah had ob-served that it was always the men who habitually fooled around on their partners who were the most jealous.

"Okay," Arlo said. "I'll have to have a little talk with

her about that. She told me she was filing books at the local library for extra money."

Savannah stifled a laugh. "Not unless she's doing some sort of naughty librarian routine for Willy and the boys."

That didn't go over well either with ol' Arlo. And Savannah was perversely pleased that it hadn't.

"But Francie's not the only one of your women who's got a problem," Dirk told him. "In fact, her wavin' her dinglebobbers in front of a bunch of guys is nothing compared to what's going on with your other gal."

"Stop messing with me, man. Which one of those stupid bitches got a problem?" Arlo demanded, not bothering to mask his bad temper.

"The one who broke up your marriage," Savannah told him, not bothering to hide her delight in rubbing some salt in his wound. "She's got a major, major problem."

"Who, Madeline? So what? Who cares?" He leaned so far back in his chair that Savannah was afraid he'd topple over backward.

She didn't particularly care if he busted his head open on the hard, cement floor, but she didn't want Dirk to have to go through all the paperwork that such an injury, occurring during an interview, would precipitate.

"You'll care," Dirk said, "once I charge you for it."

"Charge me for what? What am I supposed to have done to her?"

"You murdered her."

"Murdered?" Arlo gulped, looked at Dirk, then Savannah, his eyes wide, mouth gaping. "Are you . . . are you saying . . . Madeline's dead?"

"Very."

He appeared to quickly absorb the information . . . and deal with it. "Oh. Okay. Whatever."

Savannah said, "I'd tell you that I'm sorry for your loss, but you don't seem all that sorry yourself, so I won't bother."

"She caused me a lot of trouble, that bitch. If somebody took her out, I ain't gonna cry about it."

"I don't expect you to cry about it," Dirk said. "But I'm thinking you did it."

"I did it? How could I have done it? I'm in here!"

"I think you paid for it."

"Paid for it? You think I paid somebody to knock off Madeline? Are you serious?"

"Serious as a heart attack." Dirk leaned across the table toward him. "We've found out a lot about Madeline Aberson, and most of it isn't all that nice. I'm sure you had a good reason."

"Let's hear your side of it," Savannah said, "so that we don't think you're just a coldhearted bastard. Why did you have somebody kill her?"

Arlo shook his head. "Oh, no . . . you aren't going to get me to answer a question like that. That's like asking somebody, 'Did you hurt your hand when you smacked your wife?' I ain't falling for nothing like that."

Savannah turned to Dirk. "Arlo here's too smart for us, buddy. You can't pull the wool over *his* eyes."

Dirk's eyes narrowed as he leaned still closer to his interviewee. "Okay, then let's get real honest, real quick. You tell me who you think might've killed Madeline, and I'll check them out. And if I find out it was them, you're off the hook. Otherwise, we're gonna investigate every nook and cranny of your sorry life."

"And how much you wanna bet," Savannah said, "that we can come up with something that'll make sure

you don't get out of here until you're way too old and
feeble to do any of those 'bitches' of yours any good at
all?"

Arlo's wispy goatee trembled just a bit as he shot
them both evil looks. His hands twisted against the
manacles as he fidgeted in his chair.

"It mighta been Francie," he finally said. "Or she
mighta got some guy there at the bar to do it for her.
She really, really hated Madeline."

"Okay, who else?" Dirk prompted him.

"Maybe Madeline's old man, Ethan."

"Ah, yes, Ethan, your best friend, right?" Savannah
said. "Your bosom buddy who caught you in a compromising position with his wife."

"It was just a regular missionary position. Nothing
kinky or compromising about it."

"Well, I'm sure you explained that to him at the time
and it made everything much better." For just a moment, Savannah had a mental image of this guy and
Madeline together, and she got rid of it as quickly as
possible. With all her faults, Madeline had seemed
semi-classy. Not the sort to go for a hay roll with a guy
like this.

But there was no accounting for taste.

"Why do you think Ethan might have killed her?"
Dirk asked him.

"Well, the obvious. She left him for me . . . you
know . . . before she found out that I didn't want her.
At least not *that* way. I wasn't about to marry her or anything like that."

"*She* left *him*?" Dirk said. "Didn't he throw her out
when he caught you two together?"

"No, he didn't. Go figure." Arlo put his hands behind his head and rocked on the rear two legs of his
chair, an unpleasant, nonchalant expression on his face.

"If I'd been him, I'd have beaten the crap outta her and tossed her to the curb, but nooo. He ran off to his mommy's house and stayed there, pouting like a little boy, for a few days. And when he came crawling back to Madeline, he found his stuff in suitcases on the front porch and the door locks changed."

"That's a little hard to believe," Savannah told him.

"Hey, for me, too," he replied. "But it's what happened. She called me and told me that she'd kicked him out so that I could leave Francie and come live with her. I told her no way that was gonna happen."

"And how'd she take that?" Dirk asked.

"She gave me an ultimatum. Told me I had twenty-four hours to tell Francie about us and leave her, or she'd pay her a visit and fill her in on all the gory details."

"I'd say that'd be a good motive for murder there, buddy," Dirk observed.

Arlo nodded solemnly. "I thought about it. I admit it. I did. But instead, I told Francie, as sweet and gentle as I could."

"And?" Savannah asked.

"And she tied into me like a wildcat. Started kicking and clawing and trying to scratch my eyes out. I smacked her a time or two just to settle her down, and that's when the neighbors called the cops." He sighed. "I guess they could tell by looking at her that she'd got the worst of it, so they arrested my ass."

"So, this isn't your first domestic violence offense . . . the one you're serving now," Savannah observed.

Dirk chuckled. "Arlo's a fast learner."

"Hey, if you were married to a gal like Francie, you'd have to take a hand to her once in a while, too. She's always chasin' after other guys. And no man with any dignity's gonna take that lying down."

"Is that what this last fight was about?" Dirk asked. "The one you're serving time for now? Some other guy?"

"Yeah. I saw her making eyes at him in a bar and I couldn't let that go. I smacked her around a little bit, she acted like I was some kind of abuser or something, and here I sit."

"That's a sad tale, Arlo," Savannah said sarcastically.

"Ain't it though?" Arlo gave her a goofy half smile that made her realize he'd missed the sarcastic part of her statement.

It was no fun to insult people when your zinger flew right over their heads.

"Makes me wanna tune up and have myself a big ol' boo-hoo right here and now," she added.

He got it that time. "Screw you," he said, flashing hate from his eyes, his goatee twitching.

"No, thanks," Savannah replied. "I'll leave that to your honey bunny back in the cell."

"We have conflicting stories about what happened when Ethan caught his friend doing the hokeypokey with his old lady," Dirk remarked as he and Savannah exited the final gate of the jail and stepped into the sunlight.

No bars. No metal. Savannah was immensely grateful.

She lifted her face to the sun and breathed in the sweet, fresh air that smelled like sage and eucalyptus trees and ocean. A big improvement over sweat and urine and that indefinable but ever-present stench of stress and misery.

"Yes," she said. "Odelle says Ethan kicked Madeline out of the house the day he caught her and filed for a legal separation immediately."

"And good ol' Arlo here says that he kept trying to get her back and that he's the one who wound up with his suitcases on the porch."

"Funny how many different historical accounts there are for every major battle that's been fought since the beginning of time."

"They say the final story's written by the winner."

She thought of Madeline lying on the slab. Ethan and his parents who now had to raise a little girl without the child's mother. Odelle having to sell her beloved home. Francie clinging to Willy's pole for support. Arlo in an orange jumpsuit, looking at the world through cold, metal bars.

It was hard to spot a winner among them.

Chapter 15

"Ah, I needed this," Savannah said as she and Dirk walked, hand in hand, along the San Carmelita pier, enjoying one of the prettiest sights on earth—a southern California sunset.

The salt sea air had never smelled sweeter. In fact, she was so grateful to be on the "outside" again that she didn't even mind the squawking seagulls circling overhead, begging for treats.

"If one of those shit hawks craps on my head," Dirk growled, "I'm going to take my weapon out and shoot him."

"Oh, you would not," she said, squeezing his arm and leaning her head on his shoulder.

"I'm not as big of an animal lover as you are," he said.

"Yes, you are. You're worse," she said. "I hear you talking all mushy to Cleo and Di when you think I'm not listening. Besides, you wouldn't kill a wild animal like that bird," she said, pointing toward a particularly beautiful gull circling directly over them. "You aren't that good a shot."

He growled, but grinned down at her and placed a kiss on her forehead. "How're you feeling?" he said.

"Fine, and don't ask again."

She didn't feel fine. Just walking the length of the pier had caused the pain under her breast to flare. And her legs were a little shaky as they neared the far end.

At nearly two thousand feet in length, San Carmelita's wooden pier was one of the longest in the state. But it shouldn't have been an exhausting walk. She'd strolled it many times without giving it a thought.

But that was before . . .

"Let's sit down over here," Dirk said, guiding her in the direction of the bench at the very end. "I wanna look at the waves for a while."

"You do not," she snapped.

Her curt, angry tone surprised her. She hardly recognized the voice as her own.

But it didn't seem to faze Dirk. "Yeah, I really do," he said. "I want to sit with my girl and look at the ocean and get in touch with my inner, peaceful self."

"You've got one of those?"

"Usually it takes a few beers and listening to Elvis or Johnny Cash to bring him, out, but . . . yeah. I got one."

She moved toward the bench. "Well, then by all means, let's sit down. I gotta meet this peaceful Dirk dude."

Once they were settled, she realized how chilly the wind was out here at the end of the pier at sunset. She chided herself for forgetting her jacket.

A moment later, Dirk had taken off his old, leather bomber jacket and was wrapping it around her shoulders. .

"How very gallant of you," she said, savoring the warmth of the jacket that still held the heat of his body and the scent that was his alone . . . leather, Old Spice, cinnamon . . . and him.

"Hey, I gotta take care of my girl, especially now that she's my fiancée."

Savannah's mind reluctantly returned to another time, three months ago, when she had been lying on the floor, her life's blood flowing out of her body, her strength fading fast. And he had taken off this very jacket and wrapped it around her, just like today.

He had literally saved her life. And since that day, she had realized how precious life was.

"You've always taken care of me, fiancée or not," she said, her voice breaking a bit.

"Yeah, well, let's just say, we take care of each other."

Savannah's cell phone jingled, playing the happy little tune, "You Are My Sunshine."

"Hi, Tams," she said, answering it. "You're here?"

They both turned around and looked back the length of the pier. Even from there they could see the golden-haired beauty standing in the parking lot, near the restaurant on the opposite end. She was hopping up and down, waving her arms.

Savannah smiled. "We see you. We'll be right there." She started to stand, but her left leg buckled under her.

Dirk caught her, lowered her back down onto the bench, then took the cell phone from her hand. "We're gonna sit here and enjoy the view just a few more minutes," he told Tammy. "Why don't you go on inside and get us a table? Order Savannah her iced tea and me a fake beer, and whatever you want."

"You got it," Tammy replied.

They watched as she bounced into the restaurant.

Savannah wondered if she would ever bounce anywhere again.

Dirk handed her the phone. "Nice view, huh?" he

said, waving an arm to indicate the distant horizon, where purple islands peeked above a fluffy layer of white fog. A lighthouse blinked its beam at them across the way. A flock of brown pelicans flew by, looking like prehistoric pterodactyls. And below a bevy of surfers in black bodysuits rode waves that glistened coral and turquoise in the light of the setting sun.

"Yeah, yeah," she said. "Whatever."

As Savannah and Dirk devoured their fish and chips dinner and Tammy nibbled at her salad, they compared notes on the case.

Of the three, it seemed that Tammy was the most informed. And that didn't surprise Savannah at all.

Some little girls wanted to grow up and be princesses and fairies. A few who were more practical wanted to be doctors or movie stars. But Tammy had decided early in childhood that she was going to be Nancy Drew.

And, for all practical purposes, she was.

Often, Savannah had thought that if she were a fugitive on the run, the last person she'd want after her would be Tammy Hart. The girl had endless energy, dogged determination, and resolute resourcefulness.

Tammy had trained all of her considerable powers on Ethan Aberson for the past twenty-four hours. Unaware that he was in her crosshairs, good ol' Ethan had no idea how effectively his privacy had been breached.

"His mother says he's a highly successful businessman," Savannah said, dragging a crispy French fry through a puddle of ketchup. "But then, all mothers think that."

"She's right," Tammy told her. "He's an established, well-respected funeral director. Owns a mortuary in Twin Oaks."

"Which one?" Dirk asked.

"Perpetual Peace."

He nodded. "Yeah. I've been there. So have you," he told Savannah. "Kevin Flynn was laid out there after that undercover bust went wrong."

"Oh, right. Sad case. Nice place though," Savannah observed.

"He does a lot of business," Tammy said. "If he's a good financial manager, he should be well set."

Dirk scowled. "Wait a minute. His parents said he's at a convention in Vegas. Undertakers don't go to conventions."

"The heck they don't." Tammy grinned, looking obnoxiously pleased with herself. "I'm telling you, that's where he's been. Yesterday, he attended a lecture on the risks of formaldehyde exposure. The day before, it was a class on how to reduce your paperwork and still stay within federal guidelines, and another on protecting yourself from blood-borne pathogens."

"Woo-hoo. I wanna be an undertaker and go to cool classes like those," Savannah said, stirring an envelope of sugar into her drink.

"Hey, don't poke fun," Dirk told her. "They do a really important job . . . a job most other people wouldn't want. I still remember how good they made Kevin Flynn look after he was shot to hell. That meant a lot to his widow and his kids."

Savannah nodded thoughtfully. "You're absolutely right. I'm sorry. But you've got to admit, that sounds like a boring convention."

"Don't feel too sorry for him," Tammy said. "He's been ducking out of the seminars."

"Oh?" Savannah was all ears. "And how do we know that?"

"Because . . . we . . . have become best friends forever

with the concierge there at the Victoriana, and he told me a lot of interesting stuff."

"Spill it."

Tammy reached into her purse, took out her electronic tablet, and turned it on. "Well, he's the one who told me about the convention and the various classes. He even checked the lists to see who attended what."

"He did all that for you over the phone?" Dirk asked, astonished and maybe a tad jealous.

"He certainly did."

"How?" Dirk wanted to know.

Tammy batted her eyelashes. "If you're a girl and use a southern accent, you can get a guy to do anything for you. Huh, Savannah?"

Savannah glanced at Dirk, shrugged, and cleared her throat. "What else did this concierge tell you?"

"He told me that when a hotel guest enters their room, using their key card, the time registers on the hotel's security computer. And he told me exactly when Ethan Aberson entered and exited his room every day since he's been there."

"Okay," Dirk said. "Anything interesting?"

Tammy glanced down at her tablet's screen. "The day that Madeline was killed, he left his hotel room at nine fourteen in the morning. And he didn't return until a little after three in the afternoon."

"Maybe he was at a seminar on hair-dressing trends or a symposium on complementary shades of pancake makeup," Savannah said. She glanced at the scowling Dirk and added, "Or not. . . . Sorry."

"There were classes, but he didn't attend any of them," Tammy told her.

"He was gone from the hotel the whole time?" Dirk said, perking up considerably.

Tammy nodded.

"But he was in Las Vegas at nine fourteen and back at three," Dirk said, coming down a bit. "That's six hours. And it would take him at least five or six hours to make the drive to San Carmelita, one way. Even if he flew from Vegas to LA and then drove to San Carm . . . it'd still take too long."

"Not if he flew from Vegas to Santa Barbara and drove down here from there," Savannah said. "It would be snug, but he could have done it."

"If he didn't dally when he was doing the murder."

"Doesn't take that long to plunge a long, sharp object into your soon-to-be-ex-wife's back."

Tammy held up one hand. "Before you two get all excited, I'll tell you, I already thought of all that and checked it out. He wasn't here." She lifted her chin and grinned, looking quite pleased with herself. "I know where he was."

"The concierge spilled that, too?"

"As a matter of fact, he did. The day before the murder, the concierge arranged a car rental for Ethan and printed out directions for him to a brothel called Monique's Ranch. It's about an hour drive from Vegas. The next day—the day Madeline was killed—when the concierge asked Ethan how he liked the brothel, he said he'd had such a good time, he was on his way back, right then, for a second date."

"Wonder if he mentioned that to Mom and Pop when he called home to check on his daughter?" Savannah said.

Dirk chuckled. "Guys don't tell Momma everything."

"Gals either," Tammy returned.

"An hour to drive to the brothel. Two hours round trip," Savannah mused. "Say he stayed there an hour. That's three hours. Leaves him with several hours to spare."

"He could've gambled," Dirk suggested.

"He was at a matinee of a magic show," Tammy told them. "He had the concierge get a ticket for him."

Dirk raised one eyebrow. "I'm surprised that concierge has time to get tickets for anybody, if he spends all his time talking to women with fake, flirty southern accents."

"I was most assuredly his first," she said, pouring on the Georgia drawl. "And I dare say that young man was plum enamored by my down-in-Dixie charm."

"Hush up, girl," Savannah told her. "It's just too weird, hearing you talk like me."

"Okay, I'll drop the accent. But you don't want me to hush. Believe me . . . you're going to want to hear what else I came up with."

Casually, a smug little grin on her face, Tammy picked up her fork and began to play with her salad.

Savannah and Dirk watched, simmering with impatience, as she carefully cut a cucumber into four even, neat pieces.

Finally, Savannah snapped. "Girl, you better spit it out, or I'm gonna slap you upside the head with a French fry. With a big ol' glob of ketchup on it, too."

Tammy laughed and put down her fork. "Okay." She turned to Dirk. "You've probably already found out about the restraining order."

Dirk looked at Savannah. She shrugged.

"What restraining order?" they both said in unison.

Tammy picked a cherry tomato out of her salad and popped it into her mouth. After chewing for about a year, she said, "The one that Madeline Aberson took out a couple of weeks before she was killed."

"Madeline had an RO against someone?" Dirk said.

Savannah nearly choked on her iced tea. "Who? Who?"

Tammy laughed. "You sound like a hoot owl."

Shaking a long, floppy fry drenched in ketchup in her face, Savannah said, "Cough it up, babycakes, or you'll be wearing this."

"Threaten to do me bodily harm with trans fats! I'm sure that's a felony in forty-five states!"

"How would you feel about having some cod shoved in your right ear?" Dirk added, brandishing a piece of his deep-fried fish.

Tammy rolled her eyes. "Okay, okay. Madeline took out a civil harassment restraining order against Celia Barnhart."

Savannah and Dirk looked at each other questioningly. Then both shrugged their shoulders.

"Who the hell," Dirk asked, "is Celia Barnhart?"

"Funny you should ask that." Tammy fiddled with her tablet, then turned it so that they could each see the screen.

On it was a picture of a normal-enough-looking young woman. Conservative even. It was a simple, nondescript head shot, like the thousands used every day on Internet social sites.

"Okay." Savannah deflated a bit, like the old Disneyland balloons in her living room. "What's that supposed to tell us?"

Tammy messed with the screen a bit more and came up with another picture of Celia Barnhart. This time she looked quite lovely in her wedding gown, standing next to her groom, who was decked out in a stylish tuxedo.

Though as attractively dressed as the couple was, neither wore the happy, beaming smiles that were expected of a twosome on their wedding day. In fact, they both looked quite disgruntled.

"Looks like they had the same sort of day we had,"

Dirk grumbled. "What? Did their wedding hall burn down, too?"

"No," Tammy said. "But you two and this two, you did have something in common."

"What's that?" Savannah asked.

"The same wedding planner."

Savannah quickly added two and two and came up with a couple of couples who hadn't had the stellar weddings of their dreams. "Don't tell me she died during their wedding, too."

"No, of course not. But according to Celia Barnhart, Madeline ruined the most important day of her life."

"A bridezilla, huh?" Dirk said. "I guess women are a bit temperamental at a time like that . . . stress and all." He shot a look at Savannah.

She said, "Watch it, boy."

"Present company excepted, that is." He turned back to Tammy. "But this gal took it so far that Madeline got an RO against her?"

"Yes. According to the court documents, which I found online, she threatened Madeline with bodily harm . . . during the wedding itself, in front of all of her guests, and then daily for two weeks afterward."

"I think we need to talk to this gal," Dirk said, waving to the waitress to bring their check.

"Ah, yes," Savannah said. "If nothing else, we can compare wedding-day horror stories. If hers is bad enough, maybe it'll make us feel better about ours."

"Oh, please. Like anybody in the world has a worse wedding story than you two do." Tammy laughed and put her tablet back into her purse. "When it comes to getting hitched, you guys have the worst luck of all time."

When she had her chore done, she glanced up and saw they both had fixed her with stony glares.

She shrugged. "Well? You do."

"And you, young Miss Prissy Pants," Savannah said, "if you mention it again, I'm going to change your ring tone on my phone from 'You Are My Sunshine' to 'Rainy Night in Georgia.'"

Chapter 16

The next morning, Savannah and Dirk took a trip to Celia Barnhart's house. She wasn't home, but one of her chatty neighbors told them that she was a teacher's aide at a private day school in the neighboring town of Arroyo Verde.

As they pulled into the school parking lot, Savannah sized up the school. With its pristine green lawns, generously equipped playground, and scores of students running around in neat white shirts, blue and green plaid skirts on the girls and navy slacks on the boys . . . it was obviously a place that cost the parents a few bucks.

A place that was a far cry from the small country school that she had attended in McGill, Georgia, with its dirt play yard, one broken teeter-totter, and a single swing with frazzled ropes.

She smiled as she watched the kids slipping down their safe, bright red slide—splinter free, no doubt.

These kids were blessed. They wouldn't have to work as hard as she had to climb upward in life. They had a head start. She hoped that at least some of them would grow to realize that and make full use of it.

"See her anywhere?" Dirk asked as they got out of the car and walked past a neat queue of children all lined up and waiting to march back into the building to their classrooms.

Savannah thought of her last visit to a local public school, where the teachers did well to keep the kids from harassing, pummeling, and mugging each other. And she mentally applauded the difference.

"No," she said, as she scanned the crowd, looking for adults. "I don't. Are we sure she's working today?"

"Her sister said she is."

One elderly lady with a whistle around her neck and a firm, no-nonsense look on her face was straightening the line, cautioning those who were overly energetic to calm down.

At the end of the line was a pretty redhead who looked to be in her late teens.

But they were looking for a thirty-four-year-old brunette . . . possibly with a sunburn. According to Tammy, Celia Barnhart and her groom had recently returned from their honeymoon in Cabo San Lucas.

"Maybe she's inside," Dirk said.

Then Savannah spotted her leaving the main building by way of a side door and walking toward a large structure that might be a gymnasium or auditorium.

"There she is," she said, recognizing the woman instantly from the pictures Tammy had shown them. She was dressed in a baggy, dark dress instead of a well-designed, formal wedding gown, but she was wearing the same grumpy look on her face.

Savannah had a feeling this wasn't going to be particularly pleasant. "I'm not in the mood for drama," she told Dirk. "I'm to the point where, if anybody spouts off to me about how bad life's been treating them lately, I'm gonna give 'em an earful about my own problems."

"Nobody knows . . . de trouble I see. . . ." Dirk sang, his voice deep and deliciously bass, though a bit flat here and there.

She laughed and felt a little better, though still resolved to keep the amount of bellyaching she would hear to a minimum.

Life was just too short to listen to everybody else's whining, cursing, and raging. If for no other reason than because it seriously cut into one's own time for whining, cursing, and raging.

They caught up with Celia Barnhart just as she opened one of the large double doors. Savannah caught a glimpse of the gloriously shined wooden floors of a gym.

That was something else the little school in Georgia hadn't had either. They had played basketball on the asphalt parking lot . . . which had been a bit rough on the knees when a player took the inevitable spill.

"Celia Barnhart?" Dirk asked, showing her his badge.

"Used to be. I'm Celia Wynn now."

"Yes. Congratulations," Dirk said. "This is Savannah Reid. We'd like to talk to you."

Celia placed her hands on her hips and the anger in her eyes flared to a new, hotter level.

Oh, goody, Savannah thought. *And here goes my ocean pier Zen, swirling right down the john.*

"What about?" Celia snapped. "That stupid restraining order?"

"Yes, ma'am," Savannah replied. "That's a real good guess."

"It wasn't all that hard to figure out. It's the most ridiculous thing in the world, and I'm sick to death of hearing about it. After all that woman did to *me, I'm* the one who gets an order of protection filed against her? Get real!"

Dirk pointed to a wrought iron bench that was strategically situated to take in the view of a statue of a woman in a long dress, holding hands with a child . . . no doubt the founder of the school. "Would you like to sit down and—"

"No, I would most certainly not like to sit down. I'm on a break, the only break I get from these screaming brats all morning long, and I'm not going to spend it talking to you about some perceived threat I made toward that stupid bitch."

"Actually," Savannah said, "I'm more interested in hearing what *she* did to *you.*"

Yeah, right, she thought. *Toxic dumping ground, that's me. Lay it on me.*

"Oh, well . . . in that case . . ." Celia took a deep breath, and Savannah braced herself for the onslaught. "I don't know where to begin. Madeline Aberson is the wedding planner from hell! Don't let anybody that you know hire her! She totally ruined our day for us. It was a disaster because of her, and she won't even own up to it, let alone apologize!"

"Could you be more specific?" Savannah asked . . . knowing she could and would.

"Oh, sure. First of all, she didn't even show up on our wedding day. I didn't see her face or get as much as a phone call from her. Come to find out, she'd booked two weddings at the same time. I guess the other one meant more to her than mine."

"Okay. That's very unprofessional of her. What else?"

"Our flowers never arrived! She booked the vendor and placed the order, but she owed them a fortune, and they refused to deliver. My husband's father ran to the grocery store at the last minute and bought some supermarket roses, or my bridesmaids and I would've been empty-handed walking down the aisle."

"Ouch."

"And the hotel where she'd booked us for our first night together, before we took off for Cabo? We arrived only to find it was closed for remodeling! She should have known that! We had to spend our first night as husband and wife at my mother-in-law's!"

"Whoa, that's a bite in the butt!" Savannah said, forgetting, for a moment, her own wedding catastrophes.

"No kidding. And she never returned the money to us either. No matter how many times I called her. That's the so-called 'harassment' that she accused me of to get that restraining order. I was just calling to tell her she'd better at least pay me what she owed me, or I'd sue her. What's 'harassing' about that?"

Dirk cleared his throat. "Um . . . I read the order. It says you made threats of physical violence against her."

Celia shrugged. "I might have casually mentioned in passing that if she didn't fork over the cash, I was going to kick her ass so hard that it'd be up between her shoulder blades."

Nodding, Savannah said, "Yep. That'd be it."

"It was just a colorful figure of speech."

Savannah chuckled. "I'm from the South, so I understand all about colorful figures of speech, but can you see how Ms. Aberson and the court construed that as a threat?"

"I guess. But what the heck are you here for? I haven't gone near her or called her or contacted her in any way since I was served that paper telling me not to."

"We're working a case," Dirk told her. "And we're here to ask you where you were last Saturday afternoon."

"Why?"

"You answer my question, and maybe I'll answer yours," he told her.

She seemed to think for a moment. "Let's see . . . Sat-

urday afternoon . . . . My fianc—I mean, my husband—
and I had just returned from our honeymoon. I guess I
was home unpacking and doing laundry."

"Can anybody verify that?" Dirk asked.

"No. Not really. My husband was already back at
work. It was just me and the dogs there at home. Why?
Why does it matter where I was?"

"Because we're trying to rule you out as a suspect."

"A suspect for what?" She looked at Dirk, then at Savannah.

"Madeline," Savannah said simply.

"What about Madeline?" An ugly, most unladylike
grin spread across Celia's face. "Don't tell me . . . somebody actually did kick her butt up between her shoulder blades."

"No," Savannah said.

Celia looked deeply disappointed. "Oh, damn."

Savannah watched her closely when she said, "But
they did stab her between the shoulder blades. Three
times."

Celia Barnhart-Wynn's face suddenly turned as white
as the shirts her students wore. "Oh," she said. "Oh,
wow."

Savannah nodded solemnly. "Oh, yeah."

Later, they left Celia to return to her teacher's assistant duties, and as they walked back to the car, Savannah said, "Can you believe a person that hostile takes
care of children? Scary thought."

"Do you think she killed Madeline?" Dirk asked.

"I don't know, but one thing's for sure . . . she certainly had motive. Listening to her story, I was wanting
to kill Madeline for her."

Dirk sighed as he opened the Buick's passenger door

for Savannah. "You know, it's a lot easier when the victim's a nice person without an enemy in the world."

"Except one."

"Yeah, except one. It's a lot easier to catch a murderer if the whole damned state didn't want them dead."

Once again, Savannah and Dirk were driving along the winding streets through Spirit Hills, the posh community where Savannah intended to live when she grew up someday.

That was also the day when she won the lottery, the Miss America Pageant, and married Prince Charming.

"Oh, yeah," she told Dirk. "I'm going to have to revise my life plan. You've thrown a monkey wrench into the works."

"What?" he said. "Are you talking to yourself again?"

"Of course not. I never talk to myself. You're the one who does that."

"What were you saying about your life plan?"

"Only that I'd intended to grow up and marry a prince, so you're messing up my plans."

"I feel really bad about that."

He didn't look the least bit remorseful. In fact, he was giving her a little smirk that made her want to whack him and kiss him at the same time.

"How about just a prince of a guy?" he said. "A man among men. A studly stud. A hunk, a hunk of burnin' love."

"Whose good looks and virility are surpassed only by his humility."

"Yeah, something like that."

"Okay, I guess you'll do."

"Gee, thanks."

"Prince Charming's horse probably broke down on the way here."

"Threw a shoe on the Golden State Freeway."

"Yeah, something like that."

They had arrived at Odelle Peters's house just in time to see an enormous truck backing into the driveway.

"Uh-oh," Savannah said. "Moving day."

"That's rough." He pulled the Buick to the curb across the street from the house. "Moving's tough enough, even under the best of circumstances. . . ."

"Like when you're moving from a trailer into your new wife's cute little house?"

"Exactly. But to lose your house like that . . . I don't particularly like this gal, but I feel for her."

"A lot of people are in her shoes these days," Savannah said sadly. "I feel for all of them."

They got out of the car and walked up to the front door, which was standing wide open. Dozens of cardboard boxes were stacked in the foyer.

Farther inside the house, Savannah could see still more boxes and pieces of furniture swaddled in padded covers.

A couple of burly fellows had begun to carry the cardboard boxes out to the truck.

"You be careful with that stuff!" Savannah and Dirk heard Odelle shout from several rooms away. "Those are valuable antiques, and don't think I won't sue your boss to kingdom come if you break anything!"

A moment later she came stomping out of a room toward the rear of the house and into the entryway. "Hey, that's a mirror you've got there, buddy, and you'd better—"

She caught sight of Savannah and Dirk and stopped

abruptly. The cross look on her face deepened into something akin to loathing.

"You two again?" she snapped. "I thought we'd already said all we needed to say to each other."

"Do you know a Celia Barnhart-Wynn?" Dirk asked without bothering to exchange any mundane pleasantries.

Savannah agreed it was the right move. Odelle didn't seem to be in a "pleasantries" sort of mood.

"Of course I know her!" she returned. "She's one of the reasons I had to sell my house! I had to settle up with her, and at least half a dozen of Madeline's other highly dissatisfied customers."

"But why is that?" Savannah asked. "If they were her customers and not yours . . ."

"We were partners, remember? And when she started to go downhill, I couldn't get our assets untangled fast enough. She brought me down with her."

"I'm sorry," Savannah said, sincerely meaning it. She'd seen too many people dragged under by their associations with the wrong people.

It seemed so unfair. But then, many things seemed unfair. The older she got, the more she was pretty certain that the whole concept of "fair" was a hoax played on children, like Santa and the Tooth Fairy, only minus the magic and fun. The world wasn't a fair place, and to expect it to be only ensured disappointment.

"We just went to see Celia Barnhart," Savannah told her. "She has a lot of hatred for Madeline, blames her for ruining her wedding."

"Oh, pleeez. Celia's no different from any other spoiled, impossible-to-please bridezilla."

"Impossible to please? Madeline never even showed at the wedding. Celia had no flowers. No hotel room for her honeymoon night. That goes beyond just being spoiled, now doesn't it?"

Odelle walked past them to an oversized antique vase that was only half wrapped in padding. She began to tug the cover around it, securing it with a stretchy cord.

"Sure, Madeline was getting sloppy and Celia Barnhart probably didn't get all she paid for," she said, "but still . . . You have no idea what we put up with in this business. There are a lot of controlling, nasty women out there, and when they're about to get married, it *all* comes to the surface. They bark and expect everybody to jump. They tell you they want one thing and then throw a temper tantrum when you get it for them and they don't like it quite as much as they thought they would."

"It's a lot of stress, putting a wedding together," Savannah said, feeling the need to stand up for her sister brides everywhere.

"Yes, and a lot of that stress can come from indecisive, bossy brides. Celia Barnhart's one of them."

"Do you think she'd hurt Madeline?"

Odelle shrugged and walked over to a wall niche that held a beautiful bronze statue of a mermaid combing her hair with a sea shell. Lovingly, as though attending a baby, she started to wrap it as well.

"I suppose she could have. I don't know. Does she have an alibi?"

"Sort of," Savannah said. "Not a very solid one."

"Well, then, I guess you'd better keep her on your short list, huh?" Odelle paused, ran her fingers through her hair, and then wiped her hand across her face, as though refusing to see what was abundantly clear . . . herself moving out of her beloved home.

"We'll leave you alone now, Ms. Peters," Dirk said. "Thank you for your time . . . and I'm sorry about your home."

Odelle gave him a mildly surprised look, as though not expecting comfort from that quarter. "Okay," she said. "I appreciate that."

"I'm going to be moving soon myself," he told her.

"I hope you're moving up in the world, not down, the way I am."

Dirk gave Savannah a sweet smile and said, "Oh, I am. I most certainly am."

"Then you're a lucky man," Odelle told him.

"Oh, you have no idea *how* lucky."

Chapter 17

"**D**o you really have to do this?" Dirk asked Savannah as they pulled up in front of her house. "You can come back to the trailer with me and hide out."

"I do. I really do. They're my family, and they've come all this way to visit me. I can't keep avoiding them forever," she replied, staring at her yard, which was littered with toys. Her hedge was draped with a Minnie Mouse beach towel. Her bougainvillea had sprouted a pair of Mickey ears. A couple of *Toy Story* dolls were lying in the middle of her lawn. She wasn't sure if Woody and Jessie were doing something naughty or wrestling.

Dirk noticed her looking over the carnage. He shook his head. "Did it occur to Vidalia when she let the kids buy all that stuff that she's going to have a helluva time getting it all into a suitcase when she goes home?"

"She won't bother," Savannah replied. "I'll be the one packing it into cardboard boxes and standing in line at the post office to mail it back to them."

He reached over and took her hand. "Has it ever

dawned on you . . . um . . . how can I put this nicely . . . that you do a bit too much for your family?"

"You mean, has it ever occurred to me that I'm a doormat, an enabler of bad behavior, a flunky, and a pushover?"

"That would about sum it up."

Savannah rolled her eyes. "Of course it has. I've read the self-help books about setting boundaries and all that good stuff. I may be codependent as hell, but I'm not stupid or ill-informed."

"Then why do you do it?"

Savannah thought about it a long time before answering. It was a good question and deserved an honest answer. "It isn't what people think. It's not because I'm too weak to stand up for myself."

"Knowing you, that never occurred to me."

"I guess more than anything else, it's a habit . . . a habit that started years and years ago, and I've never changed it. When I was little, my mom was always saying, 'Watch the kids, fetch Vidalia a bottle, change Macon's diaper, get Waycross out of that mud puddle before he drowns hisself.' And, of course, if I didn't watch them close enough, and they got into trouble—which was bound to happen ten times a day with so many of them—I'd get a whoopin'."

Dirk was quiet for a long time. And when she turned to look at him, she saw what could only be described as fury on his face. And tears in his eyes.

"Your mother brought all these kids into the world and then made a child take care of them? And she gave you beatings when you didn't do it to suit her?"

"Wasn't exactly beatings. Just your old-fashioned hide tanning."

"Did it leave marks?"

"Are you kidding? After she took a switch to the back of my legs, I'd have to wear knee socks for weeks. You'd be surprised the sort of bruises and welts a hickory switch can raise."

He gently squeezed her hand and said softly, "Savannah, that's a beating. A felony. How many times have we hauled a guy outta his house in cuffs for doing way less than that to his old lady . . . a grown woman, not a kid?"

"I never thought of it that way," she said. "I guess if it's your parent doing it, it's just a spanking."

"If a stranger did that to someone's child, everybody would be up in arms about it. He'd be arrested on the spot. So, if it's your parent leaving bruises on you—the person whose job it is to protect you from harm—and not a stranger on the street, that makes it worse, not better. Acting like it's okay just adds insult to injury."

They sat in silence for a long time as Savannah thought over what he'd said. It was as if he had switched on a bright light inside a dark room in her soul.

He lifted her hand to his lips and kissed the back of it. "You know, baby," he said, "times have changed. That crap's all in the past. They aren't kids anymore. And your mom's sitting on a bar stool in Georgia, drinking her way into an early grave. She's never going to hit you again."

"No, she isn't. Nobody's ever going to hit me. Never again. I decided that years ago."

"So, nobody's going to beat you if you go in there and tell Vidalia to take care of her own kids. Or if you tell Marietta to make her own damned bologna sandwiches. Or if you tell Macon to get up off his fat ass and pick up his empty pizza boxes and soda cans."

Savannah sat, staring at him for a long time, as his

words found their way from her ears, through her brain, and down into a place much deeper.

And in that place, deep in her soul, she heard him loud and clear.

More importantly, the little girl who had been beaten because her baby brother had broken his bottle, spilling the last bit of milk in the house, heard it.

Savannah jerked the car door open, got out, and slammed it so hard that Dirk thought his windows would break.

"Uh-oh," he muttered as he watched her storm up the sidewalk to her front door. "Hell's broke loose in Georgia and the devil deals the cards."

"Where's Granny and the children?" Savannah demanded, standing in the middle of her living room and looking around at her siblings, who, from what she could tell, hadn't budged an inch from the last time she'd seen them.

"They're upstairs, taking naps. Butch, too," Marietta told her without taking her eyes off the television.

"And not a minute too soon," Vidalia said from the sofa as she flipped through her movie magazine. "I'm so tired, I'm draggin' my tracks out, just tryin' to corral 'em. It's time Butch lifted a finger to be a father to those younguns."

"Gran and the kids are upstairs? Good," Savannah said. "Then I don't have to watch my language none when I tell y'all what's what."

Jesup, who was sitting in Savannah's comfy chair, painting her toenails black, glanced up—as did the rest of them—slightly surprised looks on their faces.

"Well, boy . . . you got a nasty tone there, Sis," Marietta said. "You best mind how you address us."

"Shhh, Mari," Cordele said. "Can't you see that Savannah's experiencing some sort of anxiety attack? It's no doubt related to the post-traumatic stress she's suffered from the shooting. We all need to be patient with her as she works through her issues. She's quite fragile at this time and—"

"Oh, can it, Cordele," Savannah snapped. "The last thing I need right now is hearing your psycho-babble. I'm not fragile; I'm fed up. And if I'm stressed out, it ain't just from getting shot or having three attempted weddings go down the drain. It's also from putting up with the likes of you!"

Their mouths dropped open.

"Well, I never heard such abuse," Vidalia said, sitting up and slapping her magazine down onto the coffee table.

It occurred to Savannah that she looked downright unnatural without it, and what sad commentary on her daily life that was.

"Well, you're gonna hear what I've got to say," Savannah told them. "So listen up, all of you."

She drew a deep breath. "Vidalia, I love those children of yours to pieces, but I swear, if you don't keep them from tearing up my house, I'm gonna send you a bill that'll knock your eyeballs out. And I'm gonna expect you to pay it. So far you owe me for two African violets, three rose bushes, the plumber's bill from Jilly flushing that toy teacup down the toilet, the dry cleaning to get the peanut butter and jelly off my good bedspread—who the hell sends a kid off for a nap with a peanut butter and jelly sandwich in his hand? Oh . . . and a toothbrush."

"A toothbrush?"

"Yes. Your son decided to pee on mine. God knows why."

"He didn't!"

"He did! I caught him in the act."

Savannah turned to Marietta. "And I'm not going to tell you again that when you're in my house, you'll watch family-oriented programming on that television or not watch it at all. With children and our saintly grandmother in the house, you'll show some restraint and respect, or I swear I'll unplug the thing and hide the cord."

"Well! I—"

"And while I'm talkin' to *you* . . . from now on you make your own damned bologna sandwiches! You're over forty years old, for Pete's sake! Learn to feed yourself!"

She glanced toward the foyer and saw Dirk standing just around the corner, a big grin across his mug.

On a roll, she turned to Macon. "Haul your butt up off that floor," she told him, "and make yourself useful for once! Pick up all this food trash you've been throwin' down for the past week and drag the garbage to the curb. Tomorrow's collection day. And when you get back in here, go put on some clean clothes and throw those in the washing machine. You haven't changed since you been here, and frankly, you smell like the south end of a north-bound polecat."

It was Jesup's turn. "If you want to spend your life painting spiders and bats and blood drops and other weird things on your body, that's your business. But do it outside, 'cause you've already got that glittery makeup crap all over my couch, and if you get it on my comfy chair, you're gonna pay to have it reupholstered."

"Well! I never had anybody speak so disrespectful to me in all my livin' life!" Vidalia said, jumping up off the sofa with far more energy than Savannah had seen her display in years. "And frankly, Savannah, I'm disappointed in you that you'd speak so harshly to anyone, let alone your loved ones. I thought better of you."

"Oh, come down off that high horse before you get a nose bleed," Savannah told her. "You kept us all awake half the night, yelling at Butch because he said he likes your big butt! You've got a big heinie, Vidalia! Of course you do; you're a Reid! And lucky for you, you've also got a sweetheart of a husband who loves every inch of it. Get over it and move on! Geezzzz!"

"Well! If that don't just cap it all!" Vidalia said, as she stomped across the living room, passed Dirk in the foyer, and huffed and puffed her way up the staircase.

"Quiet down, or you'll wake up those younguns of yours," Savannah called after her. "And then poor Butch'll have to watch 'em, 'cause Lord knows, you'll be too busy reading about what nit-wit movie star's screwin' what other 'un."

Vidalia continued to huff and puff, but she did lighten her step as she disappeared up the staircase.

With a bit of effort, Macon raised his bulk from the floor and did a pseudo brush off of his sweat pants. "Well, I guess I'll go change clothes, since I've been told that I *stink*!"

"Eh," Jesup said, "ain't like it's the first time somebody told you that." She gathered up her makeup and tossed it into a skull and crossbones kit. "And I'll take my grooming supplies out to the backyard. That is, if Savannah isn't afraid I'll get nail polish on her lawn furniture."

"Actually, I am. Sit on the grass."

Jesup disappeared, too.

"Well," Marietta said, making a great show of changing the channels on the television to one with cartoons, then tossing the remote control onto the coffee table. "If this ain't a fine how-do-you-do. We come all the way out here to watch you celebrate your nut-chew-alls and—"

"Nuptials, Marietta. For God's sake, it's pronounced 'nuptials!'" Savannah walked over to her chair and plopped down in it. "When will you ever learn how to talk?"

"Well, excuuuse me! I'm sorry I don't pernounce things exactly the way that you—"

"Pronounce. It's pronounced '*pro*-nounce.' Not *per*-nounce."

"Well!" Marietta stood and flounced out of the room by way of the kitchen door, saying, "That does it! You've always been bossy, bad-tempered, and high-strung, Savannah . . . but this takes the cake!"

Only Cordele remained—a patient, condescending look on her face. "I understand, Savannah," she said. "I was expecting this. I knew it was coming, this overreaction you're having to simple, everyday family issues. You totally fit the diagnostic criteria for PTSD, that's post-traumatic stress disorder, or at least ASR, that's acute stress response. So—"

"Stop it!" Savannah said, gritting her teeth.

"So," Cordele continued, undaunted, "unlike the rest, I'm not going to take your verbal abuse personally. I'm going to take into account the stress you're experiencing with your wedding plans falling through . . . not to mention your near-death experience and—"

"Cordele, I'm warning you, girl. If I have to get up out of this chair and come over there and smack you, I'll do it twice. Do not pretend that you know me better than I know myself. It's annoying as hell. So are your stupid labels and diagnoses. Just keep 'em to yourself!"

Her chin lifted several notches, and nose high in the air, Cordele headed for the kitchen door, too, her normally ramrod-straight posture even stiffer than usual.

"That's what I get, trying to help someone who won't admit they need help. Clearly the denial stage of grieving . . . grieving for the loss of a sense of security . . . loss of . . ."

Her voice trailed away as she left the room and not a moment too soon for Savannah.

She sat there in her living room, in her favorite chair, her feet on her cushy ottoman. Even Diamante and Cleopatra climbed down from their sunny window perch and jumped up onto her lap, purring and rubbing their glossy black heads against her hands to get her to pet them.

Dirk stepped out of the foyer and into the living room. His ear-to-ear smile looked like it was going to reach all the way around his head.

"So," he said, "was it good for you?"

"I'm just basking in the afterglow," she replied, scratching behind Cleo's left ear. "And I'm going to enjoy the feeling for as long as I can. Because knowing me like I do, I'm sure I'll be second-guessing myself and feeling all guilt-ridden in five minutes."

Dirk started to reply, but his cell phone rang. He answered it, "Coulter here." He listened for a moment, then said, "Yeah, well, who're you and what do you want with me?"

She smiled. Dirk had such a great telephone persona. It was even more gracious and eloquent than his non-telephone persona.

"Yeah, all right. I'll be there in half an hour."

He hung up.

"Who was that?" she asked.

"Bambi Delight."

"Who?"

"Another stripper at Willy's."

"What did she want with you?"

"She wants me to meet her at Willy's. Says she can tell me who killed Madeline Aberson. Wanna come with me?"

Savannah sighed. "I should stay here, make amends with my siblings, spend some quality time with them, and re-cement our badly strained familial bonds."

"Yeah, you probably should. Are you gonna?"

She stood and grabbed her purse. "Hell no. Let's get going."

Chapter 18

"Ah, Willy's. How I've missed this place," Savannah said through moderately gritted teeth as they pulled up in front of the strip joint once again.

"You know you've got the hots for Will," Dirk teased her. "I saw you ogling him from across the room the other day."

"Oh, right. That leather vest really does it for me. I'm gonna get you one of those to wear for me on our honeymoon night."

"We're going to have a honeymoon night?" he asked, a bit wistfully.

"Theoretically," she replied, sounding just as sad.

Once inside Willy's Rendezvous, it didn't take them long to identify Miss Bambi Delight.

Even through the copious clouds of second-hand smoke, she wasn't hard to spot.

"She's gotta be the one over there with the plastic Rudolph antlers on her head and the deer tail hanging off her bikini bottom," Savannah said, pointing.

"What powers of observation you have, my dear,"

Dirk said, nudging her. "Ever thought about being a detective when you grow up?"

"Yeah. For a minute. Till I heard I'd have to hang out in dives like this one. Then I decided to be the Tooth Fairy, instead."

"How'd that work out for you?"

"It didn't. Went broke . . . you know, negative cash flow and all."

They didn't even have to approach Bambi. She spotted them almost instantly and hightailed her fake tail across the room to them.

She was a young, petite brunette with a nice figure that didn't appear to have been heavily augmented, like Francie's.

As Savannah gave her a quick once-over, she decided that Bambi—or whatever her real name was—would have been pretty, if she hadn't looked so darned hard and mad at the world.

"Hi," she said to them. "I heard you were here the other day, talking to Francie. I've got something to tell you."

Savannah glanced around. Big Willy, his vest, and ponytail were behind the bar, drawing mugs of beer. Francie was nowhere to be seen. And the rest of the Rendezvous crowd's attention was riveted on a particularly buxom redhead on the pole.

"So you said on the phone," Dirk replied. "You on a break now?"

"Better than that. I'm off!"

He nodded toward the front door. "Then come out to my car, and let's talk."

"Lemme get dressed. I don't want to be seen in . . . you know . . . this." She waved a hand at the almost-clothes she was almost wearing.

"Yeah, okay," Dirk replied. "Meet you out there. It's the blue Buick."

As Bambi scurried away to "get decent," Savannah and Dirk left the bar and returned to the parking lot.

"People are funny," Dirk observed. "Inside those walls, she strips off down to buck naked. But heaven forbid somebody might catch a glimpse of her out here in her bikini."

Savannah chuckled. "Hey, a gal's gotta uphold her standards, whatever they may be."

They had only been in the car a couple of minutes when Bambi came strutting out, wearing a pair of super-short shorts, an ultra-skimpy halter top, and flip-flops. She was carrying a ragged duffle bag with a pair of plastic antlers sticking out the top.

"Oh," Dirk said. "I'm so glad she got dressed up for us. That outfit's so much better than the other one."

Savannah reached around to unlock the back door for her. "Hey, I never said a gal's particular standards had to make sense to anyone but her."

The door opened, and Bambi crawled into Dirk's backseat, shoving fast-food wrappers aside to make room for herself and her bag.

"Can we go somewhere else to talk?" she said with a quick glance back at the front door of the club. "I'd feel more comfortable if . . ."

"Sure," Dirk said. "Anyplace special?"

" 'Bout a half a mile down the road there's a church with a big parking lot. Sometimes I go there to talk to . . . I mean we . . . I mean, sometimes us girls . . . talk to guys there."

The skin on the back of Savannah's neck crawled, and she was glad that Granny Reid hadn't heard that. For sure, she'd call down hellfire and damnation on anybody who dared to . . . talk . . . to customers right there on God's own property.

"Oookay," Dirk said. "Let's go wherever you're comfortable."

He gave Savannah a sideways glance.

She shrugged and said, "Standards. I'm telling you . . . standards."

Savannah could see why Willy's ladies had chosen this spot for their off-campus rendezvous. It was a large parking lot, and the far end of it was at the edge of a dense woods. A long way from the actual church and with a great view of the open space.

Most importantly, a body who was up to no good could see the law coming a mile off and get their britches hiked back up in time.

Ah, the subtleties of the world's oldest profession, she thought.

"Okay," Dirk said as he cut the key on the Buick and turned to face his backseat passenger. "Let 'er rip. Whatcha got?"

"You two are investigating a murder, right?" Bambi said. "That gal that Francie's old man was doing . . . ?"

"Yes," Dirk replied. "How do you know that?"

She shrugged. "Hey, Willy's is a small place. We know everything about everybody there."

"Everything?" Savannah said, hopeful.

"Everything worth knowing." Bambi took a deep breath that threatened to cause her to pop out of her teeny halter top, and said, "For instance, I know that Francie killed that Madeline gal."

"You do?" Savannah said, working very hard not to get excited or to let it show in her voice. She'd been led down way too many dead-end paths to get too excited too early.

"How do you know that?" Dirk asked.

Bambi looked very pleased with herself. She was enjoying this a lot, and that alone made Savannah doubtful.

Most genuine informers didn't enjoy the act of informing. They did it for any one of a dozen reasons, and none of those motives were anything to put a smile on anyone's face—unless, of course, they were getting paid for it.

"Well . . ." Bambi said. "I know that she told you that she was taking a nap in Willy's office when that gal got killed. And she wasn't."

"No? How can you be so sure?" Savannah asked.

"Because I saw her sneaking out the back door. The rear entrance is right there by Willy's office door, you know."

"Yes," Savannah said. "We noticed that."

"You saw her sneaking out." Dirk reached for his bag of cinnamon sticks on the dash and took one out. "How do you know she was 'sneaking' and not just 'going' out the door?"

"She was creeping along, like on her tippy-toes, and looking around like she was hoping nobody was watching her."

He popped the cinnamon into his mouth. "But you were watching her."

"Yeah."

"From where?"

"Just inside the door to the ladies' can. It's down the hall, out of sight. She didn't know I was there."

"That's it?" Savannah said. "You saw her tippy-toe out the door, and that's your proof that she killed Madeline Aberson?"

"Also, I heard her say something suspicious to Willy."

"What's that?" Dirk asked.

"When she came back a few hours later, she went up to him at the bar and whispered something to him. I heard it. She said, 'I took care of her, like I told you I was gonna. So, that's one problem that ain't a problem no more.'"

Savannah's neck bristled again, but this time it was a good sign. This wasn't a definitive, solid piece of evidence, but then, it might turn out to be something worthwhile.

In the past, she had solved cases with less.

"That's pretty incriminating, don't you think?" Bambi said. "It could mean something, huh?"

Dirk had his poker face in place as he gave her the briefest nod. "Might. Might not. But thanks for telling us. Anything else?"

Bambi seemed to get miffed in an instant. "What do you mean, 'anything else?' You expect me to solve your whole case for you? That's pure gold, what I just gave you."

"We don't know yet what you just gave us," Savannah told her. "We'll have to check it out."

"Well, there's money offered for information in a case like this, isn't there?" Bambi said, looking anything but innocent and doe-eyed as her stage name might suggest.

In fact, Savannah thought as she looked into the dancer's face, *she looks pretty darned predatory herself right now.*

Back in Georgia, she'd seen chicken hawks looking friendlier at a hen they were about to tear apart.

"I don't know what sort of reward, if any, is being offered in this case," Dirk told her. "But I do thank you for being such a good citizen and coming forward like this.

I'm sure there's a special place in eternity for informers like you."

Savannah nodded thoughtfully. "And especially those who do their good deeds right here on church property."

Bambi looked from one to the other, a frown deepening on her face. "I think I'm ready for you to take me back to Willy's to get my car," she said.

"Definitely that time," Dirk said, starting the Buick. "Yeah. I think we're all ready."

Five minutes later, Savannah and Dirk were watching Bambi walk from their car across the parking lot to her own beat-up jalopy.

"Do you think she did it?" Savannah asked him.

"I don't know if she did or not. Francie had a lot of hate for Madeline. We knew that after our talk with her."

"I wasn't talking about Francie. I meant Bambi there."

"What would Bambi have against Madeline?"

"Who knows. But did you get a load of the anger in her eyes when she was talking about it?"

"Yeah, I picked up on that. Some definite hostility there. But why do you think she might be the killer?"

Savannah shrugged. "I don't really. I was just saying because . . . well, you know how on *Bonanza* and *Gunsmoke*, it was always the guy who was pointing at some other dude, saying, 'He done it! He done it! Let's hang him right now!' and every time it turned out to be the one pointing the finger."

"Well, yeah." He gave her a sarcastic grin. "But I'm not sure that the same crime-solving techniques that worked on the Ponderosa and in Dodge City would apply here in San Carmelita."

"Bite me."

"I'm looking forward to the day when I can."

"Oh, yuck."

Bambi drove away, and they got out of the car.

It was time to have a talk with the man, old Willy Rendezvous himself, about his girls.

Savannah looked down at the pit bull who was standing next to her, nuzzling her hand with his big, square face, gazing up at her with a wistful look that she recognized all too well. It was the same expression that Cleo and Di used when they either wanted to be petted or fed.

She glanced over at the full bowl of doggy kibbles in the corner of the office.

"Okay, big boy," she said, dropping to one knee. "I didn't exactly come in here to scratch a dog's ears, but since you asked so nicely."

She gave the big, burly animal a nice face massage as she listened to Dirk squeeze Willy for information about his dancers. It was the same, basic routine she used on the cats, but Hercules didn't seem to mind.

"So, you're gonna sit there and look me straight in the eye and lie to me?" Dirk was asking Willy. "If you piss in my ear and tell me it's raining, we're gonna have a very rocky relationship, my friend."

Willy looked like he wasn't particularly happy being yelled at in his own office. And he didn't look like he was accustomed to it either. Apparently, most of the people in Willy's life were too intimidated by him to raise their voices in typical Dirk-fashion.

But it took a lot more than a leather vest, a chest and tummy covered with naked-women tattoos, and a long, greasy ponytail to impress Dirk.

"Don't go giving anybody an alibi who doesn't have

one," Dirk was telling him as he leaned over the front of Willy's desk, his hands planted among the papers scattered on its scarred surface. "Because that'll get you at least five to ten for interfering in the course of a homicide investigation."

"Okay, okay," Willy said, holding up one hand. "Maybe Francie wasn't here the whole time she told you she was. Maybe she went out for a while to run a little errand for me."

"What kind of errand?"

"She took care of some business for me."

Savannah left Hercules wanting more and walked over to the desk. "Take some advice from me," she told Willy. "My buddy here will work with you as long as you tell him the truth. But most of the guys who've lied to him in the past are now missing vital body parts. So, you'd better pony up quick."

"What did she do for you?" Dirk demanded to know.

"She took some money to one of my girls to take care of a . . . a medical procedure she needed done."

"What kind of medical procedure?"

"An abortion, okay? She was knocked up, and she needed to get it taken care of. We don't exactly have a medical plan for the girls here, so I take care of them. I'm sorta like a daddy that way."

"Oh, yes, heartwarmingly paternal, that's you," Savannah said.

Dirk shook his head and backed away from the desk. "When she came back from supposedly delivering this money to your damsel in distress. Where and how did she tell you it was done?"

Willy thought for a while. "I think I was behind the bar. She came up and said something like, 'I took care of her. No more problem.' Something like that."

Savannah's heart sank. Not that she'd invested a

large chunk of her life on this dead-end street, but still, she had hoped that maybe . . .

Oh, well. Life was full of disappointments. She'd file this one away as "not earth shattering."

Hercules had left his place in the corner and followed her to Willy's desk. He was nudging her hand again, trying to get a few more pets out of the visit.

"Tell me something, Willy," she said, fingering the velvety soft ear and thinking that maybe she'd have to reevaluate her stance on pit bulls. "How does Bambi feel about her?"

"The Aberson gal? I don't think Bambi knew her."

"Not Madeline. How does Bambi feel about Francie?"

"Oh, she hates Francie. Francie makes way bigger tips than her. You know . . . she's a blonde and . . . well, she's got way bigger tips."

Five minutes later, when Savannah left the office with Dirk, she had a new-found appreciation of at least some pit bulls.

But in her book, Willy was nothing more than a flea-bitten mutt.

Chapter 19

"So, where are you on the case?" Tammy asked as she joined Savannah and Dirk at Savannah's kitchen table.

"Nowhere," Dirk replied. "Absolutely, positively nowhere."

Tammy turned to Savannah. "Come on. It can't be *that* bad. You have to have *some* clues, *some* leads."

"Oh, we've got clues up the kazoo. In fact, we have too many. Unfortunately, none of them lead to any solid subject." Savannah shook her head and toyed with a coconut and macadamia nut cookie that was lying on a napkin in front of her. "I hope wherever she is on the other side, Madeline realizes how difficult she's made our job. With the kind of life she led, there are just too many people who hated her enough to kill her."

"It's bad," Dirk said. "So bad that, at this moment, these cookies are the only thing making my life worth living."

Tammy was mortified. "You can't let a cookie, especially one made with refined flour and white sugar, be your only reason for living."

Dirk bit into the cookie and closed his eyes when he chewed. "Yeah, well, you haven't eaten Alma's and Waycross's cookies."

Tammy's indignation evaporated. "Waycross bakes?"

Savannah stifled a chuckle. "He bakes, restores classic automobiles, can fix any machine on the planet, plays piano for the kids' Sunday school class, and plants Granny's garden for her every spring. Oh, and he can bench press one and a half times his body weight. Twice."

"Whoa!" Tammy's eyes were positively sparkling.

"Yep," Savannah said, "Waycross is a real Renaissance man."

To Savannah's utter shock, Tammy reached over and took a cookie off the plate in the center of the table. She fiddled with it awhile, breaking it apart and examining each piece. Finally she popped one into her mouth and chewed.

"Holy cow!" Savannah said. "I can't believe my eyes! Did I just see Miss I Only Eat Healthy Food put some cookie in her mouth?"

"It's mostly just macadamia nut," Tammy returned. "I don't want him . . . and Alma, of course . . . to think that I'm rude by not eating their cooking."

"Why not? Lord knows you've turned your healthy little nose up at my cooking ten thousand times over the years!"

Dirk nudged Savannah. "She wasn't trying to impress you. In case you haven't noticed yet, your girlfriend there's got evil designs on your little brother."

"I do not!" Tammy said, nearly choking on her nut.

"Of course, I've noticed," Savannah told him. "I just didn't think she'd go so far as to poison her own body to impress him."

Tammy's eyes narrowed. "You know . . . I don't like you two very much."

"Sure you do." Savannah pushed the plate toward her. "Here, have another cookie."

Tammy tossed her long hair back over her shoulder and lifted her chin. "I came here to see if I could help you with your case, not get insulted."

"Hey, you know the drill around here," Dirk told her. "One comes with the other."

"Case? Insults?" said a voice behind Savannah. "Can I help with the case and get insulted, too?"

She turned and saw Waycross, who had just walked in from the living room. "Sure," she said. "No shortage of insults to go around in this place."

Tammy went from "perky" to "perkiest" in a heartbeat. "I love your cookies, Waycross," she said. "You'll have to give me the recipe sometime."

Waycross shot her a look that Savannah could only describe as blatantly flirty. "You don't need the recipe," he said. "I'd be happy to whip a batch for you any time you've got the hankerin'."

Oh, yeah, Savannah thought. *Little brother's definitely the one with the "hankerin'."*

And she couldn't blame him. Tammy was lovely as she sat there, a red flush to her cheeks, ducking her head shyly, her curtain of golden hair falling around her face.

She looked across the table at Dirk and saw from his grin that he found the whole thing quite amusing.

Tammy and Waycross? Sure, why not? she thought. They were two of her favorite people in the world. Both had hearts of gold and both deserved love if they could find it. Especially Tammy. After all she'd been through, she had a good guy like Waycross coming to her.

"Drag up a chair," Savannah told her brother, "and take a load off. We wouldn't mind a fresh perspective."

Once he was settled next to Dirk, across from Tammy, Savannah said, "It's awful quiet around here. Where is everybody?"

"Sightseeing," he replied. "Alma got 'em to go to the beach for the afternoon. Fly some kites. Dig in the sand. Build castles. You know . . . tourist junk like that."

"You and Alma have been jewels during this trip," Savannah told him. "I don't know what I'd have done without you."

"Kilt the whole kit and caboodle of them?" he said.

"Probably. Or at least locked them all in the upstairs bathroom and tossed the key out the window."

"No problem," he said. "I aim to help any way I can. Now, let's hear about this case you're workin' on. We gotta get 'er done, so we can get you two hitched."

"And then," Tammy said, a sad look on her face, "you guys will all be going back home, huh?"

Waycross looked at her for a long time, a definite sweet longing in his eyes. "Well," he said softly, "let's don't go gettin' the horse before the cart." He turned to Dirk. "Now, good buddy. Let's hear what you've got."

"It's more like what we *don't* have."

"Then let's hear that, too."

Half an hour later, Waycross said, "You're right. Y'all got squat."

"Succinctly put." Savannah got up and walked to the refrigerator. "Who needs ice cream with those cookies?"

"Not me," Tammy said demurely. "They're perfect by themselves."

. "Oh, please," Savannah whispered. "Love makes liars of us all."

"Who do you think did it, Savannah?" Waycross asked her as she plunked a bowl of butter pecan in front of him.

"She thinks it's the husband," Dirk said. "She always thinks it's the husband, unless the gal had a boyfriend, then she thinks it's the boyfriend."

"But this floozy had one of each," Waycross said.

"And a business partner who hated her, and her lover's wife, and a father-in-law who acted like he was tickled pink when he heard she'd expired," Savannah said. "We've got motives for all of them and nobody's got an alibi that's worth a hoot except the husband, who's in Las Vegas."

"That's too bad," Waycross said, " 'cause it sound to me like he's the one you mostly need to talk to."

Savannah turned to Tammy. "When did that hotel concierge in Vegas tell you that he's coming home?"

"He's booked there for three more days. I'm not sure why. The convention's over tonight."

Dirk reached for another cookie . . . and took two. "I don't think I can wait that long to look him in the eye and ask him about his dearly departed wifey. Let's just say that I have powerful motivation to wrap this case up and get on with my life."

He gave Savannah a longing look. She grinned back. And Tammy giggled.

"Whatcha say, gorgeous?" he said. "Wanna go to Sin City with me? We can lean on this guy and also check out that cat house alibi of his while we're at it. It's a five and a half hour drive. I can make it in four."

Savannah scrunched up her nose. "How can a gal turn down a romantic offer like that? I'll drive, and we'll make it in five and a half."

She turned to her assistant and saw the residual pain

in her eyes, still so keen and sharp, even after three months. Tammy had lost so much—her sense of security, her innocence, her trust in others, and most devastating, her trust in herself, her judgment and intuition.

She needed something . . . badly.

"If you aren't too busy, Tams," Savannah said, "we'd really appreciate it if you'd come with us. You've done so well with that hotel concierge. It would help us a lot if you were along."

Dirk shot Savannah a quick, mildly disapproving look. She knew that he'd rather this was a trip for two, but he would also understand when she had a chance to tell him why she'd invited a third party.

For all of his griping about Tammy, for all of his bickering with her, Savannah knew that Dirk loved the kid as much as she did and wanted what was best for her.

Tammy gave a yelp of joy that sounded like she'd just discovered she had five out of five *and* the mega ball. "Really? You mean it!"

Savannah smiled. "I guess that means you're available."

"Oh, I am sooo available!"

Savannah looked at Waycross, sitting there looking at Tammy with love-struck, beagle puppy eyes.

She gave Dirk a questioning look. He gave her a little smile and a slight nod.

"But who's gonna keep this wild woman here out of trouble?" Savannah asked. "Tammy's hell on wheels when she's gamblin' and drinkin' and all those evil doin's."

Tammy snickered. "Oh, come on. I don't—"

"Well, I don't have time to walk around town with her on a leash," Dirk said. "I've got a murder case to work."

Dirk and Savannah fixed Waycross with a pointed stare, which he didn't even notice, because he was too busy watching Tammy giggle.

Finally, when Savannah cleared her throat much too loudly, he looked up. "Oh!" He stammered, stuttered, and turned two shades redder than Tammy. "You mean? I? Oh! I'll do it. That is, well, not the leash thing, but I'll come along and keep an eye on her."

He reached over and placed his hand on Tammy's shoulder. "If you want me to, that is. I know you don't really need anybody to take care of you, 'cause you're plenty smart enough to do that for yourself. But if you want some company—"

"Sure! You bet!"

More giggling. More goo-goo eyes. More blushing.

It was almost more than Savannah could stand.

"I'm going to go pack," she said. "And while I'm at it, I'm gonna try to figure out how to tell my grandmother I'm going to a place where you can commit all seven of the deadly sins in seven minutes without even getting up outta your seat."

"How'd it go over with Granny, you telling her we were taking this trip?" Waycross asked.

Savannah glanced in her rearview mirror at the tall good-looking kid in the backseat of her Mustang and wondered, not for the first time, if he was really her brother. He was the only redhead in a family of midnight brown brunettes. He was slim and trim when the rest of them were . . . well . . . not so slim and trim. He was as easygoing and peaceful of spirit as the rest were rowdy and cantankerous.

Sometimes Savannah wondered if her mother had

strayed from the straight and narrow on the night Way-cross was conceived.

And as soon as the thought went through her head, Savannah pushed it aside. It didn't matter. She was just so grateful to have a brother like him . . . no matter where he came from.

"How do you figure it went over?" Savannah said. "You know Gran. It went over like a fart in church."

Dirk shifted in the passenger seat, making a show of how uncomfortable he was. It was the exact same type of seat as the driver's, but he had to pout about something when she didn't let him drive. "Doesn't your grandmother know that we're going to be too busy to do any of the stuff she's worried we'll do?" he said.

"Oh, I don't think she's fretting about us getting arrested for public drunkenness or prostitution or raising a ruckus," Savannah said, "but when it comes to stuff like this, she always says, 'Flee even the appearance of evil.'"

Dirk sniffed. "Heck, if I did that, I'd spend all my time fleeing from most of the people I know."

"Alma's planning a day in Hollywood and Beverly Hills for everybody," Tammy piped up from the backseat. "Once your granny gets to see Lucille Ball's and Jack Benny's old houses, she'll be in a better mood."

"Don't count on it," Waycross said. "You'd be surprised how long Granny can hang on to a grudge."

Tammy rolled down her window, put her face half out, and took a deep breath. "Ah, I love the desert. It's so clean and fresh and natural."

"Yeah, this is really cool!" Waycross agreed. "I've never seen the desert before. It's awesome."

Savannah looked ahead at the straight, straight road stretching into infinity before them. And on either side, brown sand decorated with brown brush. Only the occasional Joshua tree broke the monotony.

"Eh, maybe for rattlesnakes, jackrabbits, lizards, and rats," she muttered, but not loud enough for them to hear her. No point in popping anybody's bubble.

"I like it because it reminds me of *Bonanza*," Dirk said wistfully, as he, too, rolled down his window and took a deep breath. "I can just see Hoss and Pa and Adam and Little Joe riding their horses across this very spot, rounding up cattle, shooting at bad guys."

"Dirk, you're just too old to be that obsessed with a television show," Savannah said.

"I like it, so shoot me. What's wrong with it?"

"It's kinda . . . well . . . nerdy, the way you go walking around a grocery store humming that theme."

"It's catchy. When I watch a *Bonanza* marathon, and hear it forty-eight times in twenty-four hours, it sorta sticks in your head, you know?"

"That's kinda my point. Also, you still have your Little Joe lunchbox."

"So? It's a collectors' item by now."

She sighed. How could you argue with a zealot?

"Besides," she said, giving it one more try. "The Ponderosa was in Nevada. We're still in California."

"We'll be in Nevada in an hour or so."

"I give up."

Chapter 20

"Okay, so Las Vegas is . . . um . . . big," Waycross said, as they stood in front of the Victoriana Hotel and looked up and down the street. "Not as spiffy as I thought it might be, but okay, I guess."

"Leave it to you, little brother," Savannah said as they walked to the front door of the hotel, suitcases in hand, "to be impressed with a desert full of nothing and let down by the adult vacation capital of the US."

"I'm sorry. I was just expecting really big, cool hotels and casinos, and these buildings aren't that big and most of them need a painting. I'd say, Sin City is sorta shabby looking."

"That's because you haven't seen the good parts yet," Dirk told him. "Wait'll you get a load of the Strip. And Fremont Street at night. That'll knock your socks off."

"I'm not sure," Tammy said, "because I've never been here before, but I don't think we even got into Las Vegas proper. This is sort of out in the toolies."

"Yeah, it is." Savannah looked up at the hotel façade and thought it looked more like an old haunted mansion than a hotel. And a rundown one at that. "And this place gives me the willies."

"Maybe that was the appeal," Dirk said. "Undertakers' convention . . . ?"

"Sure, that must be it." Waycross held the door open for the rest to enter. "Makes sense if you think about it. There's more atmosphere in a creepy place like this than one of them fancy, new-fangled places."

"No offense," Tammy said before they crossed the lobby, "but I want to check in alone. I don't want anyone to know I'm with you guys. It'll blow my cover with the concierge."

With that, she prissed off, leaving them to watch her sashay and chuckle among themselves.

"Boy howdy," Waycross said, "she's got a 'cover'! She sure does take this detecting stuff serious!"

Savannah rolled her eyes. "You've no idea."

"It's what she lives for," Dirk told him. "And if you make fun of her for it, she'll call you all sorts of obscene things, like she does me."

Waycross's eyes widened. "I can't imagine a nice lady like Tammy cussin'."

"Like a blue streak," Dirk replied.

"Oh, stop it." Savannah smacked Dirk on the arm. "She calls him Dirko. And if she's really mad, Pee-Pee Head or Booger Brain."

"Ewww, that's pretty bad."

Dirk nodded. "See. I told you so. Let's go check in."

Savannah turned to Dirk. "This is going to be expensive . . . four rooms. You're coughing up the big bucks, right?"

"Four!" Dirk was horrified. "How am I gonna explain four rooms to the captain? He'll never okay something like that! I was thinking two."

"Okay," Savannah said, walking in front of him. "Girls in one room and boys in the other."

"That wasn't exactly the arrangement we boys were hoping for," he replied. "And what about Tammy's cover?"

"She'll have to come up with a new one."

As Savannah joined Tammy at the counter, Dirk turned to Waycross and shrugged. "Oh, well . . . can't say I didn't try for you, good buddy."

"It's just as well. Sooner or later, I've gotta go back and look my grandma in the eye. And she can always tell when I've been up to no good."

Half an hour later, Savannah and Tammy were settled in their "girls' room." Savannah was lying on the bed, resting her eyes that were weary from the desert glare. Tammy was arranging the fresh fruit she had bought on a hand towel on the desk.

"This isn't so bad," Savannah said, enjoying the respite from having her hands on the wheel and her foot on the gas. "It doesn't smell too much like the bottom of an ashtray."

"Third-hand smoke is so dangerous," Tammy replied. "Waycross doesn't smoke, does he?"

"He did once. Then Granny bought him a big, cheap cigar and made him puff on it till he puked. That was Gran's technique for keeping all of us away from Demon Tobaccy."

"I'll bet it worked."

"Like a charm. Well, that and the threat of a trip behind the woodshed."

"Granny was strict with you guys."

"It didn't hurt us none. She dished out way more love than she ever did whuppins."

A "Shave and a Haircut" knock sounded on their door . . . with one extra little tap at the end.

"Dirko," Tammy said. "He thinks that 'secret knock' of his is so original."

"He's a man," Savannah said. "So, he suffers from delusions of grandeur. It's part of the charm of the gender. Let him in before he goes to his authoritarian police knock and disturbs the whole building."

Savannah groaned as she sat up, stretched, opened her eyes, and looked around.

No, the room wasn't that bad. It was actually sort of charming, in a haunted-house, bordello sort of way.

The dark mahogany furniture was antique, but in good condition, and the plum velvet bedspreads added a typical, overdone Vegas touch. The antique lamp with its fringed shade gave a golden glow to the room. And on the walls, the Victorian-era prints in their gilded frames added a certain ambiance.

When they had first entered the room, Savannah had decided that this was, indeed, the perfect place for a funeral directors' convention.

And with any luck, it might turn out to be the perfect place to catch a cold-blooded killer.

Tammy opened the door and Dirk entered, followed by Waycross.

Dirk took one look around the room and said, "Hey, you gals got big beds. We got twins. What's with that?"

"We made eyes at the guy who checked us in. Did you?" Savannah asked.

"Of course not."

"Then don't complain. You want the perks, you gotta put out. Besides, you don't really want to sleep in a *queen* bed, do you?"

"No, but a couple of *kings* would've been nice."

"Stop your complaining," Tammy said, offering him

a freshly washed and polished, organic apple. "And sit down over there. We've got to come up with a plan. A plan to catch this sucker so that we can go back home and you two can get married. A brilliant plan. A super plan. A sneaky plan."

"This was the plan?" Dirk asked Savannah the next morning as they stood across the lobby of the Victoriana and watched Tammy and Waycross as the two of them watched Ethan Aberson.

They had hung around the lobby in pairs, pretending to chitchat until Aberson had walked through. They'd recognized him instantly from his DMV photo. And Savannah had to admit that he was even more attractive in person.

Tall and muscular, with thick prematurely silver hair, and a deep tan, he didn't look like the stereotype of the pale, thin, black-haired undertaker.

Again, a somewhat annoyed Dirk said, "Is this the sneaky, brilliant plan?"

"I guess so," Savannah replied. "Why?"

"It seems sorta stupid. Why don't I just go up and talk to him, grill him . . . you know, the usual? Isn't that what we came here for?"

Unaware that he was being watched by a couple who were themselves being watched, Ethan strolled over to a stand that held brochures, advertising some of the many, many attractions the city had to offer.

Tammy and Waycross meandered over to the window and pretended to look outside. But it was obvious to Savannah that Tammy was observing Ethan's every action in a mirror on the wall.

"You and I might have come here just to talk to him," Savannah said. "But Tammy's all hot to trot to do some hardcore detecting first. And she might be right. Why don't we observe him for a while and see what he's up to?"

Dirk just grunted.

"Don't you have a feeling that this trip is more than just a convention for him? After all, he's staying even though the seminar's over. Why's that?"

Dirk shrugged. "It's Vegas, for heaven's sake. Maybe he just wants to do some gambling, go to some strip clubs, see some shows."

"Then why's he still staying here, out in the boonies, away from all the action?"

"I don't know."

"Well, maybe if we follow him around a bit, we'll find out."

"You mean, follow the bimbo and your brother while they follow him."

"We can't all four follow him at the same time in one big ol' lump. That'd be a bit obvious, don't you think? Duh."

"Oh, wow! Do you see that? He's picking up one of those brochures over there! Be still, my heart."

"Be still your mouth, before you get in trouble."

"I'm so afraid."

"Live in fear, my dear. Live in fear."

"Pooh."

Ten minutes later, Savannah and Dirk were walking down the street, tailing Tammy and Waycross, who were still tailing Ethan Aberson.

Their strange, clandestine parade continued for a few blocks before Dirk lost his patience, took out his cell phone, and called Tammy.

"What the hell are we doing?" he barked into the phone.

Savannah saw Tammy shoot an annoyed look over her shoulder before she answered him.

Dirk put it on speaker phone so that Savannah could hear.

"What do you mean, what are we are doing?" Tammy said. "We're surveilling our suspect."

"How many times do I have to tell you, there's no such word as 'surveilling'?"

"There is, too, I looked it up in the dictionary."

Savannah nodded. "Me, too. It's a word."

"Okay, why exactly are we 'surveilling' our suspect instead of me just interviewing him?"

"Because he's going someplace suspicious, and we want to observe what he's going to do there."

"He could be going anywhere. How do you know it's someplace suspicious?"

"Because we know. We saw which brochure he took out of that display there in the lobby. And we're just pretty sure that's where he's headed."

"Where's that?"

"You'll see."

Tammy snapped her phone closed as she shot Dirk a cocky look over her shoulder.

He growled. "One of these days, one of these days . . . to the moon."

"Yeah, yeah. She lives in fear, too."

Two blocks ahead, Ethan turned the corner, which resulted in a new view for all of them.

This was a quiet, sparsely traveled, street where the buildings were in far more need of a sprucing up than the Victoriana. The desert sun had done its damage on the walls of businesses and houses alike, causing their paint to peel and fade to pastel, no matter what their original shade had been.

Decorative bits of wrought iron were rusted,

flowerbeds were empty, and lawns were parched. The signs on the various storefronts advertised off-beat and colorful services and products, like: Lady Velma's Tarot Readings, Stinkin' Inkin' Tattoos and Body Piercings, and Lame Vanilla Washington's Voodoo Parlor.

And in the center of this eclectic block, was the strangest of them all. A large, two-story, brick structure with blackened windows and a large, white skull painted above the front door.

Ethan Aberson hurried inside.

They could hear the bells on the door tinkling as he opened and closed it.

This time it was Savannah who called Tammy. "What the heck is that place? And don't tell me it's 'someplace suspicious,' unless you wanna get beaned the next time I've got you within reach."

"It's the Museum of Death," Tammy said proudly. "Cool, huh? And suspicious, no?"

Savannah looked at Dirk. "Do you consider a museum about death out of the ordinary?"

"Not for an undertaker. You've gotta figure that anybody who's a funeral director has to be wired just a little bit different from the rest of us."

"Well, I think it's suspicious," Tammy said. "We're here investigating him for murder, and he's all obsessed with death? What are the chances?"

"Surely they have quite a few visitors to this place, and they can't all be murderers," Savannah said, knowing that her words were falling on ears that had already made up their minds.

She'd seen Tammy like this many times before. Savannah called it her Super Sleuth mode. There was no dampening the gal's passions at a time like this.

"Listen," Tammy said, "we're going in now, so I have

to hang up. Can't risk him overhearing what I'm saying to you."

"No, of course not."

"Are you two coming in, too?"

Savannah turned to Dirk. "Do you want to check out the place and tail the tails?"

"No. We're outta here. They can follow him around, while we go check out that cat house she says he went to. But while we're gone, tell her not to approach him for any reason whatsoever. He's to be considered armed and dangerous at all times."

Savannah returned to the phone. "Dirk says—"

"Yeah, yeah, I heard him."

"He means it, Tams. And I mean it, too. No contact! And if you need anything at all, call me. Okay?"

But Tammy had already hung up.

Savannah looked at Dirk and shook her head. "I almost feel sorry for ol' Ethan. With a bloodhound like her after him, he doesn't stand a chance."

Chapter 21

"More driving. More desert. Oh, goody gum drops," Savannah complained as they headed out of Vegas and once again, into the wild, open countryside.

"You've gotta leave town," Dirk said, "if you're going to find a whorehouse. Contrary to popular opinion, there aren't any in the city. Not officially anyway."

"I don't think most sex workers would approve of your terminology."

"Oh, sorry. How about den of iniquity? House of ill repute?"

"I think the appropriate term is brothel."

"Huh. I didn't think you were the type who worried a whole lot about hookers getting offended."

Savannah fixed her eyes on the road straight ahead and looked a bit grim as she said, "You and I, we've had a lot of contact with that world. How many gals, and guys, too, did we bust in our careers?"

"Way too many."

"That's for sure. I had a front-row view to how much misery it causes in this world. To the prostitutes them-selves, their johns, and the johns' families. I've seen the horrible results of the diseases that are spread, and the dangerous situations these girls put themselves in to make a buck. The abusive pimps. The drug-addiction angle. There's a heap of better ways to make a living that don't get a body beaten or killed."

"So, you wouldn't legalize it?"

"Not on your life."

"Me either."

Savannah thought for a few moments, remembering. Wishing she could forget.

"My father was into prostitutes," she said.

No sooner were the words out of her mouth than she caught her breath, shocked by her own candor. She had never shared that with anyone before.

"He was?"

She ventured a glance at Dirk. He seemed a little surprised, but mostly sad.

She nodded.

"I'm sorry to hear that, Van. Very sorry. I had no idea."

She took a deep breath. "As you know, he was a trucker. Those truck stop cuties would wave it in his face, and he'd go for it every time. Unless you believe my mother's version of the story, and then they didn't even have to wave it. He'd go after it. In fact, she said that's why he became a trucker in the first place. So he could be away from home for days on end and do whatever he wanted with anybody he wanted."

Dirk reached over and laid a hand on her shoulder. "That must have been awful for you."

"It was. And I remember lying in bed, crying, when I was little, after hearing them screaming and fighting about it. And I wanted to just get up out of that bed and go to those truck stops and tell those girls to leave my daddy alone. That he belonged to us kids and my mommy. That we needed him more than they did."

He ran his fingers gently through the back of her hair and massaged the nape of her neck. "I'm so sorry, Van."

"So, I'd have to say, no, I don't like prostitution very much."

"I don't suppose you do. And I can't blame you."

"But we're on our way to interview some, so I'm going to put my prejudices in my back pocket, and you're going to watch your terminology. Because no matter what they do for a living, we're going to treat them with respect."

"Understood."

They traveled on in companionable silence for a while, until Dirk said, "Savannah, you don't ever have to worry about me doing something like that."

"I know."

"I want to make sure you know. I'd never be unfaithful to you. I'll never break your heart."

"I know."

She turned her head, nuzzling her cheek into the palm of his big, warm hand.

"If for no other reason," he said, "I wouldn't do it because of that little girl in Georgia. I can't stand the thought of her crying in her bed over crap she shouldn't have even known about till she was a whole lot older."

The road ahead got very blurry. Savannah blinked her eyes several times and sniffed.

"Thank you, Dirk."

"You're welcome, baby."

"Wow, how romantic," Savannah said as she and Dirk pulled over to the side of the road and parked in front of what looked like a miniature, abandoned trailer park out in the middle of nowhere.

For as far as the eye could see in any direction, the dilapidated mobile homes were the only structures, the only signs of humanity. An island of faded, rusting metal, baking in the desert sun.

Savannah thought she'd never seen such a lonely setting in all her life.

"I don't think romance is an important ingredient in what goes on here," Dirk said. "What were you expecting?"

"Oh, I don't know. With a name like Monique's Ranch, I guess I was picturing something with some French flavor. A bit of New Orleans charm, balconies with fancy wrought iron. Beautiful ladies standing on them, wearing feather boas and revealing evening gowns, beckoning 'come hither' to passersby."

Dirk shook his head and laughed. "You've read way too many of those romance novels, gal. Let's go inside and get a taste of the real world . . . distasteful though it may be."

They left the car and walked across the hard-packed dirt to the door of the trailer that was front and center in the haphazard complex. Over the door hung a hand-painted black sign with the name of the place spelled out in hot pink. On either side of the name was a pink circle with a red dot in the center.

"Are those supposed to be boobs?" she said.

"I reckon," he replied. "I drew better ones than that when I was nine."

"You drew boobs when you were nine?"

He grinned and glanced down at her ample chest. "I became a boob man very early in life and never looked back."

"Apparently so."

Dirk tried the doorknob, but found it locked. He rang the bell and a loud, annoying buzz like an electric shock sounded throughout the property.

A few moments later, the door was opened by a large, Slavic-looking man. With his blond hair and light blue eyes, he might have been handsome, had it not been for the coldness in those icy eyes and the numerous scars on his face.

Savannah had seen scars from accidents and scars from fights. And she knew, this was not the face of a peace-loving man.

He glanced quickly from Dirk to Savannah and back. "Yes," he said in a heavy Russian accent. "What can I help you with?"

Dirk showed him his badge, though Savannah noticed that he flashed it a bit faster than he normally did.

No point in advertising the fact that he was out of his jurisdiction.

"I need to talk to the madam of this establishment."

The guy's eyes flickered over Dirk like a prize fighter checking out the competition before a bout. "You talk to me," he replied.

"Inside," Dirk replied, matching his gruff tone. "Now."

The doorman didn't exactly jump to obey. He stood there for several long, tense moments before he finally stepped backward just enough to allow them entrance.

Once inside, Savannah glanced around at Monique's reception area and saw that this legal brothel looked like every other cheap, illegal establishment that she and Dirk had rousted when she was a cop. The cliché, dim, red lighting, crushed red velvet, dirty chandeliers, and pictures on the walls of nude or scantily clad females set the mood.

The place smelled like it could use a good airing out,

Savannah thought. She would bet that it hadn't seen a beam of sunlight or a whiff of fresh air in years.

"I need to talk to Monique," Dirk said as he walked over to a small counter in the left-rear corner of the room and picked up a piece of paper that said "Menu" at the top.

"You talk to me," the iceman repeated.

Dirk scanned the paper, then handed it to Savannah. She glanced over it and was mildly surprised at the simplicity of the choices. For the most part, there wasn't anything on it that didn't routinely occur in bedrooms of regular old married folks the world over.

It was hard to imagine what the big deal was.

"Are you telling me that this is your place?" Dirk asked him.

"It is."

"Ah, well, then . . . in that case, Monique, you're the one I need some answers from."

"My name is Vadim. You will call me Vadim, not Monique. That woman's name."

"Okay, Vadim. I would have guessed Boris, but . . . whatever."

Savannah stifled a grin when Vadim the Terrible's nostrils flared.

At times like this, she often thought that maybe someday she could break Dirk out of his unfortunate habit of pissing off nearly everyone he met. It was a pleasant fantasy, a civil Dirk, brought into being under her gentle tutelage.

But Granny had warned all of her granddaughters, "Don't marry a man expecting to change him. It'll just annoy the daylights outta him, and wear you to a frazzle."

No, she would probably never be able to change Dirk. She was lucky if she could get him to keep his feet off her coffee table.

"What you want with me?" Vadim barked, crossing his burly arms over his even burlier chest.

Savannah hoped that Dirk had noticed these burly qualities and was taking them into account when he was taunting him like this.

Dirk reached into his pocket and pulled out the photo copy of Ethan Aberson. He shoved it under Vadim's nose.

"Vadim shoved the picture away. "No. I know nothing about him. I—"

"You look again," Dirk said, shoving it back in his face. "He was here. We know that. I want to talk to the gal who serviced him."

"My ladies do not 'serve.' They are companions."

Savannah couldn't resist the urge to enter the fray. She stepped forward and held the menu up to him. "Okay, then which one of your lovely lady companions provided one of these . . . um . . . tasty dishes for that man in that picture."

"I don't remember."

"That's too bad," Dirk said, "because that means you're going to have to blow your whistle, or whatever you do, to get your ladies to all come parading in here and line up so that I can show each one of them this picture and see who remembers him."

"They shouldn't mind too much," Savannah said. "They do it all the time, day and night, for your customers. And we'll even let them wear their clothes and retain their dignity."

Vadim wrestled with his anger, staring at Dirk with those pale blue eyes that got colder by the second.

"You have some paper to show you can make me do this?" he asked.

"No, but I can get one," Dirk lied. "And while we're interviewing all of your women, we're going to look them over really closely for any signs of bruising, any indications that they aren't happy in their work here."

"This is legal brothel."

"Oh, I'm sure it is," Savannah replied. "And I'm sure that you're abiding by absolutely every single rule regulating its operation. There are so many of those pesky laws, I don't know how you people can keep them all straight."

"And I hear the penalties are pretty harsh," Dirk said. He paused, letting their message sink in, then he said, "I need to speak to the young lady who was a companion to this gentleman at this establishment. Now. We ain't got all day."

Stoically, Vadim stood, staring at them, a muscle in his massive jaw twitching furiously.

Dirk stared back. And so did Savannah.

The only sounds were of an old regulator clock on the wall ticking and the whistling of air that was rushing in and out of Vadim's flared nostrils.

Finally, he whipped a cell phone out of his pocket and barked into it, "Come up here." Then he snapped it closed.

Less than thirty seconds later, a pretty little blonde came rushing in, wearing nothing but a bikini bottom. She had a baby face, and Savannah would have guessed she was no more than fifteen.

On that sweet face was entirely too much makeup and an obviously fake smile. When she saw Savannah, she looked mildly surprised. She turned questioningly to Vadim.

"Both of them?" she said.

"No. He just wants to talk," her boss told her.

"No," Dirk interjected. "Both of us. Her *and* me. Both of us just want to talk."

The girl motioned for them to come with her, but Vadim held up one hand.

"Stop," he said. "Pay first. Both of you. You just talk, you pay, too."

. As Dirk forked over the cash, Savannah watched Vadim and the girl and saw a look exchanged between them. Having seen that look far too many times, Savannah was familiar with the subtext it contained. "Watch what you say, or else," was the message, loud and clear.

Savannah wasn't sure how much they were going to get out of this young woman. But she was sure of two things: This professional "companion" was terribly afraid of this barely glorified pimp. And the two of them had something to hide.

When Savannah entered the tiny room with its big bed, she had to breathe deeply to avoid an attack of claustrophobia.

The small, single-wide trailer made Dirk's mobile home feel positively palatial by comparison. And the dark red walls and heavy drapes that blotted out all sunlight didn't help.

Like the reception area, it was lit with red lights and dusty chandeliers. Apparently housekeeping wasn't high on Vadim/ Monique's list of priorities. Or his customers' either.

"Do you want to shower first?" the young woman asked, waving a listless hand toward the narrow hall.

"No, darlin'," Savannah said. "We told you we're here just to talk and we are. What's your name?"

"Trixie," was the unenthusiastic reply.

Savannah gave her a sad smile. "I'd like to call you by your real name." She held out her hand to her. "Mine's Savannah, and this is Dirk."

"I'm Charlene," she said, awkwardly shaking Savannah's hand.

When she turned to Dirk, he said softly, "You can put on some clothes, Charlene, if that'd make you more comfortable."

"Thank you," Charlene said as she hurried to the back of the trailer and returned with an old, worn, man's flannel shirt that reminded Savannah of the kind that her grandfather used to wear.

She slipped it on, buttoned up the front, and then sat on the side of the bed. "You wanna have a seat?" she asked, waving toward the other side.

Savannah and Dirk glanced around, but there were no chairs and no place else to sit.

"No, we're fine," Dirk replied. "This won't take long. I just want to ask you something about a man who visited you here last weekend."

Charlene shot a quick glance up toward a dusty silk plant hanging in the corner of the room. "Yeah, okay. I don't know how much I can tell you, but . . ."

Savannah turned her back to the corner with the plant, reached into her purse and took out her note pad. She scribbled, "Camera?" on the paper, then held it against her chest so that Charlene could read it.

The girl glanced down at the notebook and gave the faintest of nods.

"You just do your best, Charlene," Dirk said, glancing down at Savannah's message. "That's all we're asking."

He took the picture from his pocket and held it up for her to see. "Does he look familiar to you?"

"Oh, yes!" she said with far more enthusiasm than Savannah was expecting. "He was here. He came to see me on Friday, and we had such a good time that he came back again the very next day, on Saturday."

Okay, Savannah thought, *that's a new one . . . a hooker who rats out her customers in a heartbeat.*

"All right," Dirk replied. "Thank you." He gave Savannah a questioning look.

And she knew just how he felt. How strange, to have an interview go this smoothly. When did an investigator ever find out exactly what they wanted to know within a couple of minutes?

But if everything was going so swimmingly, why did she have this nagging feeling that all wasn't the way it appeared?

"Honey," Savannah said, "did he treat you right?"

"Oh, yes. He was nice. Very nice."

"Did you catch his name?"

"Ethan. He said his name is Ethan Aberline or Abersomething. He said, I just can't remember exactly."

Dirk raised one eyebrow. "How many of your customers tell you their full names, Charlene?"

She shrugged. "Some of them tell me a name, but I doubt it's their real one, you know?"

"Yeah," Savannah said, "I can imagine. Did he give you a good tip?"

Something flitted across Charlene's face. Just a brief little something that Savannah couldn't categorize on the spot.

"Yes, he did," she responded, nodding vigorously. "Like I said, he was very nice. Handsome, too."

"I'll bet you don't get a lot of guys that good-looking in here, huh?" Savannah said.

"Guys are guys," she replied with a tone of exhausted resignation. "You know, they are what they are."

"Did he say anything or do anything out of the ordinary?" Dirk asked. "Anything at all."

She thought it over . . . or at least pretended to. Savannah wasn't sure which.

"No," she said. "He was just a regular, nice guy. Except that he came back the next day and asked to see me again. I don't get that very often. In fact, I think he might've been the first to do that."

She seemed to realize she was saying too much. She broke eye contact with them and crossed her arms over her flannel men's shirt.

"What time was he here?" Dirk asked.

"I'm not sure, but sometime in the late morning. He bought a two-hour date the second day."

She looked down, fiddling with the buttons on the front of her shirt, and the look on her face was one that Savannah had seen many times. It was the look of a liar. Someone who wasn't very good at it because they hadn't had a lot of practice.

"Sweetie," Savannah said, "did anybody tell you to say this to us?"

Charlene looked startled and not a little unsettled by Savannah's question. "No, of course not," she stammered.

"Did this nice man, Ethan, did he pay you to say this to anybody who might come asking?"

"No. Not at all. Is that all you want to ask me, 'cause if it is, I've got stuff I've gotta be doing," she said, shooting a quick look at the plant hanging in the corner.

"Yes, I guess so . . . for now," Dirk replied. He turned and walked to the door.

But Savannah hesitated, looking at the young woman on the bed with the lost look in her big eyes. "How old are you, hon?" she asked.

Again, Charlene looked up at the corner. "Nineteen," she said.

"You don't look nineteen. You look like a kid who needs to go home."

Tears sprang to Charlene's eyes. She wrapped her

arms tighter around herself, her fingers clutching hand-fuls of the soft, plaid shirt.

"You know he loves you," Savannah said softly.

"Who?"

"The guy whose shirt that is. Is it your dad, your grandpa?"

The tears flowed more freely. "My big brother."

"Well, he misses you and wants you back." She dropped her voice to a whisper. "Give him a call and get out of this hellhole. You can still have a life and you de-serve one."

Charlene looked down, covered her face with her hands, and began to sob.

Unable to resist, Savannah turned and glared up at the camera in the corner, then gave it her seldom-used, but skillfully delivered middle-finger salute.

As she and Dirk exited the trailer and made their way across the parched, cracked earth toward the Mustang, she said, "I hate places like that. I hate what they do to kids' families, like mine. And I hate what they do to kids like that one in there."

He reached over and wrapped his arm around her shoulders. "I know, babe. Me, too."

"And the whole legal-schmegal bullshit doesn't change a thing. You can dress a pig up in a Sunday suit and take him to church, but he's still a hog."

"I agree."

She looked up at him and saw that he was watching her with a mixture of humor, respect, and affection.

"I've done a bit of self-searching-type investigating and discovered that I feel strongly about this topic."

He kissed her on her forehead. "Yeah, no kidding."

Chapter 22

No sooner had Savannah and Dirk climbed back into the Mustang, than Savannah's phone rang. It was Tammy's sunshine song.

"Hello, Tamitha," she said, thinking how different Tammy was from the girl inside that trailer. Given a bit of sunshine and light, Charlene might have been a woman like Tammy instead of a heartbroken child. "What's shakin', sugar?"

"Oh, lots of things," came the weary but excited reply. "We watched him in the museum. He bought a creepy thing there in the gift shop where they sell all sorts of gross stuff, including antiques."

"What did he buy?"

"An old traveling undertaker's at-home embalming kit."

"Oh, goody. I want one."

"Really?"

"No. What else?"

"That's all he bought, but we kept following him around. He went to a bar called Bloody Mary's and had a—"

"Bloody Mary?"

"Yeah, how'd you guess?"

"I'm not a private detective for nothin'. What else?"

"He had a filet mignon at a local steak house and—"

"Extra rare?"

"Of course. And then he went back to his hotel room. We're down the hall, watching the door."

Savannah smiled, imagining her brother and Tammy hiding behind some giant palm or whatever. In her fantasy, they were both wearing Groucho noses, glasses, and mustaches.

"Above and beyond the call of duty," she told her. "Why don't the two of you go get some dinner, too? We're getting ready to leave the brothel now. We'll hook up with you later."

"Are you sure? We'd be glad to wait for you to get back for us all to eat together."

"Two's company, Tammy. Four's definitely a crowd. Go eat . . . if you can find an organic vegetable in Sin City."

"Oh, yeah . . . that might be a challenge."

"Talk to you later, puddin'. Thanks for all the good work."

"Happy to do it. Oh! Wait! I forgot to tell you. After we were all back at the hotel, I hooked up with that concierge . . . the one I got along with so well over the phone."

"Yes? And tell me you didn't really use that pregnant sister cover. It wouldn't work in person since you aren't—"

"Of course not. I told him that Waycross and I are cops."

"Tammy! You didn't! Impersonating a police officer is illegal!"

"Only if you get caught. Don't worry. He was really nice. Even let us look at some of the hotel security footage from the day of the murder."

Savannah scowled. "Yes. We confirmed what he told you before about Ethan going to the brothel two days in a row. We verified it with the gal he saw here at Monique's. And by the way, Monique's a big, ugly Ruskie dude."

"What?"

"Oh, sorry. Is that un-PC of me?"

"No, well, I don't know. But that's a fake alibi. Ethan was walking around the halls of the hotel here at . . . let me check my notes . . . eight oh four, nine fifteen, ten oh eight, eleven twenty-six, and then at twelve thirty-nine. And it's an hour drive there, right?"

"Yes. An hour and change."

"Then he wasn't there any time during the morning. He was here in town. Mostly here in the hotel."

Savannah turned to Dirk, her right eyebrow raised to all-new heights. "You're very sure about this, right, babycakes? Because I have a feeling this information is gonna open a big can of whupass."

"Yes. I'm sure. Who's ass is gonna get whupped?"

But Savannah had already hung up the phone and was getting out of the car.

"What's up?" Dirk asked, following her.

"My dander."

"Why?"

" 'Cause if there's one thing I can't abide, it's bein' lied to. And I'm about to give that lyin' Russian new excretory alternatives."

He stopped and stood there thinking about it as she stomped on toward the door. Then he ran and caught up to her. "Oh, okay. Gotcha. Need help?"

"No, but you can watch if you wanna."

She pounded on the door several times before Vadim finally opened it again. He looked annoyed, but not half as angry as she was.

She barged past him, nearly knocking him off his feet.

"What the hell!" Vadim shouted at her. "You again?"

"Yep, it's her again. And me, too," Dirk said, following her inside. "Apparently, she's got a bone to pick with you."

"What bone? What pick?" Vadim said, bristling.

Dirk opened his mouth. Closed it. Then opened it again. "Well, I'm not exactly sure, but I'll betcha she's gonna tell you."

"You're damned right I'm gonna tell you." Savannah stepped up to him and shook her finger in his face. "You lied to us. And you got that little gal in there to lie to us, too. Ethan Aberson didn't come back here for a second visit the next day. He was somewhere else."

"No. No. He was here."

"Don't you go lying to me again, you two-bit pimp. This isn't open for debate. We've got videos of him in Las Vegas at the same time you say he was here. Solid proof. He wasn't here. So why are you covering for him?"

Having caught up to speed, Dirk stepped forward, too, an equally irate look on his face. "Do you know what you're doing, buddy? You're providing an alibi for a guy who's suspected of first-degree murder. You know that? This here's a homicide investigation you're interfering with."

Vadim's face tightened with fury as he backed away from them and around the end of the counter. "I did nothing. I said nothing to you."

"The guy in that photo," Savannah said, "paid you and your girl to say he was here when he wasn't to give him an alibi so he could murder somebody. Now, when we prove that, you're going to be on the next boat back to Russia or wherever the hell you're from. And something tells me you might not get a warm welcome back there."

"So you'd better start telling the truth," Dirk said.

"And you"—Vadim reached behind the counter and pulled out a butcher knife that was at least a foot long— "you leave or I cut your hearts out."

Savannah reached beneath her jacket at the same time as Dirk went for his own shoulder holster. In unison, they pulled their weapons and pointed them at Vadim.

"Two guns beat a knife any day of the week and twice on a Sunday," Savannah told him. "So you put that cheese slicer on the counter there before we blow your damned lying, pimping head off."

Vadim was shaking so hard and glaring at them with such pure hatred, that for a moment, Savannah thought he might go for it. She had already calculated how many rounds she could squeeze off before he was able to get around the counter. And she was pretty sure that, between the two of them, they could drop him . . . big as he was.

Just for a split second, she felt a sick, familiar feeling deep in the core of her being, raw and potent as the adrenaline surging through her bloodstream.

She had been in a life-and-death situation like this less than one hundred days ago, and every cell in her body remembered it.

But this was different. This time her weapon was in her hand. And she knew how to use it.

"Put down the knife," Dirk said. "If you don't, we're gonna shoot you. Do you wanna die today, Vadim? Is that what you want?"

"Put it down," she said. "Lay it on the counter. Don't make things worse than they already are."

Finally, the fire of rage in his eyes subsided a bit, and a more sane, smoldering anger replaced it. With a deep sigh of resignation, as though he had been holding his breath for a long time, he laid the weapon on the counter.

Quickly, Dirk snatched it up.

But both he and Savannah kept their guns trained on him.

"Okay," Savannah said. "Now, you tell us the truth. How much did he pay you for this alibi?"

In a calmer, less aggressive tone, Dirk said, "If you tell me right now, I'll walk out of here, and we'll forget everything that just happened. We just want to know what he said to you and how much he paid you. Tell us and we'll leave you alone."

Vadim thought it over. Finally, he said, "Five hundred dollar."

"And what exactly did he tell you to say if anyone came asking?" Savannah wanted to know.

"He just said, 'Say I was here to see girl, that I like her a lot, so I come two days. Friday and Saturday, too.'"

"Okay, now was that so hard?" Dirk lowered his weapon and reholstered it.

But Savannah didn't.

With her Beretta pointed at his head, she said, "One more thing and then we'll go. Take out your cell phone."

"Why?"

"Vadim, it isn't smart to ask 'why' when somebody has a gun pointed at the middle of your face. Take it out of your pocket! Slowly. Very slowly."

Reluctantly, Vadim did as he was told.

"Now, call Charlene . . . you call her Trixie . . . and

hand me the phone. You just dial. Don't you say a word to her. I mean it!"

"Why?"

"Vadim, you just ain't right in the head, boy. I already told you to keep the questions to a minimum. Do it!"

He punched a couple of numbers, then held the phone out to Savannah.

A tentative, meek voice on the other end answered, "Yes?"

"Charlene?" Savannah asked.

"Yes. Savannah?"

"It's me, sweetie. Now listen to me. You throw whatever's yours into a suitcase or whatever you've got and go out to the parking lot. There's a red Mustang sitting there. You get into the backseat and then call me back here on Vadim's phone. Got it?"

"But . . . but, Savannah, I can't. . . ."

"Yes, you can. This may be the only chance you ever get to have a life that's worth living, Charlene. Take it!"

"Okay. I will."

"Good girl. Hurry up."

Savannah snapped the phone closed and continued to look down the barrel of her gun at Vadim, who was appearing more despondent by the moment.

"What now?" he said.

"We wait a few minutes," she replied.

Three minutes later, when Vadim's phone rang, Savannah answered it and heard a breathless Charlene on the other end. "Okay. I'm out here. I'm ready to go."

She sounded so happy that Savannah thought her heart would swell and burst, just hearing it.

"We'll be right out, honey," she told the excited girl. "You just sit tight."

When Savannah hung up the phone and shoved it across the counter toward Vadim, he said, "You cannot take my girl. She belongs to me."

"She ain't yours anymore," Savannah told him, her own blue eyes as cold as his. "She's a human being, and you're nothing but a no-good, blood-sucking pimp . . . a modern-day slave trader. And just for the record, I hate people like you."

She and Dirk backed out of the room, and she didn't holster her weapon until they were in the Mustang with Charlene and a pillowcase half full of belongings in the rear.

Savannah saw the meager bag and said, "Is that all you've got, darlin'?"

Charlene looked ashamed for a moment, then nodded. "Yes, but at my brother's house in San Francisco, I have a pretty room with a pink bedspread and a view of the bridge."

"Then let's get you back to your brother's house," Savannah said. "And with some work on your part, you won't ever have to see this stinkin' place or another one like it again."

Chapter 23

"What do you want to do first," Savannah asked Dirk as they walked into the Victoriana, "have dinner or go twist a knot in Ethan Aberson's tail?"

"Oh, the tail twisting, definitely. Just think how much tastier dinner will be if we've roasted him first."

That told Savannah all too clearly how aggravated he was that he'd been chasing his own tail trying to nail this guy. Dirk seldom got terribly, deeply annoyed when on a case. After so many years, it was all pretty routine for them both.

But this one had proven especially frustrating with so many suspects, so few alibis, and so little physical evidence.

She understood his vexation and shared it.

It was enough for her to want to go after Ethan Aberson on an empty stomach. And that was a first for her, a woman with her priorities in order. Food first and then . . . well . . . everything else.

"Then let me call Tammy and see what room he's in," she said.

"She's probably sitting outside his door, watching it like a cat watching a gopher hole."

"Probably." She punched in Tammy's number on her cell. Tammy answered right away. "Whatcha doing?" she asked.

"Still watching Ethan's door," she said, "with Waycross, of course."

"Of course." Savannah laughed and nodded to Dirk. "What number is it?"

"Three fifteen."

"We'll be right there."

"Good. 'Cause we could both really, really use a potty break."

Savannah and Dirk found Tammy and Waycross exactly where she'd said, down the hall, eyes glued to the door of room 315.

"Good Lord, Tammy," Savannah said. "You aren't guarding the president, for heaven's sake. Go pee, both of you."

As they raced down the hallway toward their respective rooms, Savannah and Dirk laughed.

"I wish there was that kind of dedication on the job," Dirk said. "If I had a few like her in the department, I wouldn't have to work half as hard."

"Yeah, but she makes me tired, just watching her." She pointed to the door. "And hungry. Let's go get this wrapped up. I want to hit one of those famous buffets."

They walked up to the door, and Dirk stretched out his hand to knock on it.

"Hey," she said. "You've been doing a lot of that lately. My turn."

As she nudged him aside, she whispered, "It'd be

better if he looks through the keyhole and sees me instead of you."

"Why?"

"I'm prettier. And if you were a guy, wouldn't you open a door faster for a woman than some dude you didn't know?"

"What do you mean, if I were a guy?"

"Shhh."

She knocked and listened. The television was on pretty loud inside, but someone turned down the volume. Then she heard footsteps approaching.

"Yes?" a male voice said. "Who is it?"

"Housekeeping," she replied, trying to sound like a tired, bored, hotel maid and not an investigator with her pulse thudding.

"I don't need anything. Thank you."

"I have to turn down your bed."

"It's down. I'm in it. Thanks anyway."

She could hear the footsteps walking away. "Damn," she muttered under her breath.

"Yeah, leave it up to you," Dirk said. "If you were a woman, maybe you'd have been able to—"

"Watch it."

She knocked on the door a second time, a little harder and a bit more insistent.

Again the steps approached. "Yes?" he said on the other side. "Really, I don't need turndown service. Thank you. Good night."

"But, sir, I'll get in trouble if I don't give you your mints; it'll just take a moment and then I'll leave you alone."

There was a pause, then the rattling of a chain.

She turned and made a face at Dirk.

When he didn't return her mug, but reached inside

his jacket to unsnap his weapon's holster, she sobered up a bit, too.

It was great fun getting to lie to strangers and outsmart them for a good cause, but they were hunting a killer. And it was time to get down to business.

Ethan opened the door, and when he saw Savannah, he gave her a warm smile and reached out his hand for the promised candy. But when he saw Dirk standing beside her, his warmth evaporated.

"Hey," he said, backing away from the door. "What's this?"

Dirk put his foot in the door before he could close it. "Not what you think. We're not here to rob you."

"Oh." He gave a nervous little laugh. "Good."

"Naw, it's not that good," Savannah said. "In fact, by the time we're done, you might even think it's worse."

By the time twenty minutes had passed, it was Savannah and Dirk who were hating the visit as much or even more than Ethan Aberson.

They had gone in the same verbal circle with him enough times that Savannah was getting dizzy.

She had decided five minutes into the interview that it was a mistake to do this on an empty stomach. Her brain never functioned at full capacity without a generous helping of carbs.

Chocolate never hurt either.

"I don't know what that man and that girl at the brothel were talking about," Ethan said for the fifth time as he paced back and forth the length of the small room. "I went there once, yes. That's perfectly legal here in Nevada."

Dirk shifted in the small chair he was sitting in next

to the table. Savannah sat across from him, equally rest-less.

"But you told them, paid them, in fact, to lie about where you were the day after that," he said. "Don't tell us that you didn't again, because my friend here doesn't like being lied to. In fact, she chewed up and spit out the big Russian guy who runs that dive for lying to us about your so-called second visit. The one that didn't happen."

"You paid them to say that you were there, when you were here in the hotel," Savannah said. "We absolutely know that. And you're losing all credibility by telling us otherwise."

"If you have solid evidence that I was here in the hotel," Ethan said, running his fingers wearily through his thick silver hair, "why are you harassing me like this? I couldn't have been here in this hotel and in San Carmelita murdering Madeline at the same time, now could I?"

It was true, of course, Savannah told herself. But there was still something very peculiar about this business of establishing a false alibi, even if it turned out that you had a better one elsewhere.

She knew bull-pucky when she smelled it, and from where she stood, she could swear she was standing in the middle of a dairy's grazing field.

"Look," Ethan said, "I'm sure that if you've been investigating my wife and her life for the past few days, it didn't take you long to find out that we didn't like each other, to say the least. But I didn't kill her. I don't know who did. I'm not the only person who was on the outs with her."

"We know that," Dirk said. "But we also know that divorces, and especially bitter custody battles, bring out the worst in people. Then we find out that you're hanging out in brothels, and bribing the prostitute and pimp to lie for you. We have to find out what that's about."

Ethan walked over to the bed and abruptly sat down on it, as though his legs had just given out beneath him.

"Listen," he said. "I'm going to tell you one more time, and you can believe me or not. I went to Monique's that first day that you're talking about. I went and . . . to be embarrassingly frank . . . I couldn't . . . you know. I'd never gone to a place like that before. I guess I was just in a weird mood because of all the stress Madeline put me through. Anyway . . ."

He stopped, took a deep breath, and then continued, "I couldn't, you know, perform. The girl felt bad and told me that if I came back the next day she'd give me a freebie. I told her I'd think about it. I gave her a big tip, because I felt sort of sorry for her. She seemed like a good kid in a bad place."

"She is a good kid," Savannah said. "A sixteen-year-old kid. And we took her out of that bad place."

"Oh, wow. Then I'm glad I didn't do anything with her. I wouldn't want that on my conscience."

Savannah watched him closely, and her intuition told her that at least that much was true. Plus, on the way to the bus station in Vegas, Charlene had told them as much about his lack of performance power.

"That part of your story jibes with what the girl told us," she told him. "But the rest of it, about the next day . . . that doesn't fly."

"I don't know why she and that Russian guy would claim that I bribed them to say I was there the second day. I did not. Like I said, I gave her a generous tip. Maybe she misunderstood and miscommunicated it to him. I don't know."

Savannah knew they had hit a wall with this guy. And

when she looked over at Dirk, she could see all over his face that he knew it, too.

All this time and effort, and this suspect was a dead end like all the others.

"Ethan," she said, "if you didn't kill your wife or have it done, do you have any notion who did?"

He thought for a while before answering. And when he did, he looked her straight in the eye with as much sincerity as the most innocent person she had ever known.

"I really don't," he said. "I've thought about it a lot. I know Madeline has enemies. Her former lover and his wife. Her business partner. Some people whose parties and weddings she ruined. Honestly, the woman had way more enemies than friends. Everyone in my life told me for years to leave her, that she was no good."

"Is that why you left her?" Savannah asked.

"No. I don't care what other people think. Believe it or not, but I loved Maddy. We had some really good times in the beginning. And with our beautiful little Elizabeth."

He broke down in tears, bowed his head, and covered his face with his hands.

Savannah looked around the room, spotted a nearby tissue box, and offered him a handful.

"Thank you," he said as he wiped his eyes and blew his nose. "The bottom line is: I finally wised up and realized that she didn't love me. She never had. Maddy had something broken inside her. She wasn't capable of love. And now"—his voice cracked again—"and now my little daughter has to grow up without a mother. It breaks my heart."

* * *

266 G.A. McKevett

As Savannah and Dirk left the room and walked down the narrow, dark hallway with its bloodred carpet, Dirk asked her, "Do you believe him?"

"About loving his daughter? About Madeline's short-comings and other enemies? Yes."

"Me, too. But about the brothel . . . no way. He was lying like a rug about that."

"Absolutely. I could practically see the smoke curling up off the back of his pants when he was talking about that."

"But why do you suppose he'd set up an alibi and then not use it?"

"I don't know. And frankly, right now, I'm too hungry to give a hoot. My stomach thinks my throat's been cut. Let's go eat."

Savannah and Dirk collected Tammy and Waycross and showed the youngsters the "real" Las Vegas in all of its glorious, gaudy, way-over-the-top grandeur. The majestic, golden hotels reaching into the black, desert sky. The strange architectural wonders—gigantic roller coasters, replicas of the Eiffel Tower, the Statue of Liberty, the Brooklyn Bridge, even a great pyramid, and a Roman palace. It was all simply too much to take in.

Even Savannah, who tried hard not to be impressed, had to admit that the lights were truly beautiful. Sparkling, glowing, flowing, shooting, exploding everywhere. She couldn't help but be completely dazzled.

And to everyone's delight, they had no problem at all finding wonderful food to satisfy everyone's eclectic tastes, from Tammy's organic vegetables to Waycross's rib-sticking steak.

They were a tired group when they finally returned to their hotel rooms.

Savannah wasted no time hitting the sheets. But the

excited, effervescent Tammy wasn't about to let her get off that easily.

"I had more fun today than I've had all the rest of my life put together!" she exclaimed as she practically danced out of the bathroom, having taken her shower and slipped into her pajamas. "It was wonderful! I got to do some real, live detecting and . . . oh, that was so exciting! My heart was pounding when we followed our subject around, and surveilled his every movement!"

"I'm happy for you, darlin'." Savannah yawned. "You can tell me all about it in the morning."

Tammy ran over to the other bed and dove into it, headfirst. "Waycross is so funny!" she said, flouncing around like a hen making her nest. "And he's so polite and sweet! I could tell he was worried that something bad might happen to me, and he was making sure I was safe every minute. Is that because he's a Southerner? Are all men down South super gallant like him or is he special that way?"

"Southern men are awesome. Waycross is awesome. Good night, honey bunny."

"And when we were driving around the city tonight, looking at all the stuff—can you believe that water fountain at the Bellagio or that volcano at The Mirage—he was holding my hand there in the backseat. Is that okay with you, if your brother and I like each other, because I like him a lot, and I'm pretty sure he likes me, too. You know him better than I do, Savannah. Do you think he likes me?"

"Yep."

"And you're okay with that? Like, if the two of us became a couple, you'd think that was a good thing? And you'd sort of support us if we were building some sort of relationship? You'd like that?"

"Uh-huh."

"Wow." Tammy laid down on her back, flung her arms and legs out, a smile as wide as the Bellagio fountain on her face. She was the perfect picture of a spirit that was open to life, to love, to hope. "This is just so wonderful. Don't you think so, Savannah?"

"Um."

"I sure appreciate us having this little talk. Our heart-to-heart conversations mean the world to me. You're like a big sister to me, and I love you so much."

"Zzzzz. . . ."

Savannah woke from another nightmare, her heart pounding, her nightgown wet with cold sweat.

But as she lay there, fighting her way back to reality, orienting and reminding herself that all was well, she realized . . . this dream was different.

As always, he had stood over her, pointing his gun down at her, telling her that he hated her and was going to kill her.

But this time, his face looked like that of the Russian in the bordello. And this time, she had a gun, too. She pointed at him and fired.

The face disappeared into the darkness behind him.

And somewhere in the blackness of the night, she heard the sound of sorrow and utter despair. A young woman crying.

Savannah searched until she found her. The girl was wearing nothing but a ragged flannel shirt, huddling there in the dark, sobbing.

"Come on, Tammy," she said, lifting her and supporting her as she walked her into the light. "I've got you, and you're going to be fine now, darlin'. Just fine."

Remembering the details of the dream made Savannah feel better. Much, much better, in fact.

She lay in the strange, hard, hotel bed, thinking about how Charlene had looked when Dirk had pressed money into her hand and they had put her on a bus bound for San Francisco. She thought about the brother who was going to be so happy to see his little sister again. He might have even thought he'd lost her forever.

Restoration and healing. Such rare and precious commodities in the cold, cruel world.

And as she drifted off to sleep, Savannah had to agree with Tammy. It had been a good day.

One of the best ones ever.

Chapter 24

Savannah couldn't remember when her table had been so full. So many loved ones around it. So much good food weighing it down. So much sharing.

So much bickering.

"Marietta, how many of those biscuits have you had already, girl?"

"I've been counting and she's on her fourth one there."

"Mari's always been a pig when it comes to bread of any kind."

"So true. So true. Any biscuit in her vicinity's not long for this world."

"That's why her butt's so big, and white and doughy looking. It's all bread."

"My bu-bu-tt's not b-i-i-ig."

It was hard to talk with a mouthful of biscuit.

Granny rapped her spoon on the table and spoke soft, gentle words of reconciliation. "Y'all shut your yaps and eat before I smack you all with a fourteen-inch cast iron skillet."

For several seconds, silence reigned. And it was pure bliss. Until Marietta swallowed her mouthful of biscuit.

"I don't think y'all are ever gonna figure out this murder case you got goin' on here. So, I reckon you're not gonna be gettin' married neither. Which means we all dragged our merry as—"

Gran cleared her throat. "Watch it, young lady."

"Our merry *bee-hinds* all the way across this country to see a lot of nothing."

"Marietta," Savannah said, fixing her sister with a baleful eye, "if you don't have anything kind and uplifting to say at my dinner table, you can take another biscuit and"—she glanced over at Gran and the children—"and shove it into your mouth. In fact, I'll do it for you."

As Alma passed Marietta the biscuit basket, she said, "I thought that trip to Las Vegas was going to solve the case. You do believe it's the husband who did it, right?"

"We honestly don't know," Dirk replied, looking far less content and joyful than he usually did, after putting away one of Savannah's fried-chicken dinners—his favorite.

"The guy seemed like a decent fella," Savannah added. "And it's for sure he didn't actually do the murder himself."

At the other end of the table, a quiet Tammy sat next to Waycross, her steamed brown rice and veggie plate nearly emptied. She gave Waycross a sweet smile and said, "Waycross and I have talked about it, and we think he hired it done. Why else would he go out of his way to set up an alibi? It's the mark of someone who hires an assassin to pay for the hit and then make sure you're out of town when it goes down."

"Yeah, but setting up two alibis?" Savannah said. "That makes you look more guilty than innocent."

Waycross took one of the last drumsticks off the chicken platter. "He's a little touched in the head, if you ask me. Preoccupied by death and dying."

In unison, everyone at the table turned to look at Jesup. Today she was wearing a black and red death-metal T-shirt and red makeup "tears" dripping from the corners of her eyes.

She shrugged. "Being real about the inevitability of death helps us to celebrate life. It's a healthy thing."

"This guy's an undertaker," Tammy said. "And he collects stuff like antique undertakers' tools. That's a little creepy, don't you think?"

"Cool." Jesup's eyes glowed. "There's a store down by the beach, The White Rose, that sells stuff like that. It's awesome. I went in there while you guys were all looking for dumb shells on the beach."

"My shells aren't dumb," Jillian protested. "I found a pretty pink one."

"Your shells are lovely, sweet pea," Granny told her, patting her on the head. "And the rest of you watch the subject matter of this here conversation. Let's keep our children children for as long as we can."

"Point taken, Gran," Savannah said. "The rest of us will use . . . um . . . alternative terminology when discussing the particulars of this situation."

"Huh?" Jillian asked, looking adequately confused.

"Mission accomplished. Follow in suit." Savannah looked over at Jesup, who was trying to get the biscuit basket away from Marietta. "This store you're talking about, does it carry, shall we say, items that could be classified as 'macabre'?"

"It's packed with stuff like that."

"Do they sell seashells and kites?" Jillian asked. "I like stores that sell fun beach stuff like that. Oh, and stuff with glitter and sparkles."

"Me, too," Gran said. "Gobble up them peas now."

Jesup thought for a moment. "I guess you'd classify them as 'cemetery chic.'"

"Hmm," Dirk said, "those are two words I never thought I'd hear in the same sentence."

"How much you wanna bet he's shopped there?" Tammy said.

Waycross nodded. "You know he has."

"I don't know what that's got to do with this miserable, rotten case," Dirk grumbled.

Jesup took a long drink of her iced tea, and with a self-important little smirk, said, "Aren't you missing a . . . uh"—she looked down at the children—"a utensil employed as an instrument of . . . say . . . annihilation?"

Dirk stared at her, blank-faced. "What?"

Savannah leaned over and whispered, "A murder weapon. Code, for the younguns."

"Oh, right. Yeah, we don't know what it was," he said. "Just a general description. Eight inches or more in length. Narrow, sharp on the end."

"There are lots of undertaker tools like that," Jesup said with all authority. "Things that they stab into the bod—"

"Jesup Loretta Reid, eat some peas!" Granny said, shoving the bowl in her direction.

"But I don't like peas."

"Eat 'em or wear 'em."

"Okay."

Savannah, Dirk, Tammy, and Waycross—the newest honorary member of the Moonlight Magnolia Detective Agency—filed into The White Rose, trying, for all the world, to look like four people who weren't just your ordinary schmucks, but cool, hip folks interested in the darker side of life.

The clerk behind the counter, whose face was decorated with the same type of bizarre makeup that Jesup liked to use, gave them a quick once-over and went back to reading his vintage edition of *Fangoria*.

Savannah glanced around the shop and decided that she wasn't likely to become one of their steady customers. The photo books of dead children, the artwork of serial killers reverently displayed on the walls, and the decorative statuary of demons raping women was unsettling to her spirit, to say the least.

She decided it was a good thing that Granny didn't know that Jesup was into this sort of thing. Otherwise, she'd be scheduling an exorcism for her at the next Wednesday-night prayer meeting.

Finally, the guy behind the counter lowered his magazine and said, "You need help or just looking?"

Savannah left a display of freeze-dried tarantulas and bats and walked over to him. "I don't think y'all have anything I'd want to buy," she told him. "But we do have a couple of questions for you."

"No, the skulls aren't real," he said with a condescending tone that made Savannah want to feed him one of his tarantulas. "But if you're into real ones, we have connections."

"I'm sure you do," Dirk said as he walked over to him. "But we're more interested in one of your customers."

"We don't reveal information about our customers. Confidentiality is an important part of shopping here."

"I'm sure it is," Dirk replied. "Who'd want to admit they buy this crap?"

"Excuse me," Tammy called from the other side of

the store. "Savannah, Dirk, could you come here for a minute?"

Savannah was a bit surprised. Tammy knew better than to interrupt an interview, so she must have something worth saying.

"Be right there," Dirk called back. To the clerk, he said, "We'll continue this conversation in a minute."

They walked to the rear of the store, where Tammy and Waycross were standing beside a full-wall display, which a sign identified as "The Mortuary." The items for sale included: casket plaques, decorative coffin buckles and keys, gravesite urns, and fancy bottles containing embalming fluids.

"Whatcha got?" Dirk asked them.

Tammy pointed to an old leather case, much the same size and structure as that which would hold some sort of band instrument, like a saxophone or clarinet. It had a lining of dark blue velvet and, lying in deep indentations in the fabric were miscellaneous, ominous-looking antique tools. A glass funnel with a heavy metal stand nestled next to giant scissors, some forceps, and something that looked like a large, curved needle.

Waycross reached down and ran his finger along an empty indentation. The outline of the instrument that had once occupied that place was very clearly defined. It was something with a handle and a long, very thin spike with a point on the end. "Looks about ten inches long to me," he said. "Your coroner lady said something eight or more."

Bells went off in Savannah's head that sounded like Tchaikovsky's "1812 Overture."

She turned to the front of the store and shouted, "Hey, we found something we're interested in back here."

"Oh, yeah," Dirk said. "Big time."

When the clerk had finally meandered his way to the back, Dirk pointed out the case with its missing instrument. "What was there?" he asked.

The guy looked at the empty slot in the lining and said, "A trocar."

"What the heck's a trocar?" Savannah wanted to know.

"It's a long, sharp instrument that undertakers use to drain blood and bodily fluids out of corpses," was the reply.

"And what happened to this one?"

"It got sold. I wouldn't have broken up the kit, but the gal that works for me took it onto herself to sell it without asking me."

"Who bought it?" Dirk asked.

"I told you . . . we've got a confidentiality policy."

"And I've got a badge." Dirk took it out and showed it to him. "Start talking, or you're going to be in the middle of a real-life homicide investigation. And that ain't gonna be nearly as much fun as all this fantasy death stuff you've got going on in this creepy store of yours."

"What do you want to know?" he asked.

Savannah smiled. "Everything."

"Sorry to leave you behind at a time like this, but . . ." Savannah said to Tammy and Waycross as they sat in the Mustang that was parked in Geraldine and Reuben Aberson's driveway.

"Hey, we understand, Sis," Waycross said. "Go do your cop business." He reached over and grasped Tammy's hand. "We'll be fine."

As Savannah and Dirk walked up the sidewalk to the

door, she said, "With my backseat full, you're going to need a radio car."

"I already called for one. It'll be waiting when we come out."

He knocked on the door, and as they waited, she looked around at the little kid toys scattered on the porch and said, "I hate this."

"Me, too, baby. Me, too."

When Geraldine answered the door, again wearing an apron and smelling of baked goods, Savannah asked right away, "Is your granddaughter home?"

Geraldine looked puzzled by the question. "No. She's down the street playing with some of the neighbor children. Why?"

"Because we need to talk to your husband," Dirk said. "Right now."

"Oh, okay. Come on inside. I'll get him."

She ushered them into the living room, where the white, fluffy dog danced on his hind legs like a circus horse.

Savannah shot Dirk a knowing look, and he nodded.

A moment later, Reuben walked in, wiping his hands on a rag. He had smudges of what looked like furniture stain on his light blue T-shirt. His face was red and sweaty.

"Yes?" he said with a neutral tone that was neither aggressive nor hospitable. "What can I do for you?"

Dirk walked over to him and stood in front of the man, squaring off with him. "Where is the trocar?" he asked.

In the same neutral tone, he said, "What's a trocar?"

"It's an undertaker's tool, long and sharp," Savannah said. "Kind of like the ice pick from hell, only hollow inside. It's used for draining blood. But then, you already know that, I'm sure."

Reuben wiped the sweat off his forehead with the rag and said, "I'm not an undertaker. My son is. I don't know what you're talking about."

"Okay," Dirk replied. "And I suppose you don't know anything about buying one at The White Rose, that gory little shop down by the beach that sells junk like that?"

Reuben glanced over at his wife, whose face had turned a terrible shade of gray. He didn't reply.

"We have the credit card receipt," Dirk told him. "The credit card with your name on it."

"And when we called the medical examiner and asked her if such an instrument could cause the sort of wound that Madeline had on her back, she said, 'Absolutely.'"

"In fact," Dirk added, "she double-checked the wounds and found that they did, indeed, have a strange, distinctive shape to them. It wasn't a round spike that she was stabbed with. Under a microscope you can see that the weapon had three long sides to it. And we only know of one thing that has a shape like that. It's an undertaker's tool called a trocar. You bought one from The White Rose two days before Madeline was murdered."

"What do you suppose the odds of that are?" Savannah asked. "And more importantly, what do you think a jury will make of it?"

When he still didn't respond, Geraldine reached for her husband and placed her hand on his arm. "Reuben?" she said. "Are you okay?"

She turned to Savannah, tears in her eyes. "He had a heart attack last year. Please don't upset him."

"Don't say anything, Gerri," Reuben said to her, his jaw clenched. "Just be quiet, honey. I'm all right."

Savannah felt for the woman and wished she could shield her from what was about to happen. She looked at Dirk, who was getting out a pair of handcuffs, and said, "You got this?"

"Yes," he said, turning Reuben Aberson around and cuffing him.

Savannah said to the woman, "Mrs. Aberson, let's you and I go out into the front yard and wait for the men to have their say. I'd be glad to answer any questions you might have out there."

Reluctantly, Geraldine followed Savannah to the door, with Reuben calling out to her, "Say nothing, Gerri. Call Frank and ask him the name of that attorney he used last year. Then give him a call."

"Okay," she said as she and Savannah stepped outside.

The woman looked like she was going to faint, so Savannah led her over to a lawn chair that was in the shade of a tree and sat her down.

Savannah squatted beside Geraldine's chair, held her hand, and patted it. "This has to be awful for you, ma'am," she said. "I'm so sorry."

"Why do you think he did it?" Geraldine asked, her eyes filled with pain and distress.

"We checked and saw that your son's birthday is in a few days. That trocar was probably a gift for Ethan, wasn't it?"

She nodded and continued to cry softly. "But . . . but . . . you can't arrest Reuben for murder just because of that thing, can you? It's not enough to charge him with killing someone."

"That's not all, Mrs. Aberson. When we were talking to the medical examiner today about the unusual shape of the wound, we were told something else. There was a wad of hair found on the carpet there in the hotel suite where Madeline was murdered."

"Hair?"

"Yes. Dog hair. White, fluffy, fuzzy dog hair. It's consistent with a poodle–cocker spaniel mix. Is your pet a cockapoo?"

She didn't have to answer. Savannah could tell by the increased sobbing that the truth was dawning on Geraldine Aberson, and her world was collapsing around her.

The cell phone in Savannah's waistband began to play Tammy's song. She stood and turned toward the Mustang, where she saw Tammy waving her over to the car.

Again, it wasn't like Tammy to interrupt something like this. It had to be important.

"Excuse me, Mrs. Aberson. I'm sorry, but I have to go over there just for a moment. I'll be right back. You just sit here and try to collect yourself. Everything's going to be okay."

Yeah, right, she said to herself as she walked away. *And why don't you just go ahead and tell the poor woman that the world is at peace and we've solved the problem of global hunger, too.*

She got to the car, where Tammy had rolled down the window.

"What's up, kiddo?" Savannah asked.

Tammy thrust her electronic tablet at her. "You've got to see this," she said. "I just found it and thought you should know. I think it changes everything."

A few moments later, Savannah walked back across the lawn from the Mustang to Geraldine Aberson, who was even more distraught than when she had left her.

Savannah knelt beside her and looked into the woman's tormented face.

"Is there something you have to tell me, Geraldine?" she asked softly.

The older woman sat silently, crying, biting her lower lip and wringing her hands. Finally, she nodded. "I can't let my Reuben take the blame for this, no matter what he says."

"No, of course you can't."

Savannah took her hand and held it between hers. "Tell me what happened. Help me understand why you did it, and then maybe I can help you."

Chapter 25

Savannah had decided that it was time to have an enormous backyard barbecue to celebrate the solving of the Aberson case. She hoped to foster familial togetherness with lip-smacking ribs, potato salad, baked beans, and the simple act of turning the crank on some homemade ice cream.

Plus, there were less things for the kids to break outside, and the backyard was considerably larger than her living room, so it served to dilute the strong brew of family togetherness.

Marietta was lying on a beach towel in the smallest bikini that Gran would allow, soaking in rays.

Cordele sat in a chair, reading the latest pop-psychology best-seller.

Atlanta was perched on the back porch, playing her guitar, a pencil in her mouth and a pad of paper on her thigh as she wrote down the chords to the mournful country song she was composing. It was about some girl who had jumped into a river and drowned herself after being betrayed by a lover. A unique and original subject for a country song, to be sure.

Dutiful Alma was carting dishes of food from the kitchen to the picnic table in the yard without complaint. She even hummed a happy little tune as she worked . . . except for when she walked by Atlanta. She had been told, "Cut it out! Your caterwaulin's interferin' with my composin' here, girl!"

Macon was snoring in the hammock, while Jillian and Jack stuck dandelions in his hair and between his toes.

Jesup sat under the magnolia tree, reading some vampire magazine with a gruesome cover. She looked contented as she reveled in death-obsessed fiction that, according to her, affirmed the joys of life.

For once, Vidalia and Butch weren't fighting. She was parked in a folding lawn chair with him sitting on the ground, giving her a foot rub. The two toddlers were racing in circles around them, laughing when they inevitably fell on their chubby, cherub faces in the grass.

The detectives of the group were gathered around the barbecue grill, where Savannah and Waycross manned the tongs, flipped the burgers, adjusted the hot dogs, and basted the ribs.

Granny had decided to hang out with them, because the conversation was far more lively and the subject matter more interesting.

"I can't get over a woman like that Geraldine killing her own daughter-in-law that'a way," she said as she adjusted her lawn chair to recline a couple of notches. "I saw her picture on the morning news, and she looked like butter wouldn't melt in her mouth."

"You might have, too, Gran, if you'd had the kind of provocation that the Abersons had," Savannah told her. "She bawled like a baby when she told me why she did it. Their little granddaughter told her that Madeline had been trying to get the child to say that her daddy had molested her. She even bribed the child with some sort of princess outfit if she'd tell the school counselor that he'd touched her inappropriately."

Granny's eyes narrowed and her face that was usually sweet and saintly turned hard and scary. "Oh . . . that woman needed a serious beatin' doing such a thing to her husband, let alone to an innocent child!"

"Yes," Savannah said. "And when she and Reuben called Ethan, who was in Vegas, and told him what little Elizabeth had said, he was livid . . . as you can well imagine."

Dirk took a swig of his root beer, which he was drinking instead of his regular beer, out of respect for teetotalist Granny. "I have to tell you," he said. "I'd want to kill somebody over a thing like that, too. I probably wouldn't have, but I would've wanted to."

Tammy looked at the grill to see how her lone veggie burger was faring on the fire. "Can you imagine the damage that would have done to that child if she'd taken her mother's bribe and made that terrible accusation . . . before she was even old enough to understand the gravity of it?"

"But the father of the child, that Ethan fella, he didn't kill her," Gran said. "How come it wound up being the grandmother?"

"Apparently, Ethan told his father that he had set up a false alibi to cover his tracks and was going to fly home, murder her, and fly back to Vegas on the same day, and Reuben talked him out of it. Reuben told Ethan that, as the husband, the cops would automatically suspect him. So he'd do it for him."

"But Reuben didn't do it," Waycross said as he adjusted the burgers.

"He was going to," Savannah said. "He had planned

to lure her someplace and kill her. But the morning of the murder, Geraldine overheard Reuben telling Ethan his plan — that he was going to do it that night. She was afraid for Reuben. He has a bad heart, and she was sure that if he went through with it, the act of actually murdering someone would cause him to have another heart attack."

"And that's when she decided to do it herself?" Gran asked.

Savannah moved to avoid the smoke that was getting into her eyes. "She said she was wrestling with it that morning. She knew Madeline was stuck at the country club with us, because Madeline had called her and asked her to pick up Elizabeth from her girlfriend's house. Geraldine was wondering how to do it, what sort of weapon she'd use . . . and that's when the package arrived."

"That's right," Tammy piped up. "You see, she was the one who'd gone into that weird store and bought that trocar thing for her son's birthday, to add to his collection. She'd used her husband's credit card, which threw us off and made us think it was him. And since she was driving a bunch of Elizabeth's friends to a birthday party right afterward, she asked them to send it to her house."

"Yes, I guess that'd be hard to explain to the kiddos, if they found something like that in the car," Dirk said.

Savannah nodded. "Exactly. And there she was at the house that day, thinking about how to kill her daughter-in-law from hell. And the delivery man drops off that thing."

Waycross looked at Tammy, beaming with pride. "And Tammy here was looking over the copy of the receipt that we got from the guy there at The White Rose. She saw that there was a shipping charge on it. So, she got to checking, and she was able to get the tracking information for the package, and she saw that a woman had signed for it, not a man."

"And that," Dirk told Granny, "is what Savannah told the woman that made her confess."

"Naw," Savannah said. "She was going to anyway. She wasn't going to let her husband go to jail for a murder he didn't commit."

"So, let me get this straight." Granny waved away some smoke that was drifting toward her. "The son was going to do it. But the father said he'd do it for him. But before he got a chance to, the wife did it for them both."

"That's right," Savannah said.

"Well, I admire their devotion to their family," Granny said. "Can't say it's ever right to take a life like that though."

"And," Tammy added, "now little Elizabeth doesn't have a mother or a grandmother."

"Her father's a decent guy," Savannah said. "Even if he is a little obsessed with the macabre."

Dirk sniffed. "I hope her father's strange hobby doesn't influence her too much. She could end up like Jesup."

They all turned and looked at the gal under the tree, glued to her magazine, oblivious to the world around her. She was running her fingers through her heavily gelled hair. As they watched, she absentmindedly began to tug on first one tuft and then the other, until it was sticking out all over like spikes.

Granny shook her head. "Heaven forbid."

Later that evening, when Savannah was saying goodbye to Dirk in her foyer, he glanced over her shoulder and, not seeing anyone, gave her a long, tender kiss.

"Marry me," he said, putting his arm around her waist and pulling her close.

She chuckled. "Okay."

"When?"

"It'll take time to put another wedding together."

He sighed. "How long?"

At that moment, Jack and Jillian came roaring through, and ran right into Savannah. They would have knocked her off her feet, if Dirk hadn't been holding her.

They tore up the stairs, screaming at the top of their lungs.

From the living room, Vidalia yelled, "Butch! Butch Allan! Go do something with your younguns! They're driving me plum crazy!"

"Oh, hush your screechin', Vidalia!" Marietta screamed back. "I can't hear my television show!"

Dirk sighed, pulled Savannah closer, and leaned his forehead against hers. "Can we just leave all of them and go back to Vegas? We can get hitched in some little chapel there by an Elvis impersonator."

It sounded so good that Savannah actually considered it.

For half a second.

"I can't, darling,'" she said. "I couldn't do it to Granny . . . or Alma . . . or Waycross."

"We'll bring them with us."

"The rest will wanna come, too."

"We'll sneak 'em out in the dead of night."

"Granny wouldn't get caught dead in Las Vegas."

"We'll put a bag over her head and throw her into the trunk till we get there."

She gave him a look.

"We'll throw her really easy," he said. "Put lots of

fluffy pillows and soft, comfy blankets in the trunk first."

"Dirk, be serious."

"I'm serious, baby. So, so serious. I can't wait anymore. Whatcha say?"

She didn't reply, but grinned up at him.

He kissed her on the nose. "That's my girl. As you Southerners say, 'Let's get 'er done.'"

The next afternoon, a silver vintage Bentley pulled over to the side of the Pacific Coast Highway. The handsome driver with glistening white hair, dressed in a tuxedo, got out and walked around to the rear passenger's side door and opened it.

"Why, thank you, John," Savannah said, offering him her hand and stepping out onto the sand that led to a wide, pristine beach.

The fellow who had been sitting beside her in the back got out as well.

She lifted the skirt of her third wedding gown—not as fancy or expensive as the first two, but lovely in its classic simplicity—and walked daintily through the dunes with John Gibson supporting her on one side and Ryan Stone on the other.

"Savannah, my love," John said, "I've never seen you looking happier or more beautiful."

"He's right," Ryan said. "You're a glowing bride if ever there was one."

"It's this darned, tight corset thing. It's squeezing all the blood up to my face," she said.

"Ah, come on, this is your wedding day." Ryan steadied her as they climbed a dune. "You must be happy."

Was she happy? she wondered. Between all the hustle and bustle of the morning, she hadn't had a lot of time to consult her own feelings.

"I don't know," she said honestly. "I haven't really thought about it."

"It's really going to happen this time, sweetheart," John told her. "Don't worry. Let yourself feel it."

They had reached the top of the dune and there, standing in a line that seemed to stretch from San Francisco to San Diego, were her loved ones. All fifty thousand of them.

Okay, she told herself, *not fifty thousand.*

Only . . . Granny, Marietta, Vidalia, Waycross, Cordele, Macon, Jesup, Alma, Atlanta, Butch, Tammy, Jack and Jillian, Peter and Wendy, and howling at the end of rhinestone-studded, white leashes, Diamante and Cleopatra.

The crowd caught sight of her and instantly erupted into cheers, waving their arms, hooting and hollering . . . making total spectacles of themselves.

Everyone except the cats.

And the minister in his long black robe.

And Dirk.

He stood at the end of the line, looking amazing in his tuxedo, his hands folded calmly in front of him, smiling at her with a face so filled with love that she nearly burst into tears.

She allowed it to wash over her, the sunshine, the ocean breeze, the beauty of the glistening water, the smell of the roses in her bouquet. She allowed it all to go straight into her heart—the shouts of happiness from her loved ones, the feel of her two dear friends' strong hands supporting her from either side, walking her toward this most important moment of her life.

And best of all . . . the pure joy on her man's face as he watched her coming toward him.

"Oh, yes," she told them. "I'm happy." She took a deep breath, filling her heart with it all, to the brim, and then overflowing. "I am just so, so happy."

"That's wonderful, love," John said, patting her arm.

"In fact," she said, "I'm so darned happy that I'm about to burst right out of this dadgum corset."

"Will you, Dirk," the elderly minister asked, "take Savannah to—"

"Yes. I will. Absolutely. Positively. I will."

The clergyman smiled. The assembled guests laughed. And Savannah looked up into the eyes of the man who, within moments, would be her husband, and knew he was the one she wanted, today and forever.

"For your lawfully wedded wife," the minister continued. "To have and to hold from this day forth."

To hold him . . . in her heart . . . in her arms. The thought flowed through her like Ryan's and John's fine, warm cognac.

"For better and for worse . . ."

Dirk had seen her at her worst, she thought. He'd been there with her through PMS with its chocolate cravings, bloating, and crankiness. He'd seen her family squabbles and understood her fierce need for independence. The guy knew what he was getting into.

"For richer and for poorer . . ."

They hadn't known much about the "richer" business. "Poorer" they had down pat.

"In sickness and in health . . ."

Stomach flu on stakeouts—they'd been there.

"To love and to cherish . . ."

She'd always loved him. It had just taken a lot of growing to realize it, to trust the happiness it offered.

"For as long as you both shall live?"

Yes, for that long and then some.

"Yes, I do," Dirk told the minister. Then he squeezed her hands, looked into her soul, and said, "I do, Van. I really, really do."

She smiled, griped his hands tightly, and said, "Me, too, my love. Me, too."

A few minutes later, after Savannah had given her vows and slipped Grandpa Reid's ring onto Dirk's finger, and he had placed the diamond band onto hers, the minister turned to the family and friends encircling them. He said, "And do those of you gathered here give your blessings to this marriage? And do you vow to Savannah and to Dirk your continued support and love?"

"We do!" was the resounding response.

"Then, by the authority invested in me by the State of California, I pronounce that they are husband and wife. Dirk, you may kiss your bride."

He did.

Very well.

And though the multitude around them was shouting joyously, the seagulls overhead were squawking, and a wayward wave was rolling onto the beach and over their feet . . . to Savannah, they were the only two people on earth.

And that was enough.

Chapter 26

"How does a newlywed couple get far, far away from her crazy family so that they can have a little privacy?" Savannah asked as they walked to the entrance of a motel that would probably be rated half a star.

"Let me guess," he said. "They get on a ferry and go to the nearest island?"

"Hey, hey, you win the prize."

He lifted one eyebrow and gave her a sexy grin. "Oh, goodie. I'm looking forward to collecting that."

For a moment, they paused and looked off to their left, which afforded them a gorgeous, sweeping view of tiny, picturesque Santa Tesla Island, which lay just off the coast, due west of San Carmelita.

Across the water they could see the night lights of the California coastline. And to their right, at the very end of the island stood its crown jewel, the Santa Tesla Lighthouse.

For over a hundred years it had stood, casting its beam out across the waters to warn ships of the dangerous channel nearby. And Savannah thought it was one of the most romantic things she had ever seen.

"Isn't it beautiful?" she said.

"I hope they give us a room where the light won't shine in and keep me awake all night."

She laughed and shook her head. "You've been married to me for a whole"—she looked at her watch—"five hours, and I haven't been able to reform that grumpy streak of yours?"

He wrapped his arm around her shoulders and pulled her to his side. "Let's go get a room and see if my mood improves."

As they walked into the tiny lobby and looked around at the basic shabbiness of the place, he said, "Are you sure you want to spend our first night here? I'm sure we could score a better place if you wanna."

"No," she said. "This place has sentimental value."

She thought back to when they had been investigating a case here on the island and had missed the last ferry home. They'd been forced to spend the night here together. And it had always been a secretly treasured memory for her.

"It's not like we did anything here," he said. "Other than sleep, that is."

She turned and saw something akin to a scowl on his face. With Dirk you couldn't always tell for sure. A lot of his expressions looked like scowls.

"I'm sorry," she said. "I didn't even think to ask you . . . Did *you* want to get a nicer place?"

He looked at her like she was some sort of alien species. "Savannah," he said, "I'm a guy. Guys don't care about 'nicer.' If it's got a bed, we're happy."

* * *

She came out of the bathroom, wearing the beautiful white negligee that her sisters and Granny had bought for her. The soft chiffon flowed gracefully all around her, the floral lace and tiny pearls were strategically placed to accent her feminine curves.

Dirk was sitting on the side of the bed, wearing a pair of simple black pajama bottoms. His chest was bare.

Over the years, she'd seen his chest many times before. And the sight, nice as it was, had never caused her pulse to quicken like this. But then, she hadn't been about to go to bed with him.

"You look gorgeous," he said. "I like the gown. Better than those Minnie Mouse jammies I've seen you in."

"Oh, thanks," she said with a shy giggle.

On the desk and the nightstands, several pink votive candles flickered, lighting the room with a soft, rosy glow.

"Where did you get the candles?" she asked.

"Brought 'em."

"You did?"

"Yeah, I had 'em in my suitcase."

She smiled. "Nice touch."

She looked over and saw that he had placed his red rose boutonnière on one of the pillows. "Oh, you darlin'," she said. "That's really sweet."

"If it's sweets you want"—he jumped up and rustled around in his suitcase for a minute—"I've got that covered, too."

He produced a gold box of Godiva truffles and handed them to her.

"Boy, you are too much."

"Nothing's too much for you, Van." He ran his hand down the sleeve of her nightdress. "I'm just so happy to be here . . . with you."

"Me, too."

He took her hand and gently led her over to the bed.

"You wanna, um, relax . . . or somethin'?" he asked.

"Yes, relaxing sounds nice."

They awkwardly climbed onto the bed. Savannah lifted the boutonnière from her pillow and stuck herself with the pin. "Ouch," she said, setting it on the nightstand.

He took her hand, looked at it, then put the injured finger to his lips and kissed it.

"Your hand's shaking, Van," he said. "Are you okay?"

"Sure," she said, feeling anything but okay. "I guess I'm just a little nervous."

"Nervous? Why?" He laced his fingers through her hair and massaged the back of her neck. "It's just me. You're not afraid of ol' Dirk, are you?"

"No. It's just that . . . we've waited so long for this and . . ."

He cupped her face in his big, warm palm and traced the edge of her upper lip lightly with his thumb. "And what, sweetheart?"

She gulped. "And I . . . I don't think I could stand it if you were . . . disappointed."

He threw back his head and laughed. And the deep, male sound of it went through her, touching her warmly in intimate places.

"Savannah, my love," he said, "you never fail to amaze me." He leaned over and kissed her on the forehead. "Sweetheart, it isn't possible for you to disappoint me. I have no expectations."

She looked up at him and said, "None?"

"Well . . . okay a few."

He kissed her, deeply and passionately, then said, "You don't mind if I do that, do you?"

"Oh, no," she said when she'd caught her breath. "Not at all."

He chuckled and eased her gently back onto the
bed, then leaned over her. "And would it be okay if I did
this?"

He trailed one finger from her cheek, down her
throat, to where the gown dipped and showed a bit of
cleavage.

"Okay," she replied.

Slowly, he untied the ribbon that held the front of
the gown closed. But when he started to brush the satin
aside, she put her hand over his and pulled it back up
to her face.

Tears rushed to her eyes. She felt like she couldn't
breathe, that she was choking. She turned her face away
from him and started to cry.

"Van . . . honey . . . what is it?" he asked, turning her
face back to his. "Please, please, tell me what's wrong."

For what felt like a very long time to her, she fought
the fear and the overpowering sense of shame and
grief.

Finally, between gasping sobs, she managed to say, "I
don't want you . . . to see . . ."

"See what, honey?" He put his arms around her and
held her close to his chest. "You're a beautiful, beautiful
woman, Savannah. You've always been so comfortable
with your body. I love that about you. Why wouldn't you
want me to see you?"

"It's," she cried, "it's the . . . the scars."

"The scars?" He pulled back and looked down at her.
"What scars? Do you mean where you were shot?"

Hiccupping, she nodded.

"But, babe, I've already seen them. I saw them that
day." He kissed her cheek and then the other one. "Savannah, they were awful when they were open and raw
and bleeding and—"

She felt a violent shudder run through his body.

Then he said, "But they've got to be a lot better now. Please, let me see them. I really need to see them . . . better."

Gathering more courage than she'd ever needed to do anything in her life, she reached down and slowly pulled the fabric back, revealing the puckered red scar above her left breast.

He reached over and picked up the votive candle from the nightstand. Holding it near her shoulder, he bent his head and looked at it closely. "Oh, wow, Van! Honey, that looks great! I can't believe how well it healed."

"Really?" she asked tentatively.

"Are you kidding? Of course. Sweetie, it was a horrible, gaping wound. It's all closed up now and healed over. It's like a night and day difference. Are they all that good?"

She gazed up at him and knew he was telling her the truth as he saw it. She could see the joy and relief on his face. And it washed over her so powerfully that she began to cry again. Only this time with soul-healing happiness.

He bent his head, softly kissed the scar, and said, "Every time I see that, I'm going to think how strong my wife is, that she could survive something like that. And I'm going to think how lucky I am that I didn't lose her that day. I'm the luckiest man in this world."

She threw her arms around his neck and held him close, wetting him with her tears and loving him with all her being. "Thank you, Dirk," she whispered. "Thank you so much."

Finally, she released him. He pulled some tissues from a nearby box and wiped her eyes.

"Now," he said, "are you going to let me see the rest?"

She nodded. "If you want to."

He laughed and said, "Oh, baby. I want to. I really, really, really want to."

"I love you," she said as he pulled her body tight against his.

"I love you, too. You don't know how much."

"Oh, I think I can feel how much." She giggled. "And I think you might be up, off and on, all night . . . with or without that lighthouse shining in here."

"Grrrr!"

Please turn the page for an exciting sneak peek of

the next Savannah Reid mystery

KILLER HONEYMOON

coming in April 2013 from Kensington Publishing!

Chapter 1

T hose darned cats were hogging the bed. Again.

As Savannah lay on her side—half-dreaming, half-waking—she felt Diamante draped—furry, warm, and heavy—across her thigh. Cleopatra was sprawled across her waist. Without even opening her eyes, Savannah knew which was which.

Since they were kittens, both had tried to sleep on her head, or at least on her pillow. Savannah had demanded they stay down by her feet. Over the years, they had negotiated this compromise. It worked, for human and feline alike.

Except for the snoring.

Cleopatra snored. Loudly.

She might be named after an Egyptian queen; her glossy coat could shine like fine black velvet, and her eyes glow like the most majestic mini-panther in the jungle. But Cleopatra snored like a cartoon bear. This morning was the worst that Savannah had ever heard. Plus she smelled like Old Spice.

Savannah woke fully with a start and tried to flip over

onto her back, but she was thoroughly pinned. With her newfound consciousness, she realized these were not simple kitty cats—not even the miniature leopard style—holding her down.

She ran her fingers over the hard, hairy arm wrapped around her waist. Then she investigated the harder and hairier object across her thigh. It was her husband's leg.

Yes. *Husband.*

She had one of those now.

The memories of yesterday's vows and the two rings on her left hand made it quite official. As did the presence of a man in her bed and the sound of his snoring that reminded her of a Georgia tornado, whirling a few inches from her ear.

Savannah Reid was a married woman; and normally, that thought might have alarmed her. But his familiar smell and the blissful heat of his body pressed against hers reminded her—it was Dirk. Not just her husband, but her best friend and partner for more years than she cared to count.

So it was okay. In fact, it was much more than okay.

"Hey, good morning, wifey," he said, nuzzling her ear, his breath tickling her neck. His arm tightened around her waist, pulling her even closer against him.

"Good morning to you, hubby," she replied with a giggle. "First time I ever said that."

He kissed a sensitive spot over her temple. It gave her delicious shivers. "Well, get used to it. This is a life sentence."

"Wouldn't have it any other way."

As she snuggled in, a feeling swept over her that she could only describe as wondrous, warm, and cozy. Better than a dark chocolate gourmet truffle savored lingeringly on the tongue. More delicious than a sip of the smoothest cognac that slid like liquid fire down the throat to the belly and then set every cell in the body to tingling.

Ah, it was heavenly.

Then he went back to sleep and started to snore. Much louder than before.

A moment later, her leg went numb. She tried to gently slip out from beneath him and couldn't. That big, hard, muscular thigh she had admired so much the night before weighed a ton.

She looked around the motel room and felt a bit homesick. She missed her lace curtains and her pink sheets. She missed Diamante and Cleo's soft, feminine purr-snores.

And Savannah realized that what her blessed granny had told her for so many years was true: Sometimes love was sacred, the most holy and powerful force in the universe. Sometimes it was a warm, fuzzy feeling. Occasionally it was a wildfire of passion that, like cognac, inflamed every cell of your body.

And sometimes it was just a decision. Plain and simple.

At that moment, lying in her new husband's arms, she knew that this big bear of a man would willingly die for her; and even more important, only yesterday, he had vowed to live for her.

With his arm and leg draped protectively over her, cutting off her circulation, she felt her soul fill to the brim with "warm and fuzzy."

And she decided, once again, to love him forever, just as she'd promised to do yesterday in front of God and everybody she knew.

Now . . . if she could only get back to sleep.

In an effort to get away from it all—"all" being Savannah's enormous family, who had decided to camp out in her house for a Southern California vacation following the wedding—Savannah and Dirk had hopped a ferry and escaped to the tiny, picturesque island of Santa Tesla. Twenty-four miles from their own native San Carmelita, and fifty-one miles northwest of Los Angeles, Santa Tesla was a world away and a kingdom unto itself.

With its lush, tropical greenery, brightly colored houses decorated with white gingerbread trim, and grass-roofed huts, the place reminded Savannah of pictures she had seen of Polynesia and Key West. While she had never been to either—poor little girls from Georgia and grown-up, but underpaid, private detectives didn't do a lot of traveling—Santa Tesla looked exactly the way Savannah had always imagined those romantic locales.

As she and Dirk left their shabby little motel and strolled, hand in hand, along the waterfront, she breathed deeply, taking in the delicate scent of honeysuckle wafting on the salt sea air, blending with aromas from the various food establishments they were passing.

She looked around her, enjoying the treats that nature had to offer, from the brilliance of the bougainvillea and hibiscus, which bloomed in profusion, to the giant palms swaying gently in the breeze, the glistening waves as they rolled onto the sand, and the white seagulls circling the beach.

Farther away, the harbor was lined with every sort of boat, yacht, and ship imaginable. And in the distance, a giant cruise ship lay at anchor, waiting while her passengers explored the island and sampled its exotic foods and drinks, hiked nature trails, went diving and snorkeling, parasailed, fished, and deepened their tans on the beaches.

She turned to her groom, gazed lovingly into his

eyes, and said, "Don't you just love it here? It's pure romance. Perfect for a honeymoon."

"I liked it better before that dude at the motel told me how much taxis cost here. What a bite in the ass!"

Okay, she thought. *So much for loving gazes and pure, unadulterated romance. It's not like you didn't know he was grumpy and cheap when you married him, Savannah girl.*

He pointed to the closest thing resembling a "transportation hub" on the island—a bicycle-rental hut. "Yeah, we're gonna have to rent a couple of those."

Looking around her at the steep, steep hills, rising from the beach area to the distant mountains, some soaring to nearly two thousand feet, she reminded herself of her early-morning platitude about love being a choice, a decision, a determination to commit.

"And sometimes it's a vow not to smack 'im silly with the nearest heavy, metal object," she muttered under her breath.

"What?" he asked.

"If you think I'm gonna spend my honeymoon pedaling all over tarnation on a bicycle, buddy, you best reconsider."

"But it'll save us a fortune!"

She turned to him with a look that was sans adoration and brimming with "Get real."

In her thickest, most deep-down-in-Dixie accent, she said, "Last night was wonderful, amazing, all I ever dreamed of, and more."

He beamed.

"But such unaccustomed activity has left me with an aching need to park my butt on a hot-water bottle, not a bicycle seat—if you catch my drift."

He stopped beaming. "Oh. Right. Gotcha."

As she looked up and down the beach with its seaward-facing shops and concessions, she spotted what she was looking for—a golf cart rental. "Now, *that* is more like it. I always wanted to drive one of those things."

He brightened as they headed toward it. "Yeah, that looks like fun, but I wanna drive."

"Nope, I thought of it."

"But I'm the husband. Husbands do the driving."

She grinned up at him, slapping him on the back. "Darlin', we need to get you the latest edition of the *Husband Handbook*. Obviously, the one you've been reading is badly out of date."

A few moments later, as Dirk was filling out the rental form for the cart and Savannah was sliding her California driver's license back into her wallet, she noticed something inside her purse. A creamy white envelope with beautiful script on the front.

Dirk walked up to her and dangled the cart's key in front of her nose. "Possession's nine-tenths of the law," he said, far too proud of himself.

Ordinarily, she would have snatched the key away from him, or at least tried. It might have even ended in an all-out tussle there in front of the tourist hordes. But she was too distracted by the envelope.

She pulled it out, turned it over in her hand, and studied the front. *Savannah and Dirk* had been written in a hand she knew very well. In all her life, she had only met one person with penmanship that perfect, and who wrote with an antique fountain pen.

"Whatcha got there?" Dirk asked, taking her arm and propelling her toward their waiting, freshly rented cart.

"It's from Ryan. I think it's a card." She paused, trying to remember. "I have a half-memory of him handing it to me in the Bentley, when he and John were driving me to our wedding. It's a little hazy. I was a bit discombobulated."

"Yeah, well, I was about to pee my fancy tuxedo pants. I was so nervous waiting for you to get there. I was already wondering how I was gonna explain it to the rental joint."

She hardly noticed when he tucked her into the passenger seat and stuck himself behind the wheel, because she was busy unsealing the linen vellum, tissue-lined envelope.

"It's from Ryan and John," she said as she pulled out the card and opened it. " 'Dearest Friends,' " she read aloud. " 'While we trust you two are having a wonderful first night, reminiscing in your motel of choice, we thought you might enjoy a more romantic venue for the remainder of your island honeymoon. Forgive us for taking the liberty of arranging an alternative, which you are more than welcome to accept or refuse.' "

Dirk slipped the key into the cart's ignition switch. "Cool. I wouldn't mind having better digs than that one we just stayed in."

"You told me you wanted to stay there," she said. "Sentimental reasons, and all that."

"Seemed like a good idea at the time. Since we didn't do anything the other time we slept there, it was sorta like making up for lost time. But I think I got a fleabite on my leg last night."

"Get used to it. You'll be sleeping with flea-bitten felines for the rest of your life."

He grinned at her and stomped on the pedal, causing the cart to lurch forward. "As long as it's Cleo and Di. They're my girls, fleas and all."

As they bounced away from the hut and onto the street, she gave him an annoyed, sidewise glance. "Driving as smoothly as always, I see."

"Hey, you're talking to a manly man here, and we manly men are hell on wheels." He nodded toward the envelope in her hands. "What else does it say?"

She continued to read, as best she could, considering the bumpiness of the road and Dirk's erratic swerving to avoid pedestrian tourists, dressed in eye-searing tropical prints. " 'Take this card to the gift shop at the base of the lighthouse and tell Betty Sue we sent you. Love and best wishes overflowing, John and Ryan.' "

Savannah closed her eyes for a moment and savored the thought of her precious friends, whose love and devotion had sustained her over the years. Tall, dark, and outrageously sexy Ryan Stone and his genteel British gentleman partner, John Gibson, had brought more elegance and charm into her life than she could have ever imagined. It looked as though they were providing still more.

"Whatever our surprise is," she told Dirk as he swerved to avoid a couple of old hippies in tie-dye, "it's bound to be wonderful."

"Knowing Ryan and John, it'll be classy. Hope it ain't too highfalutin. Us manly men have a reputation to uphold."

She pointed toward the end of the island where the Santa Tesla Lighthouse towered above all other landmarks, both manmade and natural, glistening white and stately against the perfect blue sky. "Point this jalopy in that-there direction. Let's go and find out what Miss Betty Sue's got for us in her gift shop."

About two hundred yards from the lighthouse, in a quaint little shop, Savannah and Dirk found Betty Sue standing behind the counter, amid a jungle of seashell-festooned wind chimes. She peeked out at them from between dangling starfish, bits of sparkling sea glass, and delicate sea horses, which danced on the breeze that floated through the cozy store.

Like Savannah, Betty Sue bore a name that suggested she might be a fair daughter of the Confederacy. But she was no dainty Southern belle. With her silver hair cropped to less than an inch, her skin darkly leathered by the sun, her baggy men's work shirt, and her faded denim overalls, she looked more like a deep-sea fisherman than a down-in-Dixie debutante.

But her smile was bright and her pale blue eyes sparkled when she greeted them. "I was expecting you two to pop in about this time," she said. "Ryan and John told me that the new bride would be as pretty as a picture. Shiny, dark, curly hair and eyes bluer than mine—that's the way they described you, Savannah."

She gave Dirk a quick glance. "And they mentioned you be comin' along, too."

"Yeah, we grooms tend to hang out and make a nuisance of ourselves on our honeymoons," he grumbled in return.

Betty Sue walked around the counter, winding her way through displays of kites, straw hats, and plaques with nautical themed quotes like, *Life's a Beach*. In her hand, she held a large skeleton key and a smaller one, both attached to a chain with a skull-and-crossbones medallion dangling from it. The keys and the ornament looked ancient—tarnished and rusty.

When Betty Sue placed them in her hand, Savannah felt a slight chill, of the delicious type, shiver down her back. If only her friend and assistant, Tammy Hart, were here, she would be thrilled. These artifacts were straight out of an old Nancy Drew book. In her imagination, Savannah could envision the title—*The Mystery of the Skeleton Keys* and the cover copy, encouraging the reader to: *Discover what terrors lurk behind the doors, un-locked with these sinister keys.*

"So, what're those?" Dirk snapped. "The keys to a dusty ol' crypt or some vampire coffin?"

Betty Sue chuckled. "Oh, no. Something much nicer than that. Follow me. . . ."

Betty Sue led them out of the shop and along a dirt walkway, which cut across a small field. As Savannah followed her, keys in hand, through a profusion of natural vegetation—wild sage, golden marguerites, orange poppies, and the occasional pear cactus—she could see that their path could only lead to the lighthouse itself.

She glanced back at Dirk, who was a few feet behind her, and gave him a questioning look. He shrugged, but he looked as intrigued as she.

When they arrived at the majestic tower, Betty Sue steered them toward the two-story white-stucco cottage, with a red tile roof, nestled against its base.

Both the lighthouse and the cottage appeared quite old. Their doors were arched and built of heavy, dark, distressed wood. The freshly polished brass hardware shone brightly, but looked as though it had weathered years of sea storms. Instead of being perfectly clear and smooth, the glass in the windows of the house had tiny seed bubbles, striations, and imperfections that hinted at its age.

At the upper-story windows and downstairs, as well, redwood window boxes added a graceful charm to the cottage, spilling over with salmon-colored geraniums, white petunias, and maidenhair ferns.

"This is the lightkeeper's cottage," Betty Sue told them. "It was built at the same time as the lighthouse itself, back in 1853."

"Wow, pre–Civil War," Savannah said as Betty Sue took the keys from her hand.

"Yes. President Franklin Pierce ordered it built after a notorious shipwreck on the reefs over there."

She pointed toward the water to a row of jagged rock teeth, some of which jutted above the surface, while others, looking just as sharp and ominous, lurked below.

"Wouldn't wanna run aground on those things," Dirk said. "They'd grind you up and spit you out—turn you into shark bait."

"That's pretty much what happened to the crew and passengers of the *Lillyan Suzanne*." Betty Sue stepped to the door of the cottage and fit the smallest key into the lock. "She was a steamer, transporting a bunch of guys from San Francisco to Panama. They'd just struck it rich in the gold rush up there and were carrying their fortunes with them. The ship hit the reefs, and it was every man for himself. In the melee, they were more interested in stealing each other's gold dust than rescuing the survivors."

"Tough group," Dirk replied. "Reminds me of our police department barbecues when the supply of ribs runs low."

Betty Sue turned the key and opened the cottage's door. It creaked loudly on its hinges, and Savannah thought, *What else would you expect from a door opened with a skeleton key?*

"If you choose to accept your friends' generous gift," the shopkeeper said, "this is where you'll spend the remainder of your honeymoon. I have to say, I envy you. It's as romantic a setting as you'll find anywhere."